COLLATERAL DAMAGE

ALSO BY KATHY BENNETT

THE DEADLY THRILLER SERIES

A Dozen Deadly Roses
A Deadly Blessing
A Deadly Justice
A Deadly Denial
A Deadly Beauty
A Deadly Prayer (A Novella)
A Deadly Blood Moon

THE BUCKNER THRILLER SUSPENSE SERIES

Collateral Damage

COLLATERAL DAMAGE

A BUCKNER THRILLER SUSPENSE

KATHY BENNETT

Collateral Damage

By
Kathy Bennett

The characters and events in this book are fictitious. Any similarity to real persons, living or dead, is coincidental and not intended by the author.

ISBN: 9781733758116

Published by Kathy Bennett
P.O. Box 1625
Eagle, Idaho 83616

"To my SWAT Team who has a ton of patience, and whose daily messages bring me great joy."

PROLOGUE

ROY

The LAPD black and white SUV skidded and stopped amid the hanging stink of burning brakes.

Officer Roy Buckner leaped out the driver's door and sprinted toward the muscled, tattooed beast driving the pointed toe of his pimp-daddy shoes into the ribs of a motionless working girl splayed on the sidewalk.

The pimp never saw Roy coming. His tackle from behind drove the assailant over the limp woman onto the gravel-strewn driveway of the Blue Cloud Motel.

Seconds later, Seth Farley, Roy's rookie partner, stood over the trio and watched as Roy ratcheted handcuffs tight around the pimp's wrists.

"Call an RA for the victim," Roy said.

Farley keyed the mic on his shirt and requested a rescue ambulance for the girl on the ground.

"Get this guy on his feet, searched, and into the black and white," Roy added. "Then get an FI on him." Roy stood and brushed the gravel from his uniform.

Farley shot Roy a look of annoyance, then assisted the pimp to a standing position and walked him over to their patrol car.

A sergeant arrived, and he and Roy squatted next to the victim and tried to get a story from the near-unconscious hooker.

Roy rose. "She's too loopy or high to tell us anything worthwhile."

The sergeant pushed himself to his feet. "Maybe the docs at the hospital can wake her up enough to tell you what instigated this ass whoopin'."

Roy nodded. "Hey, Sarge, FYI, I tackled the suspect to get him off the broad."

The sergeant sighed and said he'd meet them at the station later for the use of force reports. "I wish I had a hundred bucks for every hour I spend on paperwork. I'd retire next year." The paperwork was necessary to cover Roy's ass in case their arrestee made an excessive force complaint. Still grumbling the supervisor left.

The fallen woman moaned, opened her eyes, and cried that she hurt all over.

Roy knelt next to her. "An ambulance is coming. They'll take good care of you." He requested another unit to accompany their victim to the hospital. He and Farley would interview her after they booked the pimp for assault.

While Roy talked, he kept his eyes on his rookie partner, who filled out a Field Interview card while the suspect sat in the back of the police car.

Unlike most probationary officers, Farley wore the old-school wool uniform instead of the lightweight and cooler poly blend. The tailored shirt and pants accentuated the fact the new officer was no stranger to the gym. The gleaming leather gear, shiny badge, and high and tight haircut came right out of a recruitment poster. Farley looked high speed, but his first two months on the street had proven problematic for the former army GI.

The new cop had already been through two other training officers who'd found his job performance unsatisfactory. He'd made boneheaded mistakes, and instead of owning them, he'd argued with his training officers. If Seth Farley was going to make it off probation, Roy was his final hope.

In general, Farley struggled with police work—while thinking he knew it all—known in cop talk as being salty. His demeanor rubbed cops and citizens the wrong way.

Roy comforted the injured woman as the RA arrived. He'd found her ID in her purse and gave it to the paramedics. She was only seventeen. Roy asked which hospital they were taking her to so he and Farley could interview her later.

The other police unit arrived, and the female partner climbed into the back of the ambulance to ride with the victim. The paramedics placed the girl on a gurney and loaded her into the RA.

By the time Roy returned and got into their vehicle, his partner was checking emails on his cell phone.

"You searched him and double locked the cuffs, right? We wouldn't want his bracelets to tighten up around his wrists."

Farley sighed and stuffed his phone into his shirt pocket. "Yes, sir."

In the rearview mirror, Roy watched the ambulance make

a U-turn toward Mercy Community Hospital. He maneuvered the police car away from the curb and headed to Van Nuys station where their arrestee would be booked.

After a few minutes, Roy eased the black and white to a stop for a red light. Seconds later, a shot rang out.

PART I

1

SETH

Six months later...

If Seth Farley had known the destination of his quarry, he would have offed the guy at the cheap motel he'd stayed at last night—saving the added five hundred miles he'd put on his truck today. But the farther he'd gone, the more he wanted to see where his first LAPD partner, Jerry McMillan, was going. It appeared the final destination was in the Payette National Forest in Idaho. *This might be perfect—as long as he's alone.*

Luckily, Farley had readied for almost any contingency. The cab of his pickup truck held a tent, hiking boots, night-vision goggles, and if he got hungry, MREs—military meals ready to eat.

When McMillan pulled off the highway onto a dirt road, Farley drove past the turnoff so as not to arouse McMillan's suspicions. Farley continued about a half mile then cut across the median, speeding back to the road taken by his target.

Farley guided his pickup onto the bumpy byway, sweat dotting his brow and upper lip as he jounced along. "Damn, I hope I didn't let him slip away from me." His gaze shifted to the dusty path in front of him hoping to glimpse distinctive tire tracks he could follow. There were none.

However, a vehicle traveling on dirt stirred up dust. Particles from the wake of McMillan's truck danced in the midafternoon sun and allowed Farley to follow.

Deeper in the pines, he caught occasional indentations in the tall grass on either side of the road. The tracks resulted from motor vehicles delving deeper into the forest. But the glittering dust trail that Farley followed led him to stay on the main dirt trail.

After passing an offshoot byway, Farley could no longer see the dust flecks in the sun. He slammed on the brakes and cursed. He jerked the gearshift lever into reverse and backed to the flattened grass trail he'd just passed.

He didn't want to alert McMillan he was being followed, and noise from Farley's truck would warn his prey someone was approaching. He drove to a flat area and pulled his pickup between tall shrubs. The vegetation formed a perfect hiding spot. Thick leaves and foliage encased his truck. The bushes were so thick, he hoped he'd be able to get the driver door open. He did.

Better to explore on foot. He pulled a smaller backpack from a duffel bag and filled it with necessities—protein bars, water, and ammo for the handgun on his hip and the rifle he slung over his shoulder. If he didn't find McMillan in a couple of miles, he'd come back to the truck for the night and drive in tomorrow until he found his prey.

After hiking twenty minutes, Farley paused.

Someone whistled. "Don't Let the Sun Go Down On Me."

Farley snickered. He moved off the path he'd followed and into the brush and tall trees.

As he crept through the woods, Farley spotted Jerry McMillan's red SUV parked near a clearing.

Shifting his direction to the right, Farley observed McMillan setting up a tent, still whistling.

He was relieved McMillan was alone, but there was always a chance someone else might arrive. *I'd better do it and get out.*

He took a few more minutes to assess McMillan for weapons. The cop didn't have a pistol on his hip. McMillan's hardware was most likely still in the SUV.

Farley crept forward, using the trunks of the tall pines as cover. A moderate breeze produced a muffled wind-tunnel effect which calmed him.

When McMillan retrieved a bulky cooler from the SUV, Farley's heart raced with what he was about to do. He stepped to the edge of the clearing.

"Hello, Jerry."

McMillan spun, his eyes wide with recognition. Then his eyes focused on the rifle barrel pointed at him.

"Bet you never thought you'd see me in Idaho."

"What are you doing here? What do you want?"

Farley grinned, relishing the confusion and fear in the

other man's eyes. "I'm afraid I have bad news. The
sun *is* going down on you. I'm here for payback, my friend.
You were part of a conspiracy to steal the one thing in life I
wanted—my job as a cop." Farley shot McMillan center mass,
blowing up his heart.

2
______

AMBER

Amber Buckner shuffled into the kitchen, her eyes wincing at the afternoon sun streaming through the window over the sink.

Her husband, Roy, stood at the counter, whistling and slicing an onion. He looked up at her. "Good morning, sunshine," he said. "Did you sleep okay? Can I get you some coffee?"

Amber grabbed a ceramic mug from the cabinet. "It's not morning," she mumbled. "It's midafternoon. And no, thanks. I don't think my stomach could handle coffee." She set the mug on the counter then yawned and stretched.

A frown formed between Roy's brows. "You're not feeling well?"

She waved her hand dismissively. "I'm fine. Just a little

nauseous." She looked at the onion he chopped into small pieces. "What are you making?"

"I'm prepping condiments for the hot dogs and burgers. Remember? The boys are coming over for the Dodgers' playoff game."

Amber filled her cup with water then placed it in the microwave. A nice cup of chamomile tea sounded good.

"*That's* why you're in such a good mood. Your posse is coming over. I should have known."

"Well, that's part of it, but my best girl came into the room looking sexy as hell, wearing an animal-rescue T-shirt and gray yoga pants." He grinned at her. "Do we have time for a little afternoon delight before you have to be at the hospital?"

Amber shook her head and went to the canister where she kept tea bags. She pawed around until she came up with her desired flavor. "Sorry. I've got to leave for the hospital in about an hour. I have online training I was supposed to finish last night and didn't." She retrieved coffee creamer and a spoon. "When are the boys coming?"

"In about two hours. I told them four, but I know Luke or Speakeasy will show up early." Roy set the knife on the cutting board. "How 'bout I whip you up some eggs and toast?"

She smiled at him. "I was hoping you'd say that. I'll go take my shower while you make my breakfast." She pulled her steaming mug out of the microwave and made her tea.

"Are you sure we don't have time for a quickie?"

She glanced at the clock above the sink. "Not if you're going to cook me breakfast—unless you can do both at the same time."

Roy grinned. "I'm good, but not that good." He gathered

ingredients. "I don't want to send you off to work without food in your belly."

Amber smiled at him and blew him a kiss before grabbing her tea and heading to the bedroom.

"Hey," Roy called out. "When you come back remind me to tell you the crazy thing that happened last night at work."

A half hour later Amber returned to the kitchen, wearing her nursing scrubs and makeup. Her long brown hair was in a thick braid.

"Perfect timing," Roy said. He set a plate of scrambled eggs, hash browns, and an English muffin in front of her.

"Thanks. This looks great. So what happened last night? As a cop, you've pretty much seen it all."

"Did I ever mention that someone burglarized my mom's house? It happened right after my dad died."

"I don't think so." She gave Roy a thumbs up after tasting the eggs.

"Assholes broke into our house and stole jewelry, money, and the biggest loss of all—my dad's police officer badge."

"That must've destroyed your mother."

Roy nodded. "It did. Thank God she was wearing her wedding ring. She never would've gotten over losing that."

"So how does a long-ago burglary connect with your interesting day?"

He grinned at her. "I'm getting to it."

Roy stood at the counter where he'd placed a package of ground beef. He tore open the plastic wrap and made hamburger patties.

Amber's stomach roiled at the sight of him working with the raw meat.

"Yesterday I got called into the administrative office,

which is never a good thing." He took a piece of wax paper and placed it on top of the patty he'd just made. "I report to the adjutant, and he's got a shit-eating grin on his face but won't tell me squat."

Roy washed his hands and poured her more orange juice.

"Then the captain comes and has the adjutant announce on the PA there is a special presentation happening in the administration office."

"You must have wondered what was going on."

"Hell yeah. A few people wander in to see what's up. The captain talks about how my dad was a training officer at Rampart and was killed in the line of duty during a bank robbery.

"Next he's yakking how our home was burglarized and Dad's badge was stolen and never recovered. Then the boss puts his hand on my shoulder and asks me if I know Commander Keith Bushey."

"Do you?"

Roy shook his head as he reached into the fridge, pulled out a beer, and popped the cap. "I've heard of him, but never met him." He took a long swig from the brown bottle.

"Commander Bushey is an avid collector of police badges. He spotted an LAPD badge for sale on an online memorabilia site. Once the commander was sure it was authentic, he bought it."

Amber felt her eyes widen. "Oh my gosh. Was it your dad's?"

Roy grinned and nodded. "It sure was."

"Where is it? Did you bring it home?"

Roy reached into the pocket of his tan cargo shorts and pulled out the badge.

Amber pretended not to notice tears forming in her husband's eyes.

"The chief said I can wear it on my uniform." He handed her the metal shield. "I only wish my mom lived long enough to know the badge was recovered."

Amber rubbed her finger across the raised image of the Los Angeles City Hall on the heavy metal. "She knows, Roy. She knows."

3

ROY

Roy hummed to himself as he prepared for his academy classmates coming over for the ball game. Amber would be at work at her job as a neonatal ICU nurse. He was glad she'd be out of the house. She had no interest in baseball, and if history held true, he and his boys would throw back a few brews. They'd probably get loud and bawdy. Amber didn't need to be around for that.

The doorbell rang, and Roy hurried to answer it. Two of his best friends stood there: Luke Tremont, and Dawson "Speakeasy" Burnside.

"Yo, Padre," Luke said, shaking Roy's hand. "Let's hope the boys in blue can pull off this final playoff game and get their asses into the World Series."

Roy opened the door farther as his friends entered. Speakeasy held a case of cold beers.

"Come to the kitchen. I'll get these beers on ice," Roy said. The group followed him to where Amber sat at the kitchen table, looking at emails on her computer. As soon as the trio came in, she closed her laptop.

"Honey," Roy said. "You remember Luke and Speakeasy."

Amber stood. "Of course I do. It's good to see you again."

Speakeasy eyed her scrubs. "Looks like you've got to work tonight," he drawled with his southern accent.

Amber smiled. "Yeah, it's a good thing I don't follow baseball."

Both Luke and Speakeasy gasped and affected horrified faces, and then stared at Roy.

He laughed and shrugged. "She has many other fine qualities," he said, smiling at his wife.

Amber beamed back at Roy. "I've got to finish getting ready." She grabbed her computer. "I'll leave you boys to your ball game and beers. Have fun." She looked at Roy. "I'll let you know when I'm leaving for work."

Roy smiled with appreciation. She knew his friends would be reluctant to cut loose with her around.

A few minutes later his other friends, Fast Eddie and Jeremy "Cookie" Cook, arrived. The group went out to the back patio where Roy had an outdoor kitchen equipped with a television.

The pregame show droned in the background while the five friends popped the tops off their beers, cracked peanut shells, and caught up on LAPD gossip.

Fast Eddie took a long pull on his beer. "Hey, did you guys hear about Jerry McMillan?"

"Yeah," Cookie said. "A couple days ago. News said it was a hunting accident."

Fast Eddie nodded. "They found his body in Idaho—said he'd been dead about a month. Somebody shot him and left him in the forest."

Roy popped open another beer. "I knew he was on vacation and going north to do some hunting. They didn't find the shooter?"

Fast Eddie shook his head. "Nope. I guess that happens a lot during hunting season."

"I looked it up," said Cookie. "On average, ninety people a year get killed while hunting." He sighed. "Jerry was a great guy and a good cop."

Luke spoke up. "Yeah, and Paulo Delgado. He ate his gun last week."

Roy turned to stare at his friend. "You're kidding, right? He and his wife just had a baby. He was set to go to SWAT on the next transfer. Why go to the trouble to get on the SWAT Team if you're just going to off yourself?"

Luke shrugged. "No clue. Whatever the reason I'm sorry that he didn't feel that he could reach out to any of us."

"Let's say a quick prayer for our fallen brothers," Speakeasy offered. "Then we'll get down to talkin' about baseball and women—not necessarily in that order."

4

AMBER

Amber returned to the bedroom while laughter came from the kitchen. She was glad Roy's friends were there to keep him preoccupied.

After tossing her laptop onto the bed, she went into the bathroom and retrieved the completed pregnancy test wand she'd hidden in the cabinet under the sink. She gazed at the plus sign displayed in the window.

"No doubt about it," she whispered. "You're having a baby." She lifted her gaze to stare at herself in the mirror. A baby. She was having a baby. Roy would not be happy. A wave of nausea rolled over her, but she tamped it down.

She heard Roy and his friends move from the kitchen to the patio. They were lightheartedly debating the skills of the Dodgers' starting pitcher. Amber listened as they made a side bet on how many innings he would last.

Listening to their banter, her mind was distracted from her pregnancy worries. She stood in front of the bathroom mirror, fiddling with her hair. With the window cracked open a few inches, the voices outside could easily be heard.

"Roy, have things settled at work now that the Seth Farley investigation is done?" The speaker was Luke Tremont.

"I guess. After testifying that Farley missed the gun when he searched the pimp, and then how Farley forgot his own gun one day and didn't tell me till we'd hit the bricks, the Board of Rights panel saw him as a serial fuckup. One captain shook his head as I told them how I'd driven Seth to his house to retrieve his gun." Roy grabbed a peanut, shelled it, and tossed it in his mouth.

"Apparently, the academy is telling the recruits the story of how Seth missed a gun on the pimp we arrested, and how the pimp tried to kill us on the way to the jail. My last two probationers have been extremely thorough when I tell them to search suspects for weapons."

"Thank God for the bullet-resistant barrier in the black and white," Luke said. "Where's Farley now? Anybody know what he's doing?"

Cookie snorted. "Probably hiring a high-dollar attorney to sue the city to get his job back."

Speakeasy popped the top of another beer. "Who gives a shit? Let's talk about something important—like the new hot female detective assigned to the burglary table at Wilshire."

The group collectively groaned.

"What is it with you, Speakeasy? Your mind is constantly on women."

Amber thought the speaker was Fast Eddie.

"Nothing wrong with that," Speakeasy replied. "It's sure

better than worrying about the probationer who almost got the Padre killed."

Someone shushed the conversation.

The next thing she heard was the national anthem and the scraping of chairs on cement.

Curious, she stepped to the bedroom window and peeked between the curtains to see all five men facing the television with their hands over their hearts.

She returned to the bathroom to brush her teeth. In the background, she listened as the men outside discussed the game.

Once again Speakeasy brought the conversation to the new detective who'd transferred into his division.

"I'm telling you this chick is *so* fine. She has thick long dark hair, and a body that won't quit—and her ass coulda been sculpted by Michelangelo."

"How long before you nail her?" Amber recognized Cookie's voice.

"I don't know. Might take a while—maybe a week or two."

The other men laughed.

Considering the tawdry turn the conversation had taken, Amber wondered if more noise would make her presence nearby more apparent.

"You might want to find out if she's married—if you care," Luke said. "And haven't you learned it's a bad idea to get involved with somebody at work?"

"Who are you—my grandmother?" Speakeasy asked.

"No, I'm the guy who had to bail you out of several jams after you'd screwed one too many badge bunnies who thought they would be *Mrs.* Speakeasy."

"Talking about nice asses, do you guys remember the

brunette bunny with the bubble butt who was always at cop parties?" The voice was Roy's.

Amber's heart raced as she listened.

"You're gonna have to be more specific than that, Padre. There were a lot of badge bunnies at the cop parties."

Amber recognized Speakeasy's drawl.

"Her name started with an *N*. Natalie? Nadia?" Roy's voice trailed off.

"Oh, you're talking about Nookie Nadine."

"Trust Cookie to remember her name," Roy said.

"She was a gal worth remembering. One of the best blow jobs I've ever had came from Nadine."

"So, Padre, why are you asking about her?" Luke asked. "*You* never did her. Unless you lied to us. You were married to Jennifer back then."

"No biggie. All this talk of badge bunnies got me wondering what happened to her. I remember she got knocked up. Didn't she think one of you guys was the father?"

"Ha! Any of us, excluding you Padre, could have been the baby daddy. Nadine was like the community bicycle—everybody got a ride."

Amber's ears burned at the callous way the men outside talked.

"What's with the questions about Nookie?" The drawled question came from Speakeasy.

"I was wondering whatever happened with her. I mean, did she have the baby?"

There was silence. Amber wished she could see what the men were doing.

It was Fast Eddie who spoke. His voice was low, but Amber could still make out his words. "Pretty much anybody at Seventy-Seventh Division who'd screwed Nadine kicked in twenty-five bucks. That gave her plenty of money to have the problem taken care of."

"Yeah," said Luke. "We didn't mention it to you because you weren't ever with her. I never saw her with a kid afterward, so I assume that was the end of it."

"Yeah, probably so," Roy mumbled.

There was another bout of silence.

"Come on, guys. Let's watch the game. I'll start the chow," Roy said.

Hearing more than she'd bargained for, Amber knelt in front of the toilet and threw up.

5

ROY

Roy left his guests reminiscing about the good old days when they were young policemen who lived for nothing more than action on the streets and action between the sheets.

Going down the hallway, he heard vomiting coming from the master bathroom. *Amber must be sicker than she let on.*

Worried, he marched to the closed bathroom door, gave one quick rap, and then opened the door. "Amber? Are you okay?"

His wife, startled, looked at him with wide eyes. Her glance darted to something on the counter.

Roy saw a pink stick laying on a paper towel. Within seconds, his mind made the connection between the item on the counter and Amber's nausea.

He snatched the stick and held it in the air. "What is this? Please don't tell me you're pregnant."

Amber got up from her knees and grabbed a tissue to wipe her mouth. "I think the evidence proves that I *am* going to have a baby." A baby wasn't in their plans, and yet Amber felt excited and protective of the life they'd created, but she worried about Roy's reaction.

Roy blew out an exasperated breath. "How did you let this happen? I didn't want this—and you knew it."

The apprehension she'd carried about Roy's feelings was well placed. "I didn't exactly plan to get pregnant. I guess our birth control failed."

"You expect me to believe that?" Every word dripped with disbelief.

"Yes, I do. Because that's the truth."

Roy realized conversation on the patio had stopped. He clamped his lips tightly together and lowered his voice. "This is just great." He jerked his head toward the backyard. "I'm sure they heard everything. I can't deal with you right now."

He turned on his heel and began to walk out, then paused. "I came in here to see if you wanted me to make you a burger to take to work." He glanced at the toilet. "Clearly you can't keep food down."

Roy started to leave the room but turned and shook his finger at her and dropped his voice to a whispered hiss. "I'll tell you one thing. Don't get too attached to that baby. You're not having it." He stormed out.

6
____

SETH

Seth Farley was a man on a mission. He'd been maligned, mistreated, and fired. But those experiences only fueled the fire to prove wrong those who had judged him and dismissed him. He'd bring honor back to his name if it was the last thing he did.

Killing his very first training officer, Jerry McMillan, in the Idaho forest and getting away with it had only strengthened Seth's resolve. He was on the right path. The senior officer had bad-mouthed Seth after his first week at North Hollywood Division and set into motion the negative perception that had ruined his career.

"McMillan and Delgado make you two for two, Farley," he said to himself. "I wonder how long it will take those idiots at the LAPD to figure out I've come back for my revenge."

Seth looked over at Roy's academy class graduation

photo. The baby-faced officers stood on risers like an armed choir. Jerry McMillan's face was crossed off with a red marker, and Paulo Delgado's face was covered in red too. He looked at his next victims in the picture. Following them around for the past few weeks, he'd learned where they lived, where they went, and their schedules.

Thanks to his military experience as a cyber warfare officer he could easily hack into almost any computer. His specialized skills made planning the demise of his enemies much easier.

Tonight, with any luck, one of his biggest targets would fall. Seth wanted to make his detractors understand the humiliation he'd felt during their untruthful and disparaging testimony during his board of rights. Being murdered by the rookie officer they'd labeled as incompetent was the ultimate disgrace—at least in cop world.

With his truck loaded and ready to go it was time to pull off the big plan for tonight.

7

———

AMBER

It didn't take Amber long to gather up her things and head to work. Her emotions fluctuated between shock, disbelief, and disappointment with her husband's attitude about her pregnancy.

The farther she got from the house, the more she got angry. In the safety and isolation of her car, she talked to herself as though Roy were riding shotgun next to her.

"Who in the hell do you think you are to tell me I'm not having *our* baby? It's not my fault that our birth control failed. I know you've got some hang-up about being a parent—worrying we'll never spend enough time with our baby, but you're going have to get over it, pal. We're going to be parents."

It was easy to be outspoken and brave in her car, but in

front of Roy she wondered if she'd be able to say any of those things.

She pulled her car into her favorite parking space at a lot next door to the hospital. The row where she regularly parked was at the edge of the lot bordering a wide boulevard. It was rare for anyone else to park in the spaces intended for a defunct gym.

Amber had to assume anyone parking this far out was doing the same thing as her—avoiding someone parking next to them and denting their car or chipping the paint. Roy had recently bought Amber a luxury SUV for their first anniversary, and she did everything she could to keep her expensive gift pristine.

With a heavy sigh, she gathered up her belongings and trudged toward the hospital where sick and tiny babies needed her.

8

———

ROY

Before it had even started, Roy's night had tanked—and it was Amber's fault. Hers and that baby growing inside her. For the briefest instant, he pictured how Amber's belly would expand and, months later, how she'd look holding a chubby, bald baby.

Stop it. Don't go there. Don't turn the coagulating tissue in your wife's uterus into a baby. That road leads to the danger—making those cells a person...a part of you.

He returned to the patio. His friends gave him questioning looks. But what could he say? He and Amber had agreed that they wouldn't have children, and now she was knocked up, and he was pissed about it.

They already knew he was mad. He could tell because they wouldn't look him in the eye. Instead, they appeared fascinated by the ball game and shelling peanuts.

Roy didn't offer an explanation about the words he and his wife had exchanged, and the earlier jovial atmosphere on the patio dissipated. The guys sat somberly studying the game and guzzling beer.

Roy did his best to get their spirits back up, but the cheer was sucked out of their party. At the seventh inning stretch, everyone had eaten, and the game was tied. Fast Eddie, Speakeasy, and Cookie said they were leaving—tomorrow was a workday, blah, blah, blah.

Roy had no doubt the trio would head off to a bar to finish watching the game where the atmosphere wasn't tainted. He figured Luke had drawn the short straw to stay with Roy at least until the game ended.

The Dodgers' gameplay began to suffer as if they felt the toxic mood in Roy's backyard. After four extra innings, they wound up losing the game and their shot at the World Series.

Luke helped Roy gather up the trash and bottles on the patio, and the two men went inside the house.

Luke sat at the kitchen table while Roy put the remaining food away and rinsed off the few dishes they'd used.

"I couldn't help but overhear you and Amber talking before she left for work. I'm here if you'd like to talk."

Roy shook his head and waved a dismissive hand.

"Amber and I agreed before we ever got married—no kids. My dad was a cop, and he was never home. I don't want that life for my kids. She knew how I felt, and yet, somehow, miraculously, she's wound up pregnant."

"Man, I get it," Luke said. "I'm not saying you have to have the child. On the other hand, it's an important decision. You need to weigh your options." He paused. "Don't take this the wrong way, but consider how Amber feels."

Roy turned from the sink toward his friend. "Luke you're my buddy, and I know you mean well. You've got three kids who you love to death. But that's not the life I want, and Amber agreed to it. I think you should understand and respect my being upset."

Luke held up his hand in a defensive manner and nodded. "You're right, Padre. It's not my business, but give it a few days before you make any rash decisions."

Luke got up and stood in front of his friend. "I'm going to tell you something that no one other than Rhonda and I know. "Our first two kids were planned. But Tammy wasn't. We had just bought our house, and the last thing we needed was another child." A grin filled his face. "But let me tell you, my little Tammy is the kid that brings the most smiles to my face. What I'm trying to say is that we briefly considered terminating the pregnancy. But if we'd done that, I would've missed out on so much. Just something to think about, pal."

Roy looked into his friend's eyes. He saw sincerity, concern, and welled-up tears. "Hey man, that was the right decision for you and Rhonda. She's a great mom, and you're a great dad." Roy offered Luke another beer.

Luke shook his head.

"But Rhonda is home with the kids all day," Roy continued. "Amber has a career she loves, and I don't think she'll give it up. That's not fair to the child, because you and I both know the long and wacky hours a cop puts in, even when they're not working—they're watching, waiting, and preparing for the worst."

"It doesn't have to be like that," Luke said. He held out his hand. "But I understand. If you want to reach out, I'm here for you."

Roy shook his friend's hand and pulled him in for a hug. "You're speaking from concern and from your heart, Luke, and I appreciate it. You're a good friend."

Luke took a step back from his friend. "Okay, Padre. I'm going home to my family, and I'll talk to you soon. If you need to talk, give me a call."

"I appreciate it."

Roy walked Luke out to his car and waved as his friend pulled away from the curb.

He turned and started toward the front door of his house when the crack of gunfire filled the night. Down the street, Luke's pickup truck crashed into the back of a vehicle parked at the curb.

9

SETH

Right after he shot Luke Tremont, Seth drove out of the foothills to the heart of Northridge. He glanced at his watch —a little after ten. He used an app on his phone to listen to the LAPD radio traffic in Devonshire Division. As expected, officers from every station in the valley were responding to the shooting in Porter Ranch. The original call came out as "officer down."

A few patrol units running code three with their lights and sirens blaring passed Seth's pickup going in the opposite direction. Like any law-abiding citizen, he steered his truck to the side of the road until the black and whites zoomed past.

With plenty of time to kill, he cruised into a drive-thru and picked up a burger and fries. Killing made him hungry.

He grinned as he headed to Northridge Hospital. For weeks, he'd followed Amber Buckner. Long enough to know where she parked her car. She was supposed to get off work at 4:00 a.m. but she often didn't leave until almost 5:30. He hoped she was on time today.

His heart pounded anticipating the next step of his plan —the riskiest move he'd taken yet.

Seth pulled his truck into a spot a few spaces away from Amber's SUV parked in a space edging a major street. The location was at least a football field away from the hospital— maybe more.

As he ate his burger, he wondered why Roy's wife kept her car so far away from her job. She might want to drop a few pounds and figured the walk would do her good. Although, from what he remembered, she didn't look like she needed to lose weight.

The area was perfect. Enough distance away that hospital cameras wouldn't pick up his activity and an enclosed bus stop blocked any video from the 7-Eleven across the street.

Amber wouldn't get off work for three hours. With time to kill, he set his phone with an alarm to wake him and reclined his seat for a catnap.

10

KAREN

Karen Watson couldn't believe her luck. First, she'd made the semifinal cut in a contest that KABR television in Los Angeles was conducting to find a new reporter. She had one week from today to wow the station's general manager and the KABR viewers.

Her second bit of luck occurred when she nabbed the biggest story of the day—an LAPD officer shot while off duty the night before.

Her producer handed her a sheet with the known facts and told her to head to the hospital. "You and Brian hustle your asses down there and get a live shot. The wife of the slain officer is supposed to be there. A press conference is scheduled in an hour."

Karen and her cameraman, Brian, headed out in a news van. She liked Brian. She'd worked with him last week during the first phase of the contest. He knew the media business and in only a week had taught her a lot.

On the way to Mercy Community Hospital, Brian told her he'd get her there in time for the live shot at 5:00 a.m.

She had her doubts they'd make it to the hospital in time but reminded herself to trust her cameraman. He'd worked at the station for fifteen years and understood the traffic.

On her end, she'd been in LA for two years after finishing college in Iowa. She was working as a waitress in Hollywood when she overheard two customers discussing the KABR competition. She'd applied for the contest and was accepted.

Brian found a great spot and got Karen set up for the press conference. There was little time to waste.

She couldn't believe how many reporters were there. A handful of bigwigs from the LAPD and the mayor stood before the cameras.

The mayor displayed situational grief and spoke of the brave and noble police officers in Los Angeles. He then introduced the chief of police who summarized the shooting and brought up a lieutenant from Robbery Homicide Division.

"Good morning. I'm Lieutenant Sergio Solis. These are the facts as we know them. I remind you the investigation is ongoing and things could change. I'll take questions once I've read my statement. On Sunday evening an off-duty Los Angeles police officer was killed as he left a friend's house in Porter Ranch. The victim was traveling eastbound on Elmville Court when he was shot and lost control of his vehicle. He crashed into the back of a panel van parked at the curb.

"The officer was transported to Mercy Community Hospital where he succumbed to his injuries.

"The suspect is still at large, and we don't have any suspect information. We anticipate that Elmville Court will be closed for another hour or two." The lieutenant looked out over the crowd. "I'll take a few questions."

Karen watched as a well-known brunette reporter called out to the lieutenant. "Sir, there's a rumor going around that last night's victim is the third LAPD officer killed in the last six months—*and* all three deceased officers knew one another. Can you confirm that?"

Solis shook his head. "The Los Angeles police department has lost three officers within the last couple of months. At this time, it appears to be a coincidence. One officer was killed in a hunting accident in Idaho. The second officer passed due to one of the biggest dangers in law enforcement: suicide. Last night's incident does not seem to be related to either of those deaths."

A male reporter from a rival station shouted from the back of the group of reporters. "Can you confirm the three victims knew each other—and, if so, will the department provide security details for the friends of those victims?"

"I'm not prepared to discuss that."

Karen raised her hand.

Solis gave her a curt nod.

"Karen Watson from KABR. Is there anything in either of the other two officers' deaths to suggest foul play was involved?"

"At this time, the three deaths appear to be unrelated."

"Yes, sir," Karen said. "But that wasn't my question. In the other two deaths were there any indications of foul play?"

The lieutenant flashed her a look of irritation. "Both incidents occurred in other jurisdictions, and the investigations were conducted by outside agencies."

Other reporters shouted questions, but the lieutenant held up his hand. "When we have more information we will update you. Thank you."

Karen hated the fact she wasn't able to get any new information from Lieutenant Solis. To make an impression for the contest she'd have to find another angle to the story.

The mayor and police personnel shuffled inside the hospital. Through the large glass windows in the lobby, she watched as the group gathered around a man whose face was pinched with misery. Blood stained his khaki cargo pants and Wounded Warrior T-shirt.

"I bet that's the dead guy's friend," Karen told Brian. "Come on." She took a few marching steps toward the hospital entrance.

Brian grabbed her arm. "They won't let you talk to him. Let's wait until he goes home. You'll be close to the shooting scene, and we can get a few neighbor interviews."

"Good idea. You're teaching me well," she said, smiling.

The man in the blood-covered clothes tried to make his way to the exit, but arriving uniformed officers and cops in plain clothes stopped him. Handshakes and hugs were exchanged.

Through her earpiece, Karen heard the producer advising they wanted her to do a quick live-shot tease for the next hour of news.

Brian turned on the camera light as seconds were counted down in her ear.

"Good morning. This is Karen Watson at Mercy Community Hospital..."

PART II

11

———

SETH

Hours later Seth jerked awake as the alarm went off. He lifted his head and scanned the darkness.

Amber's car still sat three spaces away from his truck. Their vehicles were the only ones in this parking lot. This early in the morning the streets were nearly deserted.

The only thing that had changed during his nap was that a transient had curled up on a bus bench about thirty feet from Amber's car.

He'd have to take care of that, he thought as he raised his seat to its normal position.

Seth exited his truck, and entered the rear cab, and closed the door. He'd folded the back seats upright, so there was room to hold equipment and change clothes. After removing his shirt and jeans, he donned his LAPD uniform. He'd kept enough of his duty gear to fool any civilian into thinking he was a legitimate officer.

The item obviously missing was his badge. The department took it from him when they fired him. But he didn't worry. He'd slip on his uniform jacket. Anyone who noticed would think he hadn't taken the time to remove his badge from his shirt and pin it to the outside of his coat.

Next, he made sure he had all the components he needed when confronting Amber. During his preparation, he realized he had what he needed to render the bum at the bus stop useless as a witness. He was set. Now to wait for Amber.

It was a quarter to four. He'd better take care of the homeless guy while he had the chance. After filling a syringe with pentobarbital, he glanced around the parking lot and saw no one. He left his truck and walked to the sheltered bus stop where the transient slept on the bench.

From two feet away, Seth could smell the odor of alcohol wafting from the man who could be thirty or seventy years old. The drunk, lying on his side, wore a stained UCLA sweatshirt. A filthy red plaid blanket covered his legs. An empty bottle of Thunderbird wine rested against the man's chest.

In one swift movement, Seth rammed the needle of his syringe into the bum's upper arm and gave him the full contents. "No hard feelings, man. You're just collateral damage."

The transient slept through the whole episode.

Seth capped the needle and slipped it into his pocket. Out of the corner of his eye, he caught movement from the parking lot.

Roy's wife walked at a brisk pace across the deserted outer

edges of the asphalt lot. Was she walking fast because she was cold, or did she fear being attacked? Either way, Seth hoped his uniform would lower her guard.

From his other jacket pocket, he extracted a cloth from a plastic food bag.

Amber's gaze paused on his truck parked three spaces from her vehicle. Then she homed in on him leaning over the drunk.

Seth made a show of talking to the unconscious man, then heartily patted the transient on the shoulder. Straightening, he locked eyes with his prey.

He took out his cell phone as if checking a message and activated the app that broadcast police radio transmissions. Putting the device in his pocket, he turned up the volume. He wanted Amber to think he had a cop radio under his jacket.

He walked toward her.

She was six feet from her SUV when he called out to her. "Ma'am, can I speak to you for a minute?"

Amber's steps slowed as her gaze skimmed his uniform. He must have passed muster because she continued to her car. He positioned himself at the back of his truck bed.

"Ma'am, were you in this parking lot around this time yesterday?"

She hesitated, then stopped at the rear of her car. "Yes."

Seth walked to her. "There was a hit and run—" He sprang into action, slapping a meaty gloved hand over her nose and mouth.

She tried to scream and fight against the cloth soaked in an inhalant anesthetic but instead sagged into his arms.

Not taking time to look around, he dragged her over to the passenger side of his truck and dumped her on the seat.

He slid her purse from her shoulder and activated the lock before he slammed the door closed.

Seth pawed through the bag until he found what he was looking for—her key ring. He grunted in approval seeing less than ten keys on the ring—and only two of them looked like they were for a house. He removed them and dropped the remaining keys into the purse.

Jogging to the transient, Seth gave a satisfied smile. The bum's lips had already started turning blue. He lifted the disgusting blanket and tucked the bag underneath.

He darted back to the truck and climbed into the driver's seat. Glancing at the woman slumped next to him, he reached across her body and secured her with the seat belt. When he pushed her upper torso against the door, she looked like a carpooler catching more sleep.

After backing the truck out of the parking stall, he headed out into the darkness.

12

AMBER

Amber's head bounced against something hard. She tried to get herself to open her eyes, but she was so tired. Behind closed lids, she remembered something important had happened. Something bad.

As she bumped against cold hardness, she realized her forehead was banging on a vehicle window.

Her skin became clammy, and her stomach roiled. "I'm going to be sick," she murmured.

The car slowed, and someone reached across her body and opened the door as the vehicle rolled to a stop.

"Don't puke in my truck." A strong hand pushed on her left shoulder, forcing her upper torso outside into the predawn chill.

Amber inhaled, hoping the fresh air would quell her nausea.

"Well? Are you going to puke or not?"

Amber cracked her eyes a sliver and saw a policeman at the wheel. It all came back to her. His hand over her mouth. The chemically sweet-smelling cloth. This man had kidnapped her.

Her stomach roiled again, and she threw up into the gutter. She waited for the next wave of nausea but it never arrived. She lifted her hand to wipe her lips and gasped when she realized her wrists were handcuffed.

The man beside her grabbed her left arm and pulled her back into the truck. "Grab the door and close it."

"I can't. I can't reach the handle being bound like this."

"Bullshit." He squeezed her bicep, causing pain. "Get it closed. We've got places to go." He waited for a few seconds. "Do it!"

Leaning precariously to her right, she grabbed the armrest and slammed the door shut.

He accelerated into the increasing morning traffic.

Groggy, and with her heart pounding, she looked at the man next to her. Amber recognized the uniform, duty belt, and boots she'd seen her husband wear many times. A cop had kidnapped her. Why? Was it a sick joke? What was happening?

He saw her panic. "You have nothing to worry about. I won't hurt you. I know you're scared but everything will be fine."

"Yeah, right," she mumbled.

"No. I'm serious."

Amber placed her right arm across her stomach and pretended to rub her ailing belly, when in reality she was positioning her hand to undo the seat belt. Once she got unbuckled—disoriented or not—she'd open the door and leap out.

The good thing was her abductor stayed on surface streets, which meant that his driving speeds were lower and she might have more opportunities to flee.

As if sensing her intent, he took his hand and pushed her arms away from the clasp of the restraint. "Don't get any ideas. I don't intend on hurting you, but if you try to escape—whatever happens is on you."

The eastern horizon was showing a light band of gray. Before long the sun would rise. Amber took hope she could signal to other motorists that she needed help.

Her hopes died when he pulled into a quiet neighborhood of small homes in North Hollywood. He hit a button on his sun visor. The garage door raised on a house ahead of them. He turned into the driveway and drove his pickup inside, clicking the button for the door to shut.

He came to the passenger side of the truck and opened the rear door.

She heard him rummaging around, and then the sound of ripping startled her.

He slammed the rear door, then opened hers.

Before she could say or do anything, he slapped a strip of duct tape across her lips.

"Undo your seat belt."

Amber considered not following his order.

"I *said*, release the seat belt." His gaze bore into hers.

She pressed the lever. The securing device whirred across her torso to its resting position by the seat.

Her captor grabbed her arm, yanked her from the truck,

and propelled her unsteady feet through a door leading into the house.

He pulled her through a laundry room, down a short hallway, and into the living room, where he pushed her onto a couch. He grabbed her feet and expertly secured them with a thick zip tie.

"I'm sure you're scared. But I told you, I don't want to hurt you. You're just collateral damage from a huge injustice."

She rolled her eyes at him.

"You're a brassy broad, aren't you? That's what I don't understand. I'm being nice to you. I'm telling you that you've got nothing to fear from me, yet you're displaying a shitty attitude. You don't believe me. I don't tolerate negative mindset. While you're lying here, you'd better adjust your thinking.

"In the meantime, I've got good news, and I've got bad news. Which do you want first?" He laughed when he saw fear flash in her eyes.

"The good news is we won't be here long."

Amber fixed her gaze on his face. Something she didn't want to hear was coming next.

He sat next to her on the sofa and removed his hand from his jacket pocket. "The bad news is"—he seized her arms, extended them, and stuck her with the needle—"I'm drugging you to keep you quiet." Done with his injection, he rose from the couch.

Tears slid down her cheeks.

"What's the matter? You're a nurse. You should be able to take a shot without crying."

Amber growled at him and swung her legs, attempting to kick him.

He sidestepped to avoid her bound feet. "What the hell is wrong with you?"

She jerked her head at her arm.

"Jeez, relax. It's just light anesthesia normally used before surgery." He chuckled. "Don't worry, I won't cut on you. I just need you quiet for a while."

The man marched to a trash can in the corner and tossed the used syringe inside.

"One thing I forgot to tell you is that I expect your full cooperation. I know about your folks living in Scottsdale. If you disappoint me, we'll drive straight to Arizona and you'll watch me slit your parents' throats. Do I make myself clear?"

Amber nodded with a heavy sigh. The injection was taking effect. She shut her eyes while tears traversed the side of her face and disappeared into her hair.

13

ROY

Roy wanted to throw his stained clothes in the trash and take a shower. Instead, as news spread through the department of Luke's murder, more officers arrived to grieve and offer support to Roy and Luke's wife, Rhonda.

He was forced to recount the details of his best friend's death several times. After each recitation, Roy edged closer to the lobby doors. When he thought he'd finally get away, a man in a business suit approached him.

The guy towered over most of the cops. He had a lean runner's body and carried a black portfolio with the LAPD badge embossed on the front.

Roy recognized him as a detective he'd seen over the years at some police facility.

The man held out his hand. "Officer Buckner? I'm Detective Bud Johnson from RHD."

The men shook hands. The detective scanned the bustling lobby of the hospital. "I need to do a brief interview with you. We can try to find a place here, or we can go to Valley homicide and do it there. Your choice."

Roy shrugged. "I just want out of these clothes."

Johnson gave a curt nod. "I understand. Let me see what I can arrange. I'll see if they've got someplace quiet available. I'll get your story, then you can go home."

As the detective searched for a quiet place to conduct an interview, Roy pulled out his cell phone and tried to call Amber. The phone rang a couple of times and then went to voice mail.

"Hi, it's me. Call me when you get this message. It's 0530 hours."

From the information desk, Johnson waved for Roy to join him.

He trudged across the glitter-flecked floor.

"They're getting an orderly to lead us to a conference room on the second floor," the detective said. "He's supposed to be bringing you fresh clothes to wear." He eyed Roy's arms and legs. "They said they had a shower you could use too."

A half hour later, both Roy and Johnson had fresh cups of coffee and sat in black leather chairs positioned around a twelve-person conference table. Roy had showered and was wearing a pair of clean but scratchy blue scrubs that the hospital staff had found for him.

Johnson pulled out a small tape recorder and stated the date, time, location, and the fact he was interviewing Roy Buckner.

"Tell me what happened last night at your house."

Roy explained his friends had come over to watch the

baseball playoff game but saw no reason to tell the detective about the words he and Amber had exchanged. He did reveal that all his friends but Luke had left before the game was over.

"Why did they leave early?"

Roy shrugged. "Game was tied. I think the guys were bored."

"Did Luke have a falling out with anyone?"

"No. Nothing like that."

"Was everybody drinking?"

"It was the final playoff game. What do you think?"

"How many beers did you go through?"

Roy rubbed his hands across his face—an attempt to energize himself. "I have no idea. We were drinking—quite a bit. Four, maybe five bottles apiece."

Johnson nodded. "Okay." The detective leaned back in his chair. "What about Luke and his wife?" He scanned his notes. "Rhonda."

"What do you want to know?"

"Did Luke indicate to you he and Rhonda were having any marital problems?"

"No. Exactly the opposite. Luke told me how happy he was with his family."

"Was your wife at home when Luke left?"

"No. She's a nurse at Northridge Hospital. She was at work."

"Give me her number, and I'll call her later. I'll do her interview over the phone."

Nodding, he gave him Amber's cell number.

Johnson asked more questions then asked if he'd seen or heard the suspect before the shooting.

"I heard a gunshot, and then Luke plowed his car into the back end of the van. But what I *know* is a bunch of us officers—all from the same academy class—are getting whacked right and left."

Johnson leaned forward. "What do you mean?"

"Jerry McMillan went hunting in Idaho six months ago and was shot and killed. As far as I know, they never caught the shooter."

"Go on," Johnson said.

"The second guy was Paulo Delgado. He was found dead in his car in the parking lot of a bar in the Valley. They said it was suicide, but no one believes that."

"Why don't you think Delgado ate his gun?"

"Because his life and career were just coming together. He got married two years ago to his high school sweetheart, and they just had a baby. He finished in the top two percent to join SWAT and will be on the next transfer. Paulo had every reason to live."

The detective eyed Roy, assessing the credibility of his concerns. "While the deaths are troubling, it's possible it's just a horrible coincidence."

Roy turned away from him. "If that's what you want to believe, I can't change your mind. But if you ask me, somebody's systematically killing off my academy class. The department better get their head out of their ass and do something before we lose someone else."

14

SETH

He couldn't believe his plan had gone so smooth. Faster than a sailor with twenty bucks could date a hooker, Amber Buckner had bought his appearance in the parking lot. Her being off-guard had made his success possible.

Seth drove back to the Buckner house at breakneck speed. He didn't have much time. Once he entered the Buckners' neighborhood, he slowed and kept his eyes open for cops or lab techs from SID, Scientific Investigation Division. Fortunately, the crime scene was dismantled and the police personnel had left.

Knowing the detectives had released the crime scene meant the investigators were likely conducting interviews. They'd interview Roy first. When his former partner was interviewed would dictate when he might return home.

Seth drove to the entrance of the Buckners' street but

parked his truck on a more traveled road in the subdivision. His vehicle didn't stand out there. He parked near a concrete block wall of a corner house.

He hopped out of his pickup and strode down the sidewalk, still wearing his uniform. He kept his eyes lowered as though looking for something.

He got to the Buckners' house and started up the front walk.

The dog next door barked an excited alarm.

Seth used long strides to reach the front porch where he was more concealed.

"You-hoo," a high-pitched female voice called. The screen door slammed at the house next door. "Officer!"

An old woman crossed the driveway and stepped onto the porch next to him. *A nosy neighbor. God, more potential collateral damage.*

"Yes, ma'am?"

"May I help you, Officer? I'm Lula Hendricks." She turned to her yapping terrier. "Shhh, Sweeny. You hush now."

Seth eyed the hunched, birdlike woman with her white hair permed to what amounted to four inches of frizz. She resembled a giant dandelion. Her dark green sweatpants were topped by a goldenrod sweatshirt. The outfit was covered by a cow-print apron. He wondered why an old lady would be dressed before 6:00 a.m.

"I can tell you neither Roy nor Amber are at home. Ever since the excitement last night I've been watching their house. Roy went off with the ambulance. Haven't seen a sign of Amber."

"When did the detectives and lab people leave?"

"You just missed them. They didn't leave more than a half

hour ago." She shushed her dog. "Can I help you?"

"Thank you, Ms. Hendricks. I appreciate your help, but I'm here to pick up a few items for Mrs. Buckner. She isn't comfortable staying here right now."

The old woman's rheumy eyes narrowed. "Oh dear. I hope the Buckners don't move. They've been such good neighbors. Roy mows my lawn the same day he does his own. He's a prince, he is."

Seth gritted his teeth. "I'm sure he is."

"You want me to come in and pick out some outfits for Amber? I see her all the time. I know her favorite clothes."

The old lady was getting on his nerves. Seth pulled a paper from his uniform shirt pocket and waved it at her. "Won't be necessary, ma'am. Mrs. Buckner gave me a list of things to bring her."

"Hmph. All right. I can see I'm not needed here. I'll go on home. Tell Roy and Amber I'll keep watch of their house." She took a step away then stopped and narrowed her eyes. "How you going to get in?"

Seth reached into his pants pocket and withdrew the two keys he'd removed from Amber's purse. He'd wound them onto a paperclip. He held them in the air and jingled them at the old woman. "I have a set of keys."

Lula Hendricks worked her mouth, shifting her dentures. "Okay. Have a good day, sir."

"You too, ma'am."

Seth tilted his head from side to side getting the kinks out. He unlocked the door and entered. "Nosy old bat," he muttered, closing and locking the door behind him.

For the benefit of anyone who might be in the house, he called out, "Los Angeles Police Department." He hurried through the living room and the kitchen, verifying no one was there. He headed into the hallway. "Police." He cleared the bedrooms in less than a minute.

The old lady next door had alerted Seth he should bring clothing for Amber. He grabbed two overnight cases from out of the closet and opened them on the bed. He tossed a couple of pairs of jeans and some shirts he found in the dresser into the bags. Distracted by Amber's lingerie drawer, he pushed aside lascivious thoughts and selected sexy underwear and several bras. Next, he gathered sweatpants and T-shirts.

Striding into the bathroom, he found a makeup bag in a drawer. He took it, along with a brush and comb, and tossed them into the second bag. He didn't know how long he and Amber would be together, but he might as well give her the tools so she wouldn't look like crap. He zipped the bags and set them next to the bedroom door.

His efforts and haste caused beads of sweat to sprout on his forehead. Roy Buckner could walk through the door at any time.

Seth walked through the bedroom and into the bathroom where he turned on the shower. He spied a pair of satin panties in the hamper. Reaching in, he pinched the fabric together, feeling the smoothness of it rubbing against itself. His dick got hard. Reluctantly, he dropped the panties back into the hamper.

He stormed into the bedroom and yanked the bedspread, blanket, and sheet toward the foot of the bed. Minutes later, he'd divested himself of his uniform and everything beneath. Leaning forward, he sniffed at the pillow. He recoiled at the masculine odor on the pillowcase.

Seth padded around to the other side and again leaned

forward to sniff the pillow. The scent smelled like a coconut-based tropical drink. This was Amber's pillow.

He climbed onto the bed and rolled and rubbed his body all over. He thought of Amber in the satin panties he'd just held in his hands. The whole experience got him excited. He sat up and reached to bring the top sheet and blanket to cover him.

Under the bedding he touched himself, thinking of Amber and her husband making love in this very bed. The last thing he wanted to do was to shoot his wad onto the top sheet. At the point of no return, he rolled to his hands and knees and pleasured himself until he left an admirable wet spot in the center of the mattress.

Aware of the minutes ticking by, Seth jumped from the bed and jogged into the warm shower. He grabbed the bar of soap and rubbed it over his body, paying particular attention to his dick. Three minutes later he dried himself, got back into his clothes, and remade the bed.

Wheeling the two small suitcases, he went to the family room where he found a laptop sitting on the couch. Before picking up the device, he donned a pair of latex gloves. He opened the lid, and the screen filled with pictures of puppies and kittens. The display gave him confidence the device wasn't Roy's. He was relieved the computer wasn't password protected. Even with a password, he wouldn't have had any trouble hacking into the device, but bypassing security would cost him time he didn't have.

He gained access and downloaded files. When he was done, he double-checked his handiwork and closed the device.

It was time to get back to Roy's wife.

15

KAREN

After doing a report on the shooting for the morning news at six and seven, Karen and Brian almost missed Roy leaving the hospital. They'd been watching for a man wearing blood-stained clothing. Roy had changed into hospital scrubs.

Thanks to the wizardry of the internet and public records, Karen obtained Roy's address and also learned that his wife's name was Amber.

They'd waited to follow Buckner in case he was going somewhere other than to his house. Once they felt sure he was heading home, Brian increased his speed to ensure they'd reach the Buckner residence before Roy did.

"If you get Buckner talking, we'll stay as long as you need," Brian said, taking a corner too fast causing the van's tires to squeal. "But if he shuts us down, we'll try for neighbor interviews. Agreed?"

"You bet."

Minutes later, she drummed her fingers on the notebook sitting on her lap. "He'll be pissed we know where he lives. I won't have much time to approach him. I need to be in position so I can reach him before he closes the garage door."

"I'll do my best."

Buckner's pickup turned onto his street.

Karen had positioned herself behind a corner of the garage. She planned to ambush the officer as he exited his truck.

Her heart pounding, Karen watched as the vehicle bounced into the driveway. When the pickup entered the parking area, Karen was on the move, with Brian trailing her. She trotted around the tailgate to the driver's side as the big rolling door started to lower. Their movement caused the door to come to a standstill.

Buckner was exiting the truck. Before his feet hit the ground, he spun and pointed a gun at them. "Stop. Police."

Karen and Brian skidded to a halt.

Buckner eyed Karen's mic and Brian's camera. "What the hell is wrong with you people? You almost got yourselves killed." He lowered his pistol.

"I wanted to ask you a few questions."

"You're lucky I didn't shoot both of you. I have nothing to say to the media." Buckner motioned with his gun that they should back out.

"What's your reaction to last nights events?"

Buckner holstered his firearm. "I don't want to talk to you." He glared at the cameraman. "Turn that light off and get out of here."

"Was Mrs. Buckner home at the time of the shooting? Can I speak with her?"

"My wife wasn't here." Buckner extended his hand and pointed to the street. "Get out."

"Do you think Luke Tremont's death is connected to the other two LAPD officers killed in the last few months?"

Surprise flashed over Buckner's features then was replaced by a look as hard as stone. "If you continue bothering me, I'll arrest you for trespassing."

Karen didn't want to give up, but Brian turned off his cameras bright light as a signal to let it go.

"Mr. Buckner," Karen continued. "I'm just trying to do my job and keep the public informed."

"The story, in a nutshell, is that for no reason my best friend was murdered. The suspect is still out there." He pointed again. "Now, get out."

16

ROY

Roy watched the news reporter and her cameraman walk down the driveway. The throbbing in his head matched the beat of his heart as adrenaline coursed through him. "Stupid, stupid people," he said.

He pushed the button to close the garage door and entered the house.

He knew Amber wasn't at home from work yet because her parking spot was empty in their garage.

As much as he wanted out of his borrowed hospital clothes, he turned on the kitchen light and slogged to the refrigerator. He pulled out a brown bottle and popped the top.

Roy guzzled half the drink on his first hit. "Pretty pathetic, Padre. All alone swigging beer—and the sun isn't even up." He picked up the bottle and headed toward the bedroom.

He entered the hallway and paused as the hairs on the back of his neck rose.

With twenty years as a street cop as his guide, Roy listened to his gut instinct. Backing up, he stooped, set the beer on the floor, and pulled his .45 from the holster at his waist. He stepped silently to the master bedroom and used the tactical light on his pistol to do a quick peek into the room.

Satisfied no gunman was waiting to ambush him, he entered and cleared the room. He flung open the closet door and searched behind the clothes. Nothing appeared amiss. He started toward the bathroom.

Sniffing, he realized someone had recently taken a shower. The air was damp. "Amber?" He walked to the master bathroom. Empty.

He marched over to the rack and grabbed a towel. It was damp. He noted droplets of water on the door. Amber had showered but hadn't used the squeegee to clean the glass afterward as they always did.

"What the hell?" With his gun at a low ready, he moved farther to the back of the house. "Amber?"

He tiptoed to the office. His gaze scanned the room. Everything was in place. After checking the guest bedroom and another space they used as a gym, he retraced his steps in the hall.

As he walked through the den it was normal. The kitchen appeared as it always did—and yet his intuition screamed something was wrong.

He unlocked the sliding door leading to the backyard. Roy couldn't imagine his wife puttering around in the chilly darkness—especially since her car wasn't at home—but he wanted to cover all the bases.

"Amber," he called into the shadows, activating the light on his gun to scan the rear yard. No sign of her, but Mrs. Hendrick's dog, Sweeny, growled and barked through the fence.

Roy's niggling unease grew to anxiousness. He returned inside and phoned his wife. The call went to voice mail. He sent her a text. Now all he could do was wait. If he didn't hear from her soon, he'd contact the hospital and have them find her.

When he'd first arrived home, he'd been tired and defeated. Now he was wired and worried. *Why would she come here, take a shower, then leave?* It was out of character.

Roy stomped through the house, retracing his steps. He checked the doors and windows for any sign of forced entry. There was none. He bounced throughout the house like a ball careening through a pinball machine. He found himself back in the bedroom he and Amber shared. His internal radar was off the charts. His instinct said something was wrong.

He strode to the walk-in closet and turned on the light. The two carry-on travel bags they kept on the top shelf were gone. He felt like he'd been kicked in the gut. Why would she need luggage?

He looked at the hangers holding Amber's things. It didn't appear items were missing. But hell, he hardly knew what clothes hung on *his* side of the closet, much less the articles of clothing Amber owned.

He tried to think of a logical explanation of where she might go requiring suitcases. Why hadn't she told him?

What if she doesn't want you to know where she is? You jumped on her hard about the baby. She was scared and upset. Amber isn't manipulative or a game player. But was she angry enough to leave?

An idea came to him that made more sense. What if something had happened to one of her parents? They lived in Scottsdale, Arizona. If it was an emergency, she might have come home, grabbed some clothes, and hustled to the airport. She might've planned on calling or texting, but in her haste either forgot or didn't have time. It was a long shot, but he'd take it.

He whipped out his phone and searched his contacts for Amber's parents' number. Then another thought hit him.

If he called Amber's parents looking for her, and she wasn't there, he'd alert them something was wrong—or that he and Amber weren't speaking.

They'd love that. Cecilia and George Granville only tolerated Roy as their daughter's husband. George Granville had expected Amber to work at Saguaro Sunrise Hospital with him where he was the chief cardiac surgeon.

Ceci was on the board of directors of the Sunrise Foundation and had used her post to peruse through the backgrounds of eligible wealthy bachelors for their only child.

Roy's in-laws had never gotten over the fact that Amber, while on vacation in LA, had met and fallen in love with *him*. A hard-working, ass-kicking cop. Worse yet, six months later she married him.

What they thought of him didn't matter. He had to find Amber. Glancing at the clock, he saw it was 7:15 a.m. He shrugged and punched in Ceci's cell number—a number he'd never previously called.

"Hi, Ceci? This is Roy." He listened to his mother-in-law's response and rolled his eyes. "Buckner. Amber's husband." He continued on, not giving her time to talk.

"A few days ago, Amber and I were talking, and she said George's birthday is soon. She asked me to call and find out what he wants." Roy held his breath, hoping his mother-in-law would say that her husband was rushed to the hospital with an emergency.

She didn't. "Why isn't Amber calling me? I haven't heard from her in over a week. I think she's working too hard. Have you been promoted yet? If you brought in more money, Amber wouldn't have to work so many hours."

Roy sighed. He needed to get off the phone and find his wife. "I'll have her call you. Give my best to George," he said and hung up.

He had no choice but to call Amber at the hospital. He dialed the direct number to the neonatal ICU nurses' station.

His anxiety level climbed another notch when the nurse who answered advised Amber had left almost three hours ago.

"Did she say she was stopping anywhere?"

"I'm sorry. She didn't. Is anything wrong?"

"No. I guess we got our wires crossed. Thanks."

Roy disconnected the call and rubbed each of his temples, trying to dissipate his throbbing headache.

Irritated by the blue cotton scrubs he wore, he changed into his own clothing. While he dressed, he thought back to their conversation where he'd told her she'd never have the baby. He'd been too harsh and lashed out at her, blaming her for getting pregnant. She wouldn't lie about the birth control failing. He'd handled it wrong.

Eyeing the empty shelf, he realized she must have come home, packed her bags, and left him.

He tried texting her again.

I'm sorry. I was an ass. Your pregnancy caught me by surprise. I'm worried about you. Call or text me. I need to know you're okay.

He noticed her computer on the couch in the family room. Surprised she hadn't taken it with her, he hoped the device might give a clue to his wife's location.

He sat on the couch and opened the laptop. "If you're Amber and mad at me," he muttered, "where would you go?" He considered Amber's friends, but she had no one close. She'd join a few girls after work for a glass of wine, but he felt confident Amber wouldn't confide to any of them about marriage problems.

Maybe Ceci was lying. Maybe Amber had emailed her mother before she left the house. He pulled up her contact list. As he scrolled through the names of various friends, businesses, and work associates, one name jumped out at him.

"Seth Farley? Why the hell is the name of my former probationary officer in my wife's contacts?"

17

AMBER

Fastened into the passenger seat of her captor's pickup truck, Amber willed away the spinning in her head and stopped her stomach from churning and gurgling. She did *not* want to vomit again.

The man next to her had no qualms about kidnapping and drugging her. He was singing along to throbbing rap music on the radio.

She kept her eyes closed and slumped over to lean against the window. She tried to organize her thoughts, but as soon as she got an idea it fizzled out of her brain. She clung to the overriding impression she had to get out of this mess and save herself.

"Hey, you awake?"

Amber frowned, not wanting to open her eyes and fought

a wave of nausea. She didn't want to interact with this monster who had kidnapped her.

He jabbed her in her left arm. "Wake up. Gonna be there before long. I expect you to walk on your own two feet. I won't carry your ass like I did at the house." He shook his head. "Tsk tsk tsk. You must not drink or get high. I gave you a light shot and you crashed like a Hyundai on the freeway."

Amber tried to nod but wasn't sure if she'd completed the movement. He'd injected her with some kind of drug. What would it do to the baby? A whirring noise and the glass moving along her temple made her realize he was lowering the truck window. Cold air blasted her. She recoiled and sat straighter in her seat.

"How do you feel?"

Amber raised her hands and rubbed them over her face to wake herself. Wait. Her hands. They were free! New energy coursed through her veins.

No. No. Don't let him see your excitement or he'll tie your arms again.

"Forget any big ideas just because your hands are free and there's no tape on your mouth. I had to do that in case we got stopped. We're so close to our destination I'm not worried we'll be pulled over now."

Amber forced her eyes open and looked out into the twilight before dawn. Lights blinked out in the distance, evidence of dwellings.

At least he hadn't bound her hands and feet again. She didn't know where she was, but the twinkling in the dark, although far away, gave her hope of a possible escape. One thing for sure, she'd have to let him think she was so frightened that she wouldn't try to get away. Who was she trying to kid? She *was* terrified. But not to the point where she wouldn't run if given a chance.

The truck jostled along a rocky dirt road between yucca trees and dried tumbleweeds. The headlights cut a wide path in the darkness. Before too long a small windowless structure built out of concrete blocks came into view. Attached to the side of the building was a wooden carport.

"Here we are," the man said. He pulled in front of the flat-roofed hovel and turned off the engine. "Like I said, don't think about trying to run. There are houses out there, but although they appear closer they're miles away. There's nothing out here. Even if you took off walkin', you'd come across a rattler or a pack of coyotes. Mountain lions roam out here too. There's no phone service, and nobody to hear you scream."

Amber nodded and opened her door.

"And if the animals don't get you, I will." He lifted his shirt showing her a pistol in a holster on his hip.

"I understand," she slurred.

"Get out and grab your luggage. It's in the cab behind your seat."

Unsteady, she slid out of the passenger side of the truck and stood on her own feet. Holding onto the truck, she shuffled to the rear passenger door. She grasped the handle to steady herself, opened the door, and pulled out her suitcases.

He'd grabbed his duffel bag and stood at the front of the squat building to unlock the door. He pushed it open and motioned her inside.

Using the two extended handles of her luggage for

support, she inched her way across the dirt to a cement pad that served as a porch of sorts. She didn't have the strength or balance to lift the suitcases over the threshold.

The man lifted and pushed them on their wheels into the dwelling.

The interior smelled dank and dusty. She couldn't see in the inky darkness.

He entered with his flashlight and cast it around the room.

Amber swallowed. The shack was hardly habitable. Cheap linoleum squares covered the floor. There was a cot against a far wall. An old wooden table was centered to the left of the door on a rectangular piece of gold shag carpet along with two chairs. The wall to the right was taken by a workbench holding two buckets—presumedly used as a sink. There was no sign of a bathroom. "You can't possibly be thinking of staying here," she said.

The man gave her a maniacal grin. "What? You don't fancy your new home?" He closed the door and secured the four locks.

He strode to the table and reached his hand underneath. Within seconds there was a noise. The dining set lifted from the floor along with the ugly rug.

Amber gasped and took a step backward. "Oh," she said. From where she stood, she could see stairs leading into the ground.

He made a sweeping flourish with his arm, indicating she should embark down. "Notice how the lights come on when the table is raised? Go on. I think you'll appreciate the accommodations below more than these here."

Nervous, Amber shot him a look.

"Don't worry, I'm coming too."

Scared she was walking into the depths of hell, Amber moved reluctantly to the opening and started down the steps.

18

———

ROY

Roy sat on his couch with Amber's computer on his lap. He couldn't believe what he was reading. In the trash folder, he'd found several emails between his former rookie partner, Seth Farley, and Amber.

The first one read:

Dear Mrs. Buckner,

Thank you for reaching out to me via Facebook. I was surprised to hear from you and wondered if I was being set up.

You sounded as upset and disbelieving as my mother was with the outcome of my probationary time with your husband, Roy.

I appreciate you telling me Roy is demanding and overbearing with unrealistic expectations. It bolstered my self-esteem that his perceptions of my abilities at work might be more about him than me.

Again, I thank you, and I wish you the best. And if you ever need someone to talk to, I'm always available. I've included my phone number below my name.

Take care,

S. Farley

"This is a crock of BS." Roy clicked on the next email from Farley.

Hi Amber,

(Thanks for telling me I could call you Amber.) I was shocked when you called and asked to meet with me. I'm glad we got together for coffee. You're much younger than I thought—no offense!

I appreciate the advice to not abandon my career as a policeman. You gave me such hope with your own story of how hard it was to earn your nursing credentials.

I was so glad you suggested we meet for lunch. I can't wait.

I haven't asked you, but I assume you're not telling your husband about our friendship. I think that's wise. He wouldn't approve.

Roy snorted. "Damn right I don't approve." Roy continued reading the infuriating email.

· · ·

Text me next week, and I'll see you at the restaurant we discussed.
Take care,
Seth

Roy looked away from the computer screen and stared out the front window. "This makes no sense," he said out loud. He returned his attention to the laptop and searched through Amber's sent emails.

Seth. I can't tell you how much I enjoyed having lunch with you today. I haven't laughed so hard in months. The stories you told regarding your time in the service, and the men and women you served with sounded similar to incidents Roy has mentioned involving his coworkers. They aren't far off from my hospital experiences either, lol!

I've given more thought to you fighting the unsatisfactory performance evaluations Roy gave you. I know little about police bureaucracy, but Roy told me the LAPD does everything they can to keep a new hire on the force. The department has invested a lot of money to train you, and they don't want it wasted. So, you've got nothing to lose.

Occasionally, I run into officers at the hospital. I'll ask them if they've worked with Roy, and if they witnessed how rough he was with probationers. Maybe I'll get information useful to clear your name.

I had a good time. I hope we meet again soon.
A.B.

. . .

Again Roy looked away from the computer. He searched his mind for any clues he'd missed that Amber and Seth were communicating. Roy shook his head in disbelief that his beautiful wife would seek dirt to use against him. He clicked another email from Farley.

Dear Am,

I'm so relieved you agreed to meet with me and heard me out when I told you how my feelings for you had grown into something more than friendship. Kissing you and having you kiss me back made me realize I do have worth, I do have value, and I should be loved.

We were both shaken by our emotions and how fast they developed. We must decide where to go from here. We don't have to stay in Los Angeles. We could move to Arizona to be near your parents. I'm sure you'd be able to find a job at a hospital, and I'd be hired by a local police department.

Think of it. In just a few months we might live our lives together and be happy at last.

Roy slammed the screen of the laptop closed. *This can't be true.* Amber couldn't have developed feelings for that loser Farley.

His frustration took him into the bedroom where he prowled through Amber's drawers in the dresser. He didn't know what he searched for, but there must have been something that pointed to his wife's infidelity. Yanking the drawer where Amber kept her nightwear, he pulled out pajama bottoms and tank tops. Digging further, he found the two sexy nightgowns Amber wore as a signal to Roy she was in the mood. There was no new sleepwear. *If she's sleeping with Farley, maybe she sleeps naked.*

Rage started in Roy's gut and worked its way up until he feared his head might explode. "I'll kill that SOB."

The fury he experienced wasn't unknown to him. He'd experienced the same anger while working the streets. It appeased his wrath when he put the bad guy in handcuffs. He needed an outlet now.

Storming into the garage, he stood in front of a punching bag secured to the ceiling. He donned his boxing gloves and spent the next thirty minutes battering the leather at lightning speed.

At the end of his bout, he realized his rejection of Amber's desires to have a baby might have pushed her even closer to Farley. Then an awful notion filled his mind. What if the baby Amber carried wasn't his? What if Farley was the father?

There was only one thing to do. Go to Farley's house, beat the crap out of him, and bring his wife home.

Roy entered the house and confirmed he'd locked the front door and returned to his truck. As he backed out of the garage he saw the reporter and her cameraman talking to his neighbor, Mrs. Hendricks.

As he blew past them, Roy gunned his engine. He looked in his rearview mirror and observed the newsies running to their van.

He turned off his street and thought about what he'd do once he reached Farley's home. He decided to wing it.

Twenty minutes later he arrived. The road was narrow, with battered Hondas and minivans parked at the curb. It was a working-class neighborhood, and the street was lined with small bungalow homes built in the 1940s.

The sun was up, and people were on the move. A man carrying a lunch pail and wearing painters' coveralls eyed Roy's shiny pickup as he passed by.

Out of habit from work, Roy parked two doors away from Farley's house.

There was no sign of life at the small bungalow but that didn't prevent Roy from exiting his truck and knocking on the door. When no one responded, he walked around the front perimeter of the dwelling, glancing in the windows. It was hard to view inside, but it didn't appear that anyone was home.

Not to be dissuaded, he went to the side gate. It was unlocked. He entered the backyard and looked for signs of a dog. Not seeing any, he made short work of peeking through the rear windows. No lights were on, and everything seemed in order.

Once he'd exited the backyard, he was walking back to his truck when he noticed the KABR news truck parked down the road. Inwardly, he was impressed and wondered how the girl reporter and her cameraman had followed him. Outwardly, he spat onto the asphalt and muttered. "Damn reporter."

19

─────

KAREN

Karen Watson had promised her cameraman, Brian, a case of beer if he could follow Roy Buckner. She'd need to pay up later.

"Who do you think lives there?"

Brian shrugged. "I don't know. Why are we following him in the first place?"

Karen wasn't sure why she'd urged Brian to catch up to Buckner. But she had good instincts, and they told her the man was distressed by something more than his classmate being murdered.

"Oh, look," Karen said. "He sees us. He's getting back into his truck."

Brian started the van. "If I keep up with him, do I get more beer?"

Karen laughed. "Let's just see where he goes." She

watched as Roy pulled from the curb and drove away. She jotted down the address of the house he had visited, then researched on her phone.

Brian followed Buckner's truck. A few minutes later it appeared the cop was returning home. "Do you want me to keep following him?"

Karen glanced over the dashboard. "Nah. With the neighbor interview and what we got at the hospital, we have plenty of footage for the midday show." She tapped the address she'd written. "The house belongs to somebody named Seth Farley." Her thumbs danced across the surface of her phone. "Now all I need to do is figure out the relationship between Roy and Mr. Farley."

20

AMBER

As she reached the bottom of the wooden stairs, she realized her captor was right. The accommodations underground *were* better than the shack upstairs. She spotted beanbag chairs and some makeshift shelves holding books.

He'd followed her down the steps. Midway he pulled out his phone and tapped the screen. The opening overhead closed. He grinned at her as he jogged to the bottom of the stairs. "Pretty trick, huh?"

Amber nodded while fighting off another wave of nausea. She moved farther away from him.

"I bought this property specifically because they built it as a bomb shelter in the 1960s. Let me show you around." He motioned for her to follow him. "The footprint for the bunker is twenty-five feet by twenty-five. The walls are concrete block, just like the building upstairs. I added the structural support to the ceiling with those struts on the perimeter and attached to the crossbeams. Those poles running across the middle of the room are adjustable steel column joists." He turned and smiled. "Even if we get the big one—meaning an earthquake—we'll be fine here. In fact, not much would bring this baby down."

As Amber took everything in she realized this lunatic had been planning her kidnapping for a long time—unless she wasn't his first captive. As he boasted about their accommodations, all she saw was an underground prison meant to hold her indefinitely.

He was proud of the dungeon he'd created. For her self-preservation, she should try to feign enthusiasm. "Impressive," she murmured.

"Over here," he said, moving to one side of the support poles. "This is the kitchen. We've got a makeshift sink here with these two large dishpans, but there's no running water or drainage." He pointed. "Those two container's hold five gallons of water each. Here's the propane camping stove. That ice chest over there serves as the refrigerator. The table and folding chairs are used for eating."

He moved deeper into the space. "We can relax in the beanbag chairs. I hope you like to read. There isn't a TV."

Amber's eyes locked on a photo attached to the wall behind the beanbag chairs. It was a picture she knew well. The same image hung in the office of her home. It was Roy's academy class proudly wearing their formal uniforms and shiny badges. This one wasn't in a frame. Bright red *X's* marred two of the faces of officers in the picture.

The man caught her looking at it and nudged her in the arm. "Come this way."

As they walked toward the back of the room, Amber saw the "bedroom" contained a double bed and nightstand. There were several plastic drawer units holding clothes.

A cabinet on the wall got her attention. The wood looked new, and several locks told her something of value was inside. She shot furtive glances at the cupboard but didn't stare.

It surprised her to see what appeared to be a hallway in the corner. "What's that?"

"The generator room is back there. There's also a self-contained shower and toilet in its own enclosure." He turned to her, displaying a smirk. "Well, I don't know about you, but this has been a tiring day. I think it's time we go to bed."

Amber fought to keep her face neutral. What did he mean by that?

"Now, we can do this all friendly-like, or we can do it with you tied to the bed frame. What's your pleasure?"

She took a step backward as her gaze searched for an avenue of escape.

The man laughed and shook his head. "There's nowhere for you to run. I'm tired, but not so worn out that I don't have the energy to get you to comply. Of course, if I have to *persuade* you, you'll pay for my extra effort. I generally prefer my women to be willing." He took a step toward her. "Now, what's it going to be?"

PART III

21

———

ROY

As he drove home, Roy kept his eye on his rearview mirror until he saw the news van turn at a cross street that connected with the freeway.

His phone rang. He recognized the number as belonging to the LAPD.

"Buckner."

"Hey, Roy, this is Sergeant Smyth from the captain's office. Sorry about your classmate Tremont. I worked with him at Wilshire, and he was a good guy."

Since he was alone, Roy allowed tears to fill his eyes. "Yeah, he was."

"I'm calling because the department is assigning a security detail to everyone who was in your academy class. With three of your classmates dead in less than six months under questionable circumstances, the chief thinks it's prudent."

"I don't need protecting. I can take care of myself. I'm hoping the asswipe who killed Luke comes after me."

"Look, I understand your feelings, but I wouldn't say that out loud to anyone else. You never know what might happen." There was a slight pause. "The protection team is mandatory—an order from the chief."

Roy cursed.

"This is how it'll go down. There will be a two-man unit deployed at your house 24/7. We're asking you and your family to curtail any outside activities until we make an arrest. You'll be assigned to work from home."

"Jeez, I'm a cop. I want to find this asshole. In fact, is there any way I could get loaned to RHD to work with the detectives handling Luke's murder?"

"Not a chance. The department is emailing the affected officers a year's worth of e-instruction videos. You're expected to do the training from home."

"What about my wife? She's a nurse at Northridge Hospital."

"We're encouraging the spouses of employees, if possible, to stay home. If that's a no-go, the security detail will call for another unit who'll follow your wife to work and return to escort her back to your house." The sergeant sighed. "We're hoping this situation doesn't take too long. It's straining our resources."

"When can I expect to see the unit?" Roy asked.

"They'll start with the midday watch—especially for you since Luke was shot coming from your house."

"Okay, roger that."

"Hey, Roy? Take care, and watch your six, buddy."

Roy glanced into the rearview mirror at the sergeant's suggestion to guard his back. "I am, Sarge. I am."

He disconnected the call and worried what he'd tell the security detail about Amber. Roy didn't want the news to get out that his wife had left him. He hadn't given up hope she'd just wanted space and gone to a motel—not run off with his probationer, Farley. Roy needed to talk to her calmly regarding her pregnancy. He knew they could work something out. All he had to do was find her.

22

AMBER

Amber lay curled on the mattress in a fetal position. Her head rested on her left arm which was extended with a heavy steel handcuff attached to her wrist. The other end of her restraint held fast to something connected to the bed. Her right forearm was crossed protectively over her stomach. She ached all over, and hopelessness filled her heart.

She'd probably die in this man-made hell hole and never have her baby—the baby she hadn't planned on but loved more than life itself the moment she knew she was pregnant.

Would Roy be relieved to be rid of her and their baby? Surely not. But a niggling in the back of her mind said her husband might be glad to dodge the responsibility of a family. Tears dropped onto the sheet.

Beside her, her captor slept. Intermittent sawing snores grated on her nerves as she tried not to sink into a mental hole of despair. She worked her jaw side to side to see if it was broken. Her movements increased the headache that had started with the first smack to her face. He'd pummeled her good. She'd stopped fighting when his blows moved from her head to her body. She couldn't let him hurt her baby.

When she stopped resisting, he'd made her wash her face before raping her, saying "the blood all over her was a turnoff."

With her back to the monster beside her, Amber wondered what time it was. Underground, she didn't know if it was day or night. What was she going to do? What if he woke and wanted to rape her again? She couldn't bear it. What if she lost the baby? She had to do something to keep him away from her.

He began to stir.

She closed her eyes and lay still, hoping he'd leave her alone so she could plan an escape or get an idea to avoid being violated again.

He stretched and groaned.

A quick peek through her slit eyelids showed him extending his arm into the air as he let out a noisy yawn. She sensed him turn his attention in her direction. She kept her breathing slow and steady as if she were asleep. *Please don't touch me.*

He jerked upright and yawned again. He got to his feet and shuffled toward the toilet.

As soon as he was out of sight, she shifted her body to see how she was connected to the bed. *Let there be a way for me to free myself.*

Disappointment filled her when she saw that the other handcuff was secured to a rod attached to the frame. While she could slide her cuffed wrist the length of the mattress, she'd come to a stop at the crossbar at the foot of the bed.

She heard him flush the toilet. Amber resumed her position on her left side.

He came back into the sleeping area. "Hey. Wake up."

She kept her eyes closed.

"I said wake up." He extended his leg and jiggled the mattress with his foot.

After doing what he asked, she did her best to avert her gaze from his nakedness.

"You look like shit. I wish you'd behaved better." He pawed at his genitals and shook his head. "I was gonna have another go-round, but I'd either have to put a bag over you or screw you with my eyes closed."

He walked over to the kitchen and washed his hands using a spouted water container on a shelf over the two wash pans. He grabbed a paper towel and sauntered back to where she lay. "Sit up."

Amber struggled to a sitting position with her nakedness against the cold concrete block of the wall behind her.

He reached out and took her chin. He moved her head left and right. "Your cheek is swollen. I should get you some ice, and maybe even makeup so you can fix yourself up. I don't want to look at you with your face so busted."

What a bastard. He beats the crap out of me and then wants me to put on makeup so he finds me attractive? Not going to happen. I need a reason for him not to rape me again. What if I told him I had an STD? That won't work. He'll get mad and beat me again. Think, Amber. Think.

"You want to use the head?"

She nodded. She did need to pee.

"Okay, I'll uncuff you. But if you do something stupid, you'll know our earlier bout was just the preliminary round. Understand?"

Head lowered, she looked at the floor. "Yes."

He retrieved a set of keys from his pants that had been discarded on the floor. He unlocked the handcuff on her wrist.

Amber got to her feet and worked her left shoulder. It was stiff from the awkward position she'd been forced to take. A wave of dizziness swept over her. Using her arms to cover herself as best she could, she padded back to the toilet. She was relieved when he didn't follow.

He'd said he was going somewhere for ice. *There must be a store or gas station not too far away. Would he leave you here alone?* She might be able to escape. *It's a nice thought, but don't count on it.*

"Hey, unless you're dropping a deuce, get your ass back out here."

What a class act. His mother would be proud.

With her arms still covering herself, she returned to the bedroom. An idea clicked in her mind. It was a long shot, but if she could pull it off, it might keep Farley away from her.

He was crouched over her two suitcases. He'd pulled the contents out and was searching through them.

"Looking for something?" She tried to control her anger. Her stomach roiled at the sight of him rummaging through her belongings.

"Just checking your luggage. I was in such a hurry to grab your clothes, I want to check that I didn't miss anything like weapons hidden in these bags."

Oh, how I wish I had a gun. "May I get dressed?"

"Sure. And then we'll eat. I've got bacon and egg MREs. I'll start the generator, and you can cook them in the microwave."

"MREs?"

"Meals ready to eat."

"Are you going to tell me your name and why you're doing this?"

He inhaled as he rose. Then a grin filled his face. "Why I'm doing this is none of your business. But call me Victor."

Amber didn't believe he'd given his real name, but she nodded.

A short time later, after a distasteful breakfast, she was hand-washing the dishes they'd used.

"That was great. I've got things to do today. I'll be out for a while, so I'm securing you again."

"What if I need the restroom?"

"You'll have to wait until I get back."

"What if I can't?"

"Then wet your pants. Just be prepared to clean up your mess."

"Can't you attach a rope or something to the handcuff on my wrist so I can move around a little more?"

His eyes narrowed. "Don't tell me what to do. I have a plan, and I'm sticking to it."

Amber raised her hands as a sign of surrender and for him to stay calm. "Can I at least sit on the floor? It'd be easier on my arm and shoulder."

After considering her request, he agreed. It didn't take him long to reaffix the restraint to her wrist. He set a canteen of water next to her.

Once done, he checked his pocket for his wallet, grabbed

a baseball cap and stuck it on his head, and turned to her. "Before I go, do you want a book to read?"

"Thank you."

He picked a book from a shelf and brought it to her.

"Um, could you get something for me while you're out?"

Surprise filled Victor's face. "What?"

"A pregnancy test and some mineral oil. I'm fairly certain you got me pregnant."

23

———

SETH

Seth stared at Amber who still sat on the floor. "Huh?"

"I said I'm quite certain you got me pregnant."

He laughed. "Like it happens that fast and you immediately know." He chortled some more.

Her hardened expression indicated Amber didn't find it funny that he doubted her. In fact, even with her battered face, he saw a muscle jumping in her jaw as her gaze seared into him.

He shifted on his feet. "You're punking me, right?"

She shook her head. "No. I'm not."

"That's ridiculous. I've never heard of anyone finding out they got knocked up right after they had sex."

"It's not widely known yet. I work as a neonatal nurse, and new breakthroughs usually get leaked before they're announced to the public. Last week, someone told me a group of doctors at one of the major colleges in LA discovered a way to tell if a woman is pregnant within the first twenty-four hours of having intercourse."

"How?"

"You take an ordinary pregnancy test in the first twenty-four hours after sex. After urinating on the stick, immediately pour a tablespoon of mineral oil over the wand. It will indicate if you're pregnant or not."

"That's just stupid. I don't believe you."

His captive's gaze bore into his. "You've heard of the morning-after pill?"

He nodded.

"The discovery came while they were doing research for it."

Seth felt uneasy with his earlier mocking. "What college discovered this?"

"No one is saying."

He couldn't believe such a big breakthrough hadn't been publicized or hit social media.

"They're still gathering data," Amber continued, "but the accuracy numbers are staggering."

Seth crossed his arms over his chest. "Yeah, but just because we had sex doesn't mean you got pregnant."

Amber stared at the ground. "True, except I've been trying to get pregnant for eight months. I've tracked my ovulation dates for the past year. Roy and I have had no luck." She looked at him. "I was tested, and everything is okay as far as I go. Roy won't take the test." She stared at him. "I'm at the peak of my ovulation cycle today."

She reached up and took his hand.

"I know it in my bones that I'm going to have a baby. You

got me pregnant, Victor. You're a better man than my husband."

Seth didn't know what to think. Could it possibly be true? Did he impregnate Roy's wife the first time he tapped her? Oh, the irony. There was only one way to find out. He'd buy a pregnancy test and the mineral oil and see what developed.

24

ROY

It was almost noon, and despite being exhausted, Roy had driven to Northridge Hospital where Amber worked. He'd cruised every row in front of the medical center, along with the crowded parking garage, looking for her SUV. No luck.

He spent the next few hours driving through the parking lots of hotels and motels. He started with those closest to her job and then made his way to locations closer to their neighborhood. His efforts ended with negative results. He drove home.

Ticked off by the fact he couldn't find Amber and she hadn't responded to his many texts, he stormed into the house. "Amb," he called out. "You here?" *Of course not, you idiot. You wouldn't even listen to her, and now she's God knows where—probably with that flunky Farley.*

He marched to the fridge, grabbed a beer, popped the cap,

and chugged half the bottle. Lord, he was tired. "What a screwed-up day," he said. His upper body was so tight his shoulders were at ear level. He'd take a shower to relax and then nap until the security detail arrived.

He carried his drink to the bathroom and got the water running, adjusting the stream to a forceful pulsing spray. Setting the bottle on the counter next to the sink, he caught sight of the damp towel he'd touched before. He was so upset when arriving home it hadn't occurred to him that the bath sheet he'd felt earlier was *his*. Amber would have used hers. He checked hers and recognized slight remnants of moisture. Two people had showered?

A familiar rage built as he turned off the water and stomped into the bedroom. He grabbed the corner of the bedspread and whipped it back. Next came the blanket and the top sheet. He snagged his pillow and brought it to his face. It smelled the same as always. He reached across the bed, snagging Amber's cushion. Recognizing his wife's sweet scent, he noticed there was something else—a spicier smell. His gaze searched the fitted bottom sheet. He wasn't sure what he was looking for—a forgotten sock, an errant pubic hair, a used condom? Then he saw it. The stain. Dried, but it was plain as day.

The rage he'd built drained from him like blood from a murder victim collecting in a gutter.

As the reality of the situation hit him, not for the first time today, his eyes filled with tears and he let them fall. There was no one to see his disappointment, his grief, his shame. No one. He moved to the bar in the family room, and grabbed his favorite whiskey, and poured himself four fingers.

25

KAREN

At the studios of KABR News, the morning producer came to Karen as she sat at her desk.

"You did a great job giving the live shots from the hospital. Stay with the Tremont murder story, but if something else breaks, be ready to switch gears."

"Thank you. I will. I've got research to do on Tremont's friend—the cop whose house he'd left before getting shot."

"Good. I had to send Brian out in the field to get video of a warehouse fire, but he should be back within the hour. Keep me posted of any new developments in the cop murder."

Karen nodded as the producer walked away. Looking at one of the studio computers, her eyes widened when she saw the results of a Google search for the name Roy Buckner.

"Well, well, well," she whispered. "Buckner and Farley have a strong bit of history between them." She reviewed newspaper articles and videos detailing the shooting death of a pimp and Farley's ensuing termination by the LAPD.

Excited, Karen asked the producer if she could go in the field to follow up her research. To her dismay, he refused.

"Just sit tight until Brian gets back. When he returns, if you're not busy, you two can go out and rattle cages. It's hard to do a live report if you haven't got a camera with you."

Karen nodded and returned to her desk. She needed to talk to Buckner and find out why he'd been prowling around Farley's house. Being the catalyst for the probationer's firing, and the primary defendant in the subsequent lawsuit, it was strange he'd seek out his disgraced former partner.

After arranging for an Uber driver to meet her outside, Karen texted Brian where to meet her after he'd finished filming the structure fire. Her car in the parking lot was insurance. If someone noticed she wasn't around, she could say she'd been elsewhere in the studio—but she prayed no one took note of her absence.

Thank goodness for hired drivers, Karen thought as her chauffeur weaved through traffic from Hollywood to the San Fernando Valley.

A half hour later she stood on the sidewalk in front of the Buckner home. A moment of trepidation filled her. There were no signs of activity in the neighborhood or the house.

As the Uber car drove away, Karen stepped to the door and knocked. She realized she wasn't nearly as confident without Brian, his camera, and bright light. She rang the bell in case the cop or his wife were asleep—which would be understandable. Buckner had been awake over twenty-four hours, and his wife worked evenings, too. Karen knocked on the door—hard. Still no response.

Did she dare go to the backyard to see if she could rouse someone? *Karen, you snagged the best story of the week. You've got to capitalize on it, or your competition will win the reporter job. Winter is coming to Iowa. Do you want to go home?*

Karen backed from the front porch and moved around the building. Letting herself through a side gate, she eyed the manicured rear yard and admired a covered patio, in-ground spa, and fire pit.

Go big or go home. A pair of French doors sat centered in the back of the home. She held her hand against the glass and peered inside. It took a second for her eyes to adjust.

Her heart leaped to her throat. Roy Buckner was sprawled facedown on the kitchen floor.

26

AMBER

From the corner of her eye, Amber watched to see how Victor made the above-ground table rise so he could exit the bunker. To her dismay, he activated a fob on his key ring which caused the opening to appear.

Even through her disappointment, she noted that it took seven seconds for the secret passage to open and the same time to close. It was valuable information to know.

Once her captor had lowered the table, Amber got to work. Thanks to her story of being pregnant, Victor had attached a heavy chain to the bed frame, then hooked the last link through the handcuff on her left wrist. The arrangement allowed her the footage she needed to access the portable toilet.

She walked to the picture of the police officers and examined it. A third red X disfigured the image. The newest mark was inked across Luke Tremont's face. She didn't need to be a detective to know Victor had probably killed the two other officers with X's on their faces.

Dragging the links with her, she stepped over to the wooden cupboard. Three keyed locks on the cabinet indicated the contents were valuable to her captor. She suspected the unit held guns and ammunition and wondered if she'd be able to pick the locks.

She moved to the kitchen looking for items suitable as a probe. It occurred to her that with Victor gone, she should find and hide a knife or something. But the chain didn't extend far enough for her to access the box holding the cooking utensils. She could reach the sink, and that was it.

"Damn."

Next, she hobbled over to the plastic drawers that held Victor's clothes. Maybe he'd hidden a pistol between his clothing. She rifled through the compartments, being sure not to disturb the contents. No gun.

Frustrated, she extended the tether its entire length, then did her best to circle the room looking for objects she could use as a weapon. She wanted to cry. There was nothing.

For a moment she wondered if the chain would work. She'd wrap it around Victor's neck and strangle him. She lifted the links to gauge their weight. The restraint was too heavy for her to manipulate fast. Besides, he was trained to fight, and she wasn't.

She sank onto the bed. "What am I going to do?" She picked up the book he'd given her, and opened it, but the next thing she knew, a whirring sound caught her attention.

Victor. He'd returned.

Her captor, carrying several plastic bags, jogged as he

descended the stairs. He used the fob on his key ring to close the entrance to the bunker.

"You haven't been gone long," she said.

"I came back to see if you were telling the truth." He went to the makeshift kitchen and set his purchases on the workbench. He opened two large bags and dumped ice into the insulated chest used to keep food cold.

"I got the test and the oil." He produced the products from another bag. "I want to watch you go through all the steps."

"I'm not sure I can urinate on command—especially with you watching."

"Well, try—hard. I've got things to do today." He walked toward the bathroom. "Come on."

Amber followed him, her heart firing like a jackhammer in her chest. *Please, God, let me pee.*

Victor handed her the box containing the test.

She ripped it open. She'd taken three at-home pregnancy tests before but read through the instructions to convince Victor the story she fed him was true. She unwrapped the stick and looked at him.

"Be sure you've got the mineral oil ready to go. If I remember correctly, it must be applied right after I'm done urinating."

Victor nodded and twisted the cap off the bottle, then he removed the foil leakage barrier glued across the top. "Okay, I'm set."

After glancing at her kidnapper, she did her business. "Quick, give me the oil."

He thrust it into her hand.

She poured ten drops on the wand and then set it flat on

the floor. "It will take three minutes. Start timing." She adjusted her clothing and dragged the chain with her to wash her hands.

When she returned, Victor was bent at the waist, staring at the pink object on the ground.

"What does it say?" Her words were brave, but she was fighting to keep a tremor out of her voice. What if her ruse didn't work?

"I'm not sure what I should be seeing. There's just two pink lines." He picked up the stick and showed it to her.

The irony of her current situation brought tears to her eyes. "Congratulations. You're going to be a father." Then she placed her hands against her captor's chest. "And thanks to you, I'll finally be a mother."

27

———

KAREN

Karen knocked on the French door. "Officer Buckner. Roy Buckner, are you okay?"

The prone body on the floor didn't move. She pounded harder on the wooden frame. "Hello, are you okay?"

What to do? Should she call the police? An ambulance?

She banged again.

This time the man moved his leg.

She hammered again. "Officer Buckner, are you all right?"

He lifted his head and then dropped it to the floor.

"Come unlock the door. I'm here to help."

He raised his head again, looking in her direction. He attempted to focus.

Karen waved. "If you're able, please come here so I can help you."

Moving with the speed of a sloth, Buckner pushed himself to his knees, got to his feet, and stumbled toward her.

There was no blood or any sign of injury to him as he fumbled with the lock.

When he opened the door, the sour odor of alcohol—and lots of it—assaulted her nose.

"I already told you I've nothing to say."

She pushed her boot-clad foot inside. "Fine. You don't have to talk. Let me in, and I'll make you coffee."

"Don't need no coffee."

Karen chuckled. "Yeah, you do. That, and a ton of water. Open up." She looked beyond Buckner into the interior of the house. "Is your wife around?"

Roy reared back his head and glared at her. "That's none of your damn business." He tried to close the door, but it bounced off her boot. "Get your foot out."

Sensing a story in the drunken man's condition, she shoved hard, and to her surprise, he let her into the house. She closed the door.

He pulled away from her and placed his hands on each side of his head. "Shit. I drank too much."

"Why don't you take a seat? I'll make the coffee."

He turned back to face her, keeping his fingers positioned on his skull. "Who are you again?"

"Karen Watson from KABR News." She motioned for him to sit at the table. She went to a cabinet, found a drinking glass, filled it with ice, and then water. She touched Buckner's arm to guide him to the kitchen table where he flopped into a chair and released the grip on his head. She placed the water in front of him.

"Thank you," he said.

Unsure whether she should bring up his wife again, she opted to avoid the subject. "Where do you keep the java?"

He pointed at the pantry.

It didn't take her long to get coffee under way. "What caused your...um...over indulgence?"

"I don't want to talk about it."

"Is it because you're distraught over the death of Luke Tremont?"

Buckner looked surprised and sad in a matter of seconds. It was as if he'd forgotten his friend was dead.

"If you tell me what's wrong, maybe I can help."

He lowered his head so he couldn't look at her. "I'm fine. I don't need you. What time is it?"

She pulled out her phone. "Almost two thirty in the afternoon." She found mugs in a cabinet. "Do you take cream or sugar?"

He shook his head. "Black."

She poured him a steaming brew and one for herself. "Is your wife home? Maybe she'd want some too."

Before he could respond, the doorbell rang. Although hungover, he got to his feet and hurried to the entryway.

She trailed behind him.

Roy opened the front door. Two LAPD patrol officers stood in front of him.

Karen watched as Buckner's facial features sharpened and he straightened his spine.

"Oh, hi, guys. I forgot you were coming. Come on in."

It was the older officer who spoke. "Our orders are to stay outside and keep the house under surveillance." He laughed. "I'm sure the department is afraid they'll be paying us for watching TV or playing video games if we're not outside."

Roy smiled and managed to nod. "Yeah, you're right. If you need anything, let me know. I'm getting a late start to my day. I was about to make breakfast. You guys down with eggs, bacon, and toast?"

Both officers grinned. "You bet," said the older one. "Let's exchange cell numbers. We can reach each other without traipsing back and forth."

After doing so, the younger officer looked past Roy and at her. "Is it just you and Mrs. Buckner?"

Roy turned to see her standing behind him. "Oh…"

She propelled herself forward, extending her hand. "Karen Watson—Roy's friend."

A flash of curiosity crossed both officers' faces. "So, Mrs. Buckner *isn't* here?"

She couldn't wait to hear Roy's answer because Amber's location was something she wanted to know too.

"Uh, no. Amber is visiting a girlfriend out of town." He smiled at the officers. "With everything going on, I thought it was a good idea she get away." Roy rubbed his hands together. "Let me clean up, and I'll have that chow out to you pronto."

Apparently satisfied with his answer regarding his wife's whereabouts, the officers gave a brief wave, stepped off the porch, and headed back to their patrol car.

It surprised Karen they didn't question Roy's condition…*and* his wife's location.

He shut the door, looking worried.

She whispered. "Where is Amber, Roy?"

He turned his gaze to hers. His eyes were watery. Booze? Tears?

"I have no idea."

28

SETH

"I can't believe it." Seth shook his head. "You're not yanking my chain, are you?"

"Look for yourself," Roy's wife said. She held out the pregnancy stick to him, then gave him the test instructions showing what the results meant. "Two pink stripes...pregnant."

"This changes things." His mind raced through the complications, scenarios, and potential outcomes of the situation.

He looked at the woman before him. Everything was different now. She was no longer Roy's wife. She was Amber, the mother of his child. He was going to be a father. It was like she'd waved a wand and was now vital to him. It made how he executed his overall plan much more crucial.

Seth didn't want Amber to see how rattled he was. He

must stay in control and continue with his work for the day. As he took care of business, he'd decide how fathering a child altered his plans.

"I'm going out again." He looked at her. She carried his child. She smiled at him and seemed happy with that fact. "You need something? Are there foods you're craving?" He chuckled. "Or is it too soon for that?"

Her eyes widened in surprise. "I'd love saltines." A blush filled her cheeks. "Even at these very early stages, women get morning sickness. The crackers are bland enough to eat."

"Okay. That it?"

"Could I have a bit of chocolate? I have a terrible sweet tooth."

He didn't want to appear soft. He should refuse the candy, but she *was* carrying his child. "I'll think about it."

He took the test stick and placed it in the drawer of the bedside table. He tossed the remaining packaging into the trash. "I'll be gone for several hours. There are frozen TV dinners at the bottom of the ice chest."

He glanced around the space to be sure he didn't forget anything. "I'll bring you fresh fruit and milk." He smiled. "We gotta keep our little guy healthy."

She grinned back at him. "I agree...and I hope it's a boy too."

"Good. I'll return as soon as I can."

"Okay. Victor? I want to say thank you again. You've given me the greatest gift a man provides a woman—a child."

He sucked in a big breath of air with pride. She might be so grateful with a baby, she wouldn't be upset when she learned who he really was.

29

———

ROY

The shower made Roy feel halfway human again. What the hell had he done? Telling a reporter he wasn't sure where his wife was. What was he thinking? As much as he wanted to, he didn't linger in the hot water in case the woman was snooping around his house.

A few minutes later he returned to the living room where Karen leafed through the photo album on the coffee table.

"What island is this?"

"Kauai."

"This was just last year?"

"Yeah."

"What happened between your marriage in Hawaii and now to where your wife is missing?"

"I gotta get the food ready. I told those guys…"

Karen rose from the couch. "I'll give you a hand." She walked toward the kitchen.

Roy hated the fact he was so out of control. A day ago, he wouldn't have let a reporter inside his home, much less have her help to make breakfast for himself and two street cops. He was sure she'd ask more questions.

She handled the eggs and toast while he fried the bacon. They made enough for themselves too. Once everything was ready, he placed the food on paper plates and took the meal, along with plastic utensils, out to the officers parked in the driveway.

As soon as they saw him, they exited the police car. "Go back inside," they directed. "We'll come to you."

The younger officer jogged around the black and white and relieved him of the food.

"Okay, if you need a head call just let me know," Roy said.

The older cop gave a lascivious grin. "Don't worry about us calling first. Your *friend* is quite a looker."

Roy frowned but couldn't be too mad. It certainly appeared that he'd sent Amber away and then invited a gorgeous blonde over to keep him company—if not more. He hurried back to the house. He needed to get rid of her.

Karen had found plates and dished out their food. She was more than halfway through her meal.

He sat at the table across from her.

She swallowed whatever she'd been chewing. "What happened with your wife? Aren't you worried that, with someone killing cops, that maybe she's in danger?"

He cocked his head. It never entered his mind that Amber might be a target of a serial killer. But why would it?

He possessed evidence with their emails that she and

Seth Farley were having an affair. It was sloppiness on their part that he'd discovered they'd had sex in the bed he and Amber shared. He couldn't imagine his wife being so callous. But then he remembered how he'd reacted to her announcement she was pregnant. He'd yelled at her and told her he expected her to terminate her pregnancy.

"I'm certain she's fine."

"How can you be sure if you don't know where she is?"

Why did he let this bitch into his house?

"There's something you're not telling me. What is it?"

"You need to leave."

"Why? Because the questions are getting hard?" The reporter's gaze bore into him. "Did you hurt her?"

He wanted this Karen woman out. "Amber has left me. Okay? She packed her bags last night and took off." He turned a maniacal smile on her. "Satisfied?"

Karen narrowed her eyes, crossed her arms, and leaned toward him. "So do you think your wife has run off with Seth Farley?"

30

AMBER

As soon as she heard Victor's truck pull away, Amber was on the move. She tried to find something useful to escape or to utilize as a weapon against her captor.

Although Victor's demeanor had changed for the better after learning she was pregnant, his eyes held a wariness Amber didn't trust. How could such a methodical planner believe her fabricated story of an instantaneous pregnancy test?

She hadn't known she was such a convincing liar. Should she use her new skill to gain Victor's faith in her and then escape? Or should she kill him and then set herself free? Either way, baby or not, she knew he wouldn't hesitate to kill her.

He'd pulled the ice chest within her grasp but kept the bin holding cooking utensils out of her reach. If she got the chance to boil water, she could throw it in his face. She could use pages torn from the books to form a stabbing tool for his eyes.

Her ideas were good but risky. If she didn't incapacitate Victor, he'd kill her in return. She had to be mindful of her baby and how to keep it safe.

It might be better to bluff her way into his confidence where he trusted her enough that she could escape. She'd wait and see how things played out.

Freeing herself from the handcuffs or separating the manacle attached to the bed frame would be huge—even more so if Victor didn't notice until she made a move for her freedom.

On the sly, she'd tried to free herself from the handcuff affixed to her wrist. With him gone, she had time to concentrate on contorting her hand to the narrowest of proportions. She worked until she noticed her hand swelling from her efforts.

Next, she dropped to the floor and crawled halfway under the bed. With so little light from two battery-operated bulbs, it was hard to see. She soon realized Victor had welded a special rod of rebar onto the frame. He'd thought ahead in giving her the ability to slide the cuffs the length of the mattress.

She grabbed the handcuff attached to the metal bar and pulled with all her weight. The rod wouldn't break.

Think, Amber, think!

She'd have to pick the lock. She had more mobility than the first time she'd searched. There must be something she could use. She had no idea how to force open a handcuff but had seen it done on television and in the movies. She had to try. After searching around her underground prison, her problem remained—there was nothing useful within reach.

It seemed Victor had been gone for a long time, but without a clock she couldn't be sure. The stress, coupled with her pregnancy, exhausted her.

She fought off her desire to take a rest and made her way over to the cabinet holding books. Maybe someone had used a paperclip or hairpin as a bookmark. She took every book one by one from the shelf and leafed through the pages looking for anything useful to her. Carefully she placed the novels back in the same order as she found them. Instinct told her Victor was the kind of guy who'd notice a volume out of place.

Discouraged and drained after searching for a lock-picking device for at least an hour, she gave in to her frustration and let her tears fall.

She needed to rest for a few minutes. With luck, she'd wake refreshed, and find a way to escape—all before Victor returned.

PART IV

31

SETH

A father. He was going to be a father. Seth shook his head as he drove back to the LA basin. The Lord sure worked in mysterious ways. But he put that out of his mind. He had work to do. He turned on the radio to get the latest news.

The reports said security details were being assigned to some LAPD officers in light of recent "suspicious deaths."

"They ain't suspicious, you idiot," he yelled. "The dead cops are systematically being eliminated—just like they did with me. One after another they reported on my *supposed* poor performance when, in actuality, they all lied. Every single one. They couldn't stand that I was smarter than them. I'd been in the war and seen more combat than they'd ever see on the streets of LA."

The fact that the department realized officers were being

targeted made his job that much harder. "But I'm up to the challenge, assholes."

Next on his hit parade—he chuckled at the pun—was the baby-faced officer they called Cookie. *What a stupid nickname.* Why a person would be degraded in that manner was beyond him.

Jeremy "Cookie" Cook was working the Vice Unit at Mission Division in the San Fernando Valley. Thanks to his posts on social media, Seth knew that every Monday, before reporting to work, Cookie ate at a fast-food joint. The Burger Pit Stop was a stone's throw from the Mission station. Even better, the drive-thru was right next to the Golden State Freeway.

His pregnancy chat with Amber had him off schedule. He might be too late to get into position.

Seth pulled his truck onto the shoulder of the freeway. He got out and walked to the rear, slapping a yellow highway patrol sticker on the back window as he passed. The neon paperwork showed passing police units and highway troopers the vehicle had been checked out and was disabled. The last thing he needed was a CHP officer snooping around his ride.

Chippy interference wasn't likely—he'd heard LAPD officers say that CHP stood for Can't Handle Police work. He smirked to himself.

He waited until there was a lull in traffic and then removed his rifle wrapped in a blanket. He concealed the weapon using the open passenger door, stepped into the tall trees and bushes, and lay the bundle on the ground.

Returning to his ride, he shut the truck's door and locked it. He knelt as though he was checking his right front tire, and when the cars were scarce, he moved back into the shrubbery. He picked up his rifle and descended twenty feet away from the speeding vehicles.

His peripheral vision caught movement to his side. He froze, then turned. It was hard to see through all the vegetation, but he recognized the form of a homeless man hunkering down.

"Wrong place, wrong time, buddy," he whispered. He drew the Glock pistol at his waist, pulled a noise suppressor from his pocket, and screwed it on. The first shot went into the back of the man's head. The second one followed the same trajectory. Seth sighed. "Collateral damage," he muttered as he removed the silencer.

He moved farther along the embankment, finding the perfect spot to shoot Cookie while the unsuspecting officer was in the drive-thru. Seth's only concern was if there was a security detail assigned to his prey. They might offer to pick up his food for him.

Looking back at his truck, he felt secure that he was well concealed. He'd take care of his business and return to his pickup before the folks waiting for a burger even knew what had happened. He settled himself in the dry grass and shrubs. It was time to wait.

He used the scope on his rifle to check his settings and get them right. For about the hundredth time he looked at his watch. He sure hoped he hadn't missed Cookie.

Seth had no problem sitting among the bushes, ants, and spiders. He'd sat for longer times and in harsher conditions than these waiting to strike an enemy. He had to be patient.

The steady stream of cars zooming along the freeway above him calmed him. He allowed his mind to wander back to Amber in the bunker. What should he tell her? Her glee in finding out she was pregnant indicated she wasn't as committed to her husband as Seth had imagined. Could she see *him* as a potential mate? She'd said it herself—he'd given her the best gift in the world. A baby. He'd done that. No one else but him.

Knowing she was having a child, there was no way he was giving Amber back. Their relationship had started out unconventionally, but what if it was kismet they meet and be together? They'd raise their child together—with a mother *and* a father—the way family life was supposed to be.

A disruption to the traffic noise above him caused Seth to turn and check on his truck. A black and white police car had pulled behind his pickup. Gold reflective letters on the cruiser's doors read California Highway Patrol.

Shit! Was he going to have to kill a cop who just couldn't drive past a 'disabled' vehicle on the shoulder? He slowly removed the pistol from his holster again.

Seth only saw the khaki-clad lower legs of the lawman as the officer walked around his pickup. Then the cop disappeared from view. A few seconds later Seth heard a car door, and soon after, the CHP unit rejoined the traffic chaos.

He let out another long sigh. *Where the hell was Cook?* He reholstered his pistol. The smell of fresh burgers wafted his way, and he realized he was hungry. He was undecided if he should break out the protein bar he'd stuffed in his pocket or not. He didn't have time to decide.

A two-man police unit pulled into the drive-thru lane. A plain wrap tan sedan was in front of the black and white. Seth recognized Jeremy Cook as the driver of the tan car. "You guys deserve to be dead," he muttered to himself. "Weren't you taught in the academy *never* go into a drive-thru because you're sitting ducks?"

He raised the rifle to his shoulder and peered through the scope. "It would be so easy to take out you uniformed goons. But you'll live with the guilt you should have protected the schmuck in front of you—and didn't. You should both get fired. Good riddance."

Yes, he could kill all three officers. But Seth was sending a message. Cookie was getting the message instead of his burger and fries—in fact, the message was going to end his life. Seth forced himself to stop laughing at his own joke and raised the rifle.

32

———

AMBER

After her nap, Amber used the toilet and searched the bath-room area for something she could use to open the lock on her wrist. She lowered herself to her hands and knees. Sliding her fingernails along the thin crevices in the floor, she hoped to discover a discarded piece of wire suitable as a pick. No dice.

Dragging the chain with her, she shuffled to the photo by the bed. Her eyes focused on her husband's face and silent tears rolled down her cheeks as she touched her fingertips to his image. She tried to find Roy's friends and saw them with relative ease. Speakeasy, Jeremy, and Eddie. She examined every face but couldn't find Luke Tremont anywhere, which only confirmed her suspicions that Luke's picture was beneath the most recent jagged red X.

Why was he doing this? What was the point?

The sound of a car driving over gravel reached her ears. She realized the noise came from the rear portion of the bunker. She hustled to the generator room and saw a pipe going into the ceiling. "It must be an exhaust duct," she murmured to herself. *If I can hear vehicles, whoever is out there might hear me if I screamed.*

A vehicle door slammed. She assumed Victor had returned. She didn't want him to catch her wandering around and hurried to the bed. She picked up the book he'd given her and placed it on her chest, pretending to sleep.

Seconds later, the whirring started and the opening above the stairs appeared. Victor descended the steps carrying several plastic bags.

She opened her eyes and saw his gaze scanning the bunker.

"Ah, you were taking a nap," he said as he deposited his purchases on the card table.

She pushed herself up onto an elbow and yawned. "Yes. I started reading, and before I knew it, I was asleep."

He motioned at the table. "I brought you vitamins and a book about pregnancy." He looked at her for a reaction.

"Thank you so much," she gushed. She got up off the bed and made a big show of how hard she worked to move while lugging the chain. She feigned eagerness to leaf through the prenatal paperback and examine the vitamin bottle. "It was nice of you to think of me...and the baby."

He nodded at her. "I take my responsibilities seriously." He frowned. "Not everyone does."

"That's true."

"I'm kind of hungry. I bought lunchmeat, cheese, bread,

and lettuce and tomatoes. Can you make us some sandwiches?"

As long as you don't plan on killing me...or raping me again. "Sure." She set the book aside and looked through the groceries. "Good, you got mustard and mayo." She hesitated. "Victor, would you remove the chain attached to the handcuff? It's heavy, and I'm straining my belly to move around." She put on a woeful expression. "I've miscarried four times. I don't want to lose this baby."

A funny look came over his face. She worried she'd pushed too far.

"I'll remove the chain after you make the food. You'll be handling a knife. I've been thinking how we'll proceed from here. We can discuss it while we eat."

How we'll proceed? What did that mean? She made three turkey sandwiches—two for him and one for her. He'd also bought baked beans and chips. She hadn't realized how hungry she was until she brought the food over to the table. She was about to call out and tell him it was time to eat, but the words died in her throat.

He was standing in front of the academy picture, holding a red marker.

She watched as he made an *X* across another face.

33

KAREN

"Why are you asking about Seth Farley?" Roy demanded.

"Because after seeing your friend get shot and then being up all night, you came home for a short while. Then you hightailed it to Farley's house to snoop. You don't know where your wife is, so it makes perfect sense you might consider they're together." She sighed. "So, who is he?"

"Your detective skills are way off, Nancy Drew. He has nothing to do with Amber."

"Well then, who is he?"

"Someone who has nothing to do with anything." Roy stood, and grabbed her plate and his, and took them to the sink. "Our conversation is done. I'm going to lie down." He gave her a hard look. "It's time for you to go."

Karen rose while trying to form a question leading him to identify his relationship to Farley. Her phone chimed, showing a text. It was from Brian, her cameraman. He advised her he was on his way to meet her at Roy's. She texted back not to bother—the lead she'd followed was a dead end. She'd catch an Uber ride and connect with him at KABR.

Wondering what the cops in front of the house might do if they found out she was a reporter and Roy was throwing her out worried her. She didn't want to get banned from access to him. She had no choice but to leave.

"Thanks for breakfast. I think you believe Seth Farley and your wife are together. I'll be looking for both of them. If we joined forces, you'd find Amber and I'd get my story. Give it some thought." She handed him her business card.

Later, at the news station, Brian was busy editing the video he'd taken at the warehouse fire. Karen sat at her desk and researched Farley online. After entering his name into a search engine, she could have kicked herself. She should have looked him up last night.

He was suing the City of Los Angeles for wrongful termination—and listed in the lawsuit, along with the police chief and a few other names, was none other than Roy Buckner.

34

SETH

Using a thick red permanent marker to cross out Jeremy Cook's face in the academy photo was a letdown. Seth wasn't sure if it was because of the homeless guy he'd smoked or that soon they'd come after him for being behind the cop killings. He put the top on the marker and shuffled to the card table.

Amber must have sensed his mood because she didn't acknowledge his marks on the picture. She slid the paper plate holding his two sandwiches across the table to him along with a can of soda and chips.

She sat in her seat.

He took a bite of his sandwich and chewed. "It's time we talked."

Her eyes grew wide, and she nodded. "Okay."

"My name is not Victor." He swigged his drink. "I'm Seth Farley." He paused, waiting to see if she reacted.

She frowned.

He watched her trying to place how she knew of him.

"Did you work with my husband, Roy?"

He smirked. "Yeah, I did. What did he tell you?"

Her gaze locked on his. "Nothing. He didn't bring his work home with him."

"That's a real good answer, but considering I'm suing the City of LA *and* your husband, he must have *mentioned* me."

A flash of recognition crossed her face.

"Ah, so now you remember."

She gave a casual shrug. "Not really. My husband said he was being sued. He didn't offer details, and I didn't ask." She took a sip of her soda. "Why are you taking him to court?"

"You expect me to swallow that Roy said *nothing* about me?"

"I told you. Life at LAPD wasn't mentioned at home. We agreed on that when we got married. He wasn't interested in my job as a nurse, and I had no curiosity regarding his career as a cop. It worked for us."

He sat back in his chair. It hurt that his training officer didn't find him worthy of discussion with his wife. "Well, let me put it this way. Your husband was an asshole."

Amber pursed her lips and crossed her arms in front of her chest.

"What? You don't believe me?"

"I do. More than you know."

Could it be that she understood?

She moved her hands and placed them over her belly. "I told you, Roy and I were having difficulties in the bedroom."

She grabbed a chip and popped it into her mouth. "We couldn't get pregnant, and he got mean. His frustration made him find fault with everything I did."

He snorted. "Yep. When things don't go right, he blames everyone else."

Amber nodded, and he wanted to kiss her—not out of sexual desire, but because she'd heard him and understood. She, too, was wrongly disrespected and blamed.

"There was a time," he said, talking fast, "we worked till dawn. I had traffic court that morning. After I got home from the courthouse, I took a nap. I overslept with only twenty minutes to drive to work and put on my uniform." He gave Amber an embarrassed grin. "I was in such a rush I forgot my gun. I hid that I didn't have it by wearing my jacket into roll call. No one saw that my holster was empty."

"Good thinking," she said.

"*I* thought so. But not him. I told him while we gassed up the black and white. He went bat-shit crazy. The whole time we drove to my house to get my firearm, he called me names. He told me I'd better take my head out of my ass or I was gonna get myself or someone else killed."

"That sounds like him. He did the same thing with me."

"That was *one* incident where I made a tiny mistake, and he blew it up into a big deal."

"Does your lawyer think you've got a good chance of winning your case?"

He frowned. "I don't know. My stupid-ass attorney doesn't answer my calls anymore."

"That sucks," she said. "What's the lawsuit about?"

"The morons at the LAPD fired me. It was based on lies that Roy and other officers made up." He tossed the last bit of his second sandwich into his mouth, crumpled his plate, and threw it across the room into a large trash can.

"That punk-ass husband of yours had the nerve to email his friends and laugh and joke about me."

He caught the glance she gave to the picture on the wall. The image with the red *X*'s. "That's right. Those guys. I got another one today."

She let out a long sigh. "If you don't mind me asking, why didn't you start with Roy? You blame him the most, don't you?"

"Yeah, I do. These other guys are just collateral damage—payback for laughing at me. But for Roy, I have something special planned for him. I needed you as a lure to be sure he'd come to me." He reached across the table and motioned she should hold his hand.

She did, and he took it.

"We'll be parents together. I'll get to tell him I'm more of a man than he is. He can think about that as we watch him die—together."

35

ROY

Not a heavy drinker, Roy regretted getting sloshed after going to Farley's house and driving around looking for Amber.

Right after the reporter left, he threw up his breakfast.

The cops out front came to the door, asking for more coffee. Roy's hands shook as he filled the officers' cups. Hopefully, they didn't notice.

Being confined to his home for any length of time only made him want to leave more. He wasn't a guy who sat around waiting for things to happen—he *made* them happen.

His phone rang. He recognized the number belonging to the LAPD. "Buckner."

"Hey, Roy, this is Detective Johnson from RHD. I wanted to do a quick interview with your wife. I've got a couple of questions. Can I talk to her? I've been trying the number you gave me this morning, and it goes to voice mail."

No way was he sharing with a pencil-pusher that his wife had run off with his former probationary partner. "Before the security detail arrived, Amber decided to stay with a friend."

"She didn't want to be with you?"

He bristled at the question. "No. Being locked in your house for hours on end isn't all it's cracked up to be." He dialed back his sarcasm. "Look, Amber wasn't even here when Luke was shot. She can't add anything. Besides, she felt safer at her friend's. I mean, there's no reason to think family members are in danger, is there?"

"With this kind of nutjob, who knows?" There was a pause.

Roy swallowed hard. Maybe he should just come clean. But Johnson didn't give him a chance.

"Where is your wife staying? If she's local, I'll go to her."

Shit. "Her friend lives up near Frazier Park. You'd have a better shot at calling her."

"Yeah, I don't want to drive that far, even though the air is cleaner in the mountains. Do you have a name and number for the friend?"

"The friend's name is Sandy, but I don't have a number for her. I'm sure Amber will call soon. I'll have her call you. I'll send her a text too."

Over the line, he heard the detective sigh. "I've texted your wife. It's not a big deal since she isn't a witness to the Tremont death, but it *is* an *i* I have to dot. Have her call me, and I'll keep trying."

Roy put his cell phone in his pocket and considered his options. The fact he'd lied and said Amber had gone to visit a gal pal meant he must locate her before Johnson did. How to find her while being confined at home was a problem.

The one bright spot was that the reporter wanted to talk to his wife too—why, he didn't know. But Karen was his only hope now.

36

AMBER

The sandwich Amber ate gurgled in her stomach while Farley recounted his demented story. Her skin crawled as he held her hand. The guy was unhinged.

She remembered the stories her husband had told of his unsafe probationer, Seth Farley. Every shift it was something worse. The first night they'd worked together they received a radio call of a man with a gun. While he drove to the location, he explained what he wanted Farley to do if they observed someone matching the suspect's description. Roy directed his partner to be the cover officer, while, as the senior officer, he would take the lead ordering anyone they stopped in what to do.

Arriving at the call, they both saw a possible suspect. Farley, with his pistol still holstered, leaped from the car and ran to the man, ordering the suspect to face him.

Roy had emphasized to her that Farley's actions directly opposed the academy training. The man *did* have a firearm and was wanted for an armed robbery.

To improve his partner's abilities, Roy had created situation simulations to teach his partner some street smarts. One thing she remembered was her husband didn't understand how Farley could be such a rock. He'd been a sergeant in the military. In fact, Roy had said he was intelligent but lacked common sense—an essential aspect to being a cop.

During the two months Roy and Farley had worked together, her husband was irritable and had trouble sleeping.

While Farley droned on to her of the injustices he'd experienced, she fought the compulsion to snatch her hand from her captor's grasp.

If she wanted out of this alive, she needed to gain his trust. She recognized that being a father was a big deal to him, and she knew to play into that belief.

"You're not saying much," he said.

"There've been a lot of changes for me in the past twenty-four hours." She took her plate and soda can and dumped them in the trash. She moved back to the table and sat. "I understand what you're doing and why. I'm sure Roy trashed me to his friends as well."

Farley frowned. "I don't think so. When he talked about you, he was complimentary."

She fought to keep tears from her eyes. She couldn't let this psycho see how much she loved and missed her husband.

"He didn't speak of you often. He was too busy making me do these pretend radio calls and searches and shit. I hated that. None of the other boots did that crap."

"Seth, I need to use the bathroom. Are you comfortable enough to take the chain off me?" She almost gagged using his name, but she had to build his confidence. For her baby, she had to get through this nightmare.

He sat motionless for a few seconds, then gestured for her to come over to him. "I'll free you, and I'll even remove the handcuffs. But if you do anything to get away, I'll kill you and throw your body out for the coyotes to eat. Then I'll kill your parents in Arizona. Are we clear?"

Although horrified that he knew where her mom and dad lived, she kept her face passive. "I understand. You don't have to worry."

He retrieved his key ring from his pocket and thumbed through until he found the handcuff key. He took mere seconds to release the restraints.

Movement never felt so good. She longed to stretch out her arms and twirl but didn't dare. No telling what could send her captor over the edge. Instead, she shuffled off to the bathroom.

Once she was out of Farley's sight, she stretched and raised her hands in the air. "Little baby, I promise you I'll get you out of here," she whispered.

When she returned to the main room, she paused.

Farley appeared to be asleep on the bed.

Amber's heart rate bumped to triple time. Could she find a knife and stab him? Did she have the nerve? Was there time? What if he overpowered her? Too many thoughts and no time to decide.

He opened his eyes. "Hey, Mama. Why don't you come over here and lie beside me?"

37

KAREN

Excited by her find, Karen read articles detailing Seth Farley's lawsuit. He claimed he'd been wrongfully fired as an LAPD officer four months ago. Through his attorney, Farley declared he was hazed and terminated without merit. One reporter had snagged an interview where Farley asserted his training officer, Roy Buckner, "had it in for me from the first day." When asked by the journalist why Buckner singled him out, he snorted. "Roy couldn't tolerate the fact I'm much more intelligent than most new officers on probation."

"Hmm, an ego as large as the Grand Canyon," she mumbled to herself, closing out her search engine and opening Facebook.

Brian entered her cubicle and sat on the edge of her desk. "What happened at Buckner's this morning?"

She gave the cameraman the rundown of her earlier activities—including that Roy didn't know where Amber had gone. Then she told him of her online discoveries regarding the lawsuit.

"Jeez, this guy has no luck. His best friend gets murdered, his wife leaves him and you're speculating she's run off with this wayward cop, and Buckner's turning into a drunk. It's a shame I wasn't with you. It would have made great video."

She shook her head. "He wouldn't have opened up with a camera there. I think I've gained his trust."

"Are you going to help him look for his wife?"

"Yeah, but now she's secondary. My intuition says the big story will come from Farley."

Brian got to his feet. "Carry on. I'm grabbing a sandwich from that place on the corner. Want anything?"

"I ate at Buckner's a while ago but pick me up a small turkey sub—no onions. It's better to be prepared than go hungry."

She returned to her online investigation—this time on Facebook. She started her search looking for LAPD officers. She found a young officer, and by culling through police friends and other police officers, she located Farley's profile. He'd set up his username as LA Blue Boy but she recognized his photo.

As she read his most recent post, Karen's heart pounded. It was long and rambling. She skimmed along, not believing what she was reading and trying not to jump out of her chair and yell, *"I've got the story of the year here!"*

38

ROY

Still nursing his hangover, Roy flopped on the couch and turned on the TV. The low volume provided ambient noise while he dozed. Loud banging jolted him from sleep. Confused, he rolled to the floor.

Roy's cell phone rang. "Buckner," he snapped.

The veteran officer from the security detail spoke. "There's a Detective Johnson from RHD out here. We don't recognize him, but he showed us his ID. Do you know him?"

Shit. This isn't good. "Yeah, he's okay. Thanks." Ending the call, he went to the door, looked out the peephole, and confirmed it was the lanky detective, then unlocked and opened it.

Johnson didn't waste words. "Let me in. We need to talk."

He swung the door wider and motioned Johnson into the house. "Have a seat."

"No. I'll stand."

"Can I get you something to drink? Water? A soda?"

"Cut the crap, Roy." Johnson's eyes pierced into his. "Where is your wife?"

"I told you—"

"What you told me is bullshit. I've called her every hour on the hour. Her phone just rings and rings. We've pulled her records and tried pinging it, and her cell is not on. The last location documented was here—at your house. I'm asking you again. Where is Amber?"

He hesitated. He was unsure what to say.

"On second thought, I will sit," said Johnson. "You should take a seat too." The detective settled at the end of the sofa.

Roy sank into one of the two club chairs opposite the couch.

"Let me lay this out for you, Roy. I've been trying for twelve hours to contact Amber. I want to interview her, but she's disappeared. This afternoon, I hear rumors you've got a hot blonde who *isn't* Mrs. Buckner having breakfast with you."

Roy shook his head. "Those guys out front jumped to the wrong conclusion. She's just someone I know. Nothing is going on there."

"Do you see how it looks?" Johnson ran his hand through his hair. "I need you tell me the truth, and you need to start right now."

39

AMBER

Bile rose in Amber's throat. Farley was sprawled on the bed. She knew what he wanted.

He patted the mattress again. "Come on. Our first time wasn't ideal. But you didn't really know me. This will be better—for both of us."

"I'd like nothing more, Seth, but it's too dangerous for the baby."

A scowl formed on his face while his hands closed into fists.

He'll beat you again. Think of something. "We'll do other things to be...intimate."

The furrows around his eyes eased. "What have you got in mind?"

"I can give you a long relaxing massage, and I'm sure I'll be able to relieve any tension you have."

He snorted. "You sound like a street whore enticing a john." He sat up, peeled his shirt over his head, and tossed it on the floor. Next, he stood and stripped off his pants and underwear. "I'll take the massage, but I've got something different in mind for getting my rocks off," he said, rubbing his index finger around his lips. He flopped onto the rumpled sheets, his arousal on full display. "Come over here and make Daddy happy."

She rubbed lotion over his skin, paying attention to what excited him. The more eager he became, the more she talked to him—detailing what she was doing and how his body was reacting—and how those reactions turned her on. She had him turn over to his stomach and massaged his back. Moving her hands lower, she teased him to where he groaned in impassioned agony. At the height of her performance, she directed him to flip over again. He was straining to keep from coming.

"Look at me," she said. With one hand on him, her gaze seared into his, she slid her other hand under her shirt and massaged her breasts. She increased her speed and pressure on him, and he came, shooting his cum over his chest and her arm.

He was not happy. "That's not what I wanted. You made me come too fast."

"We have a lifetime together. There's plenty of time to share pleasure." She marveled how she thought up such garbage on the fly. She rose and went to the makeshift sink where she washed her hands and arm. While she cleaned herself, she looked around the kitchen. He must have hidden the carving knife she'd used to cut the sandwiches.

She brought several wet paper towels to clean his ejaculation from his skin. Her ministrations calmed him.

He sighed and pushed himself to a sitting position. "Get the chain and bring it here."

She did as he asked.

He reached out to her, fit the links around her waist, and secured it with a padlock. Then he pulled her to lie next to him. Devastated by the disappointment that he'd chained her again, she rolled onto her side.

Not much later, Farley snored and didn't stir.

Oh, how she wanted a hot shower. At least he hadn't raped or beaten her again. She wondered if he'd wake up if she took a shower. The water would be cold but better than nothing.

She eased herself off the mattress. Once on her feet, she looked back at Farley, who slept. Amber carefully placed her footsteps so she wouldn't make noise. She didn't want him to wake and expect to be serviced again.

While examining how the shower worked, she heard a noise from the generator room vent. It was a car in the distance. *Please come this way! Find me!*

Farley's phone emitted an alarm sound. The springs protested as he sprung from the bed.

"Amber," he yelled in a stage whisper.

"I'm in the bathroom," she hissed.

He ran to where she stood. He held a gun by the side of his leg. "I'll see who's out there."

While he talked, the sound of tires stopping on the gravel filled her with hope.

He nodded toward the mattress. "Sit there and don't make a sound."

Hesitating, she wondered if she should scream.

He raised the pistol and pointed it at her face. "Hurry, or I'll kill you right now and then take care of whoever is in the car."

She darted to the bed and curled up in a fetal position.

He threw on his clothes and hurried to the stairway, activating the device on his key ring as he walked. The opening to the underground chamber creaked wide.

40

———

KAREN

Karen minimized the screen on her computer and went to find her producer.

Naturally, just when she was sitting on a huge story, her producer was meeting with the news director. Should she break into their conference? She paced outside the door for a few seconds, then knocked.

A voice came from behind the door. "Enter."

She turned the knob and poked her head into the meeting room. To her dismay, the producer, news director, and the station manager were meeting. She noted the surprise on her producer's face. "Can I speak to you for a second? It's urgent."

He rose from his chair and cleared his throat. "Excuse me. I'll be right back."

She inwardly cringed at his tone. He planned on reaming her as soon as they were out of sight and sound.

He stepped out into the hallway and closed the door. "This had better be good."

"I know who's killing the cops—and why."

"Who? And how did you find out?"

"It's a guy named Seth Farley. Formerly an officer with the LAPD. Fired for poor performance, he's got a long rambling statement he put on Facebook. He says he's smarter than current officers and picking them off one by one is his way of proving his point. He's starting with those who took part in getting him booted off the LAPD. He sounds like one sick puppy. You need to read it for yourself."

"Show me," the producer urged.

She walked him to her desk and brought up Farley's post.

The producer made quick work of skimming the document. "I'll tell the director, and get on the phone with LAPD. Good job, Karen." He started back toward the conference room. "Grab something to eat because we'll be working late."

PART V

41

SETH

Thank God for the alarm device he'd buried in the road.

On his phone, Seth looked at an app connected to a series of cameras hidden in Joshua trees at different vantage points on the property. A county sheriff's black and white vehicle had stopped fifty yards from the block building where he stood. He zoomed in on the SUV. He recognized that the law officer was using his in-car computer, probably to run the license plate on his truck.

After closing the phone app, he glanced around the upper bunker. Everything needed to look legitimate. He'd staged an open duffel bag with clothes. He'd even crumpled fast-food wrappers and tossed them into a cardboard box. He hurried to the camping lanterns and turned them on.

Taking a deep breath to relax, he opened the door to greet

his visitor. He stepped out onto the cement stoop and shaded his eyes with his hand.

The deputy climbed out of his SUV. Dark shades hid the lawman's expression. His relaxed manner suggested to Seth a wanted alert about him hadn't gone out yet.

"Howdy," said the lawman.

"How's it going?"

"Good." He closed his door, assisted by a robust breeze. The cop walked toward the shanty.

Seth noted the video camera clipped to the cop's uniform shirt.

"Can I help you?"

"I'm Deputy Howard from the Los Angeles County Sheriff's Office." The officer came and stood a few feet from him.

Seth noticed he'd left himself room to take cover behind the corner of the hideout. The guy was at ease but tactically sound. He wondered if the lawman was stalling and waiting for another deputy to arrive.

"We got a call from a local there's new activity at this property. They asked us to check it out."

He smiled at the deputy, but inside he seethed. *Stupid desert rats. Why couldn't they mind their own business?* "I understand. It's true. I just bought the place."

Deputy Howard held up his finger and keyed the mic on his shirt. "A114, roger."

He must have another unit coming.

"We ask people to call us if they see something unusual. In today's world, we can't be too careful."

"I'm setting up a weekend place where I can bring my boys and get them away from their damn electronics for a while." Seth laughed.

"I hear ya, brother. I've got a couple of teenagers myself. They're always looking at their phones."

Seth opened the building's door. "Come on in and look around."

The cop propped his sunglasses on top of his head and followed him into the block structure. "Wow, this is primitive. Your boys are in for a culture shock."

Seth laughed and nodded, praying Amber wouldn't make noise or do something stupid—like scream. He didn't want this deputy to become more collateral damage. "Tell me about it. It'll be good for them."

He pulled out a card that Seth equated with the LAPD's field interview cards. "Do you have your ID? I need to jot down who I spoke to out here."

"Sure, no problem," he said as he got his driver's license out of his wallet.

Deputy Howard documented the information and handed him back his ID. "Thanks. I'll let the neighbors know you own the property and they don't have to worry drugged-out tweakers will blow up the area."

Seth grinned and walked the officer out to his vehicle. "Stop by if you're out this way again."

The deputy laughed. "You don't even have the means to make a good cup of coffee. Maybe next time I'll bring you a Venti from Starbucks." He climbed into his patrol unit and started the engine.

Seth gave him a wave and sauntered back inside.

42

———

ROY

Roy looked back at Johnson, realizing the detective was inferring he'd done something to Amber. "Wait a minute. You can't think I hurt my wife."

Johnson just stared at him.

"You've got to be kidding. I love her."

"Then it's simple. Either produce her or put me in touch with her. Right now." The detective's gaze bore into Roy's.

He sighed. "I can't."

"Why not?"

"I don't know where she is. She may have left me." He related Amber's revelation of her pregnancy and his response. "I was too hard on her. When I got home from the hospital, the house was empty, and two of our suitcases are missing."

Johnson sat silent for a few seconds. "Is her car gone?"

"Yes. I searched the parking garage and the lot in front of the hospital, but her SUV wasn't there." He recounted his conversation with his mother-in-law and that she hadn't heard from her daughter.

The detective made a note on his notepad. "I'll get an APB out for her vehicle. Other than the fight yesterday, have you two been getting along?"

"Yes. At least I thought so."

"What does that mean?"

"I never expected that she'd leave me."

Johnson looked at the floor and then turned his gaze to him. "Could there be someone else?"

Roy ground his teeth together. "Absolutely not." He refused to air his dirty laundry to a stranger. The LAPD *family* extended only so far.

"What about you? Have you been cheating on your wife?" The detective's unwavering gaze had Roy squirming.

"I'm not a player. If I wanted other women, I never would have gotten married."

The detective sighed. "You need to file a missing person's report." Johnson's cell rang. He pulled the phone out of his pocket and looked at the display. "Excuse me, I need to take this."

Roy grew uneasy as Johnson listened without saying much. The detective's eyes narrowed. The news was not good.

"No need. I'm with him now. I'll tell him."

Something awful had happened. Not for the first time during the day, he worried he'd vomit. He knew what was happening. As soon as Johnson got off the phone, the detective would tell him Amber was dead.

43

———

AMBER

As soon as Farley lowered the secret door to the bunker, Amber jumped off the bed. She ran to the generator room where the vent disappeared in the dirt ceiling to the outside. She craned her neck to hear anything aboveground.

Sounds were lost in a stiff breeze blowing across the opening, causing a whistling sound. Frustrated, she jogged to the stairs at the secret opening and crept to the highest step where she could sit without hitting her head on the floor above her.

Two men talked—one of them Farley. She made out an occasional word, but most were muffled. She heard Farley laugh. Who was this second guy? Did Farley have an accomplice? A partner in crime didn't seem likely. He hadn't indicated he was working with someone else.

What should she do? Scream for help? Tap out the Morse

code for S-O-S? She knew what would happen. If Farley wasn't conspiring with the guy upstairs, he'd kill him then murder her too. She'd gain nothing and cause the death of an innocent bystander. *This might be your only chance. He can keep you here for months or even years.*

Shuffling of feet sounded above her. Another laugh from Farley and then the topside door closed, leaving silence.

Scream. Do something!

Tears welled in her eyes and rolled down her cheeks. Above her, the sound of footsteps had her dashing to the bed. She got herself back to the mattress and curled in a ball as the opening to her dungeon rose.

Her captor descended the steps two at once. "Get up! Gather your things." Fury filled his face, from his blazing eyes to the severe downturn of his lips.

"Why? What's wrong?"

"Just do it. There's no time to explain."

She wasn't sure what he wanted her to collect. Her suitcases packed with her belongings were still against the wall. She knelt next to her luggage and sifted through them, more to stay out of his way than anything else.

Being moved to another location was unsettling. Was anyone looking for her? What must Roy think? Had he reported her missing? Did he have any idea his probationary partner, Farley, had kidnapped her?

"Zip those bags up and get started in the kitchen." He marched to the bookshelf and pulled out two pieces of flattened cardboard stored behind the shelving unit. He tossed them on the floor. "There's packing tape on the shelf below the sink. Make the boxes and pack the food. I'll handle the perishables in the ice chest."

She did as he directed.

Meanwhile, he muttered to himself as he used several keys to unlock the cabinet on the wall—the one she assumed held weapons.

She formed the cartons, using her teeth to bite through the tape to tear strips off the roll. While working, she glanced as he opened the cupboard, and sure enough, there were rifles, or maybe they were shotguns. She didn't know much about firearms. Besides the big guns, there were at least four handguns and colorful boxes of ammunition.

He caught her eyeing his actions. "Do what I told you and keep your nose out of shit that doesn't concern you."

Her cheeks flamed at being discovered gawking at his arsenal.

"Once you're done with the food, roll up the bedding. You'll find twine under the sink. Tie it up and don't forget the pillows."

"How am I supposed to cut the rope?"

He glared at her. "You chewed through the tape, didn't you?"

As she rummaged around on the shelf, her gaze searched for a knife or another weapon-worthy tool she could tuck away. "Are you planning to take everything with us?"

"No. We don't have time for that. Stupid fucking neighbors couldn't mind their own business. Worried I'm cooking drugs or something." He retrieved a nylon gun case from under the bed frame and positioned the long guns in it, and then situated the handguns inside, too.

"I'll run these up to the truck. Don't do anything dumb

while I'm up there. You did the right thing by keeping quiet while we had company."

She nodded.

With a grunt, he lifted the black nylon container and carried it in two arms, as if it were a body, and started up the stairs.

Oh, how she wished she had a knife to drive into his back. Once he was topside, she searched the kitchen area for anything to use against him.

Something had spooked him. The only thing that made sense was the visitor lived nearby or was a cop. She couldn't keep herself from second-guessing her decision to not scream for help. But at least she was still alive. Maybe she could escape once they left.

44

———

KAREN

Karen's mood was darker than the midnight blue of the uniforms worn by the LAPD officers who stood with her in the auditorium at the Police Administration Building.

Her big story regarding Seth Farley had aired during the evening news. The anchorman had given her credit for discovering Farley's declarations on social media. Piqued, she griped to Brian how she should have been the one to announce Farley's connection to the cop killings.

He told her to get used to it—that's how the business worked. Meanwhile, they were assigned to police headquarters for official updates on the investigation and the hunt for Seth Farley.

In her gut Karen felt Amber's disappearance and Farley's reign of terror were connected. But did Roy realize that? Was he aware Farley was the cop killer? She wanted to talk to Roy, but she didn't have time before the press conference got underway.

The mayor's speech was concise and to the point. There was an update on the investigation of the recent murders of police officers, and the chief would provide additional information.

Even with her short tenure in Los Angeles, she had the top cop pegged as someone who liked to aggrandize his importance. For a man in his sixties, he was in excellent shape and wore the uniform well. His boyish features were enhanced, she was sure, with Botox injections. His high and tight haircut was longish on the top and spiked unevenly— giving the impression of someone trendy and hot.

"Good afternoon. I will read my statement, and I won't be taking any questions." He cleared his throat. "It was brought to our attention that a former officer with the LAPD had posted a lengthy document on social media. We've since had the posting removed. In the writings, Seth Farley disputed his termination from the department which occurred four months ago. He blamed several employees for his shortcomings and mentioned some officers by name. In his writings, he made criminal threats against LAPD personnel and indicated a possible involvement in the deaths of several officers. Currently those claims are unsubstantiated, but we *are* looking into them. We're looking at Farley as a person of interest and encourage him to turn himself in for questioning. When we have any new information, we'll give an update. Thank you very much."

As the chief stepped from the podium, reporters shouted out questions, but he and the mayor and their respective entourages kept walking.

Brian had shot the press conference live, and afterward, Karen filmed a quick wrap-up to air during future news broadcasts.

Once they'd finished, she tried contacting Roy, but her call went to voicemail. She left a message asking him to call her.

She found Brian lounging in a camping chair and playing a game on his phone. "I'm going to find a restroom. Want me to bring coffee or soda or something?"

He didn't even look up. "Nah, I'm good. I've got a cooler in the van with drinks and snacks. You're welcome to help yourself."

"No thanks. I'll be back in a few."

She walked to the lobby. On her way to the ladies' room she saw a cluster of uniformed officers, including the chief, walking toward the front door.

Without thinking, she hurried to the group. "Chief, Karen Watson from KABR. Farley's manifesto didn't reference kidnapping or harming family members of officers. Yet I have it on good authority that the wife of an LAPD officer is missing. Can you comment on that?"

The whole pack stopped short and stared at her.

The chief moved to the front. "Who are you, again?"

"Karen Watson KABR News."

"We're happy to hear any relevant information you have." He motioned to the only guy in their bunch wearing a suit.

"Yes, sir."

"Detective Carlisle, please escort Miss Watson up to RHD. She mentioned she possibly has knowledge of the Farley case we need. If it turns out to be worthwhile, you'll notify me, right?"

"Roger that, Sir."

The detective stepped out of the cluster and motioned for her to walk toward a pair of turnstiles. He used his ID card to allow her to pass through, and he followed.

She glanced back at the lobby. The chief and his group had moved out of the building, and Karen realized she'd made a tactical mistake.

45

———

SETH

Months ago, when Seth had found the block building in the desert, he'd never dreamed anyone would notice his comings and goings. He'd lied to the sheriff's deputy. He didn't own the property. His research had shown the land belonged to the county. Apparently, the owner had forfeited ownership instead of paying taxes—or died and had no next of kin to pay.

Seth had felt comfortable removing the lock on the front door and installing his own, then adding more locks to keep vandals at bay. From appearances, no one had visited in years. It was a huge bonus to find the building had an underground bunker—probably built as a bomb shelter in the sixties.

It was the perfect hideout and he'd been so confident it wouldn't be discovered, there was no plan B. Now he was heading out on the road with his quasi-kidnapped girlfriend with no idea where he was going. Even worse, a news alert on his phone had said the LAPD had held a press conference where they announced the discovery of his personal proclamation. They'd named him as a person of interest in the deaths of officers. He was on the run—just as the shit had hit the fan.

Next to him in the pickup, Amber sat deep in her own thoughts. He wondered if she had any idea how much trouble they faced.

He reached his hand across the center console of his truck and wormed his fingers into hers.

She looked at him with a questioning stare.

"Things are getting crazy," he said. "I'm glad you're with me."

"Seth, we're having a child together. I'm scared. I don't know what's happening, but something is wrong if we're running. Where are we going?"

He sighed. "Yeah, well, that's the problem. I'm not sure." He shrugged. "I thought the desert property was a perfect place to hide. I figured I'd use you to lure Roy there, kill him, cut him up, and let Mother Nature do the rest."

He glanced at her for a reaction and there wasn't any. Further evidence her marriage to Roy wasn't that strong.

They rode in silence for a few minutes.

"Maybe..." she said, drawing the word out, "I tell Roy that he and I are through. We turn ourselves in, and the police do their investigation. They'd have to produce evidence that you'd done something to those other officers, and they've already declared one death accidental and the other a suicide." She gave him a small smile. "You've been so smart no one can prove you shot Luke Tremont *or* Jeremy Cook."

He withdrew his hand from hers and slapped her across the face. "You are out of your friggin' mind if you think I'll turn myself in. I thought you were on my side. Apparently, you're not. Now I've got to worry about you running off and doing something to get us caught."

As if he didn't have enough problems. He'd been counting on sending Amber out for supplies or fast food. His face would be all over the media before long. Stupid bitch! Why couldn't she go along with the program?

He drove up the interstate, his thoughts tumbling over one another. She was a liability. He'd have a much better chance of evading capture if he was on his own. She might have to become collateral damage. But there was the baby to consider.

Decisions, decisions.

46

———

ROY

Sitting on his couch, Roy wanted to cry with relief when Detective Johnson hung up his phone, and told him they had a break in the cop-killer case.

"Then Amber's body hasn't been found?"

Johnson gave him a puzzled look. "What makes you think she's dead?"

"The phone call. The way you were talking, I thought they'd found her body and you'd make the death notification."

The detective shook his head. "No. But the news I have isn't much better. A hotshot reporter dug around on Facebook and came across a posting taking responsibility for the deaths of Jerry McMillan and Paulo Delgado. You'll never guess who wrote the post."

"Who?"

"Your former partner, Seth Farley."

"What?" Thoughts ping-ponged through Roy's brain like a bullet ricochet.

"Apparently he's coming after everyone he feels caused his firing." The detective looked at him pointedly. "That includes you."

Roy couldn't process the information rushing through his mind. Was it possible that Farley had brainwashed Amber and started an affair with her as part of a scheme of revenge? To him, considering the emails and the evidence in his bed, infidelity seemed more likely than his wife being kidnapped by his former partner. But how to be sure? There was always the outside chance that Farley had taken her against her will. *No. He's killed off cops one by one. What's the point of taking Amber?*

Should he tell Johnson about the emails and the intimate stain? *No.* He feared the love notes and bedding told a story he wasn't ready to face. It wasn't information he wanted to share with anyone else—at least until he was sure his suspicions were right.

He had to get rid of Johnson, then ditch the security detail out front. He needed to find Amber. Sitting straighter, he turned to the detective. "I'm ready to report my wife missing."

47

AMBER

Amber had screwed up. Suggesting that Farley turn himself in was a stupid move. She'd unraveled whatever trust she'd built since persuading him he'd gotten her pregnant. Now she had to fix it.

She needed to offer a place for them to hide where he'd feel comfortable but one that allowed her the possibility of escape. If she could figure out a location, she'd take back some control while convincing Farley she was helping him. But where?

They rode in silence for at least five minutes when an idea finally came to her.

"I know where we can go and be safe until we decide what to do," she said, intentionally using the word *we*. It was a signal she was part of his team.

"Where?"

"Before they died, my grandparents owned an old cabin in the woods near Big Bear Lake. My parents were trying to sell it, but I begged them to hang onto it. They've been renting it out. No one would look for us there."

"Really? What about Roy? Has he been to the cabin?"

She tilted her head, feigning consideration. She and Roy had spent a romantic week in Big Bear the previous winter. But had Roy mentioned that trip to his partner? Was Farley testing her loyalty to him? She'd have to take a chance. "No. We've never discussed it." She held her breath waiting for his response.

"How do we know the place isn't rented now?"

She shrugged. "We don't."

"No matter," he said. "We'll deal with whatever we find when we get there. It's a good idea and will give us a place to develop a plan."

She worried what he meant by *dealing with* what they found at the cabin.

He rolled his shoulders to release tension. "We need new license plates for this truck." For the first time since they'd left the bunker, he smiled. "I'm driving north. It's unexpected. I'll take Highway 58 out to Barstow and switch plates there. We'll blend in because it's a transient town with lots of people passing through. From there we take Route 247 to Highway 18 and to the cabin."

Yes, go to Barstow. Maybe a trooper or local sheriff's deputy will catch you in the act of stealing license plates and rescue me.

"It's smart you're staying off Interstate 15. The CHP is always on the interstate giving tickets to speeders heading to Vegas." She shifted in her seat. "I realize we're in a hurry, but I need to use the restroom."

A look of irritation flashed across Farley's face. "You can go on the side of the road. I won't risk taking you into a restaurant or something."

"How about a gas station? I can't relieve myself in public. I've tried before."

"You didn't think you could pee on the pregnancy test stick in front of me, but you did."

"Okay. I'll try, but it will probably take me a while." She threw worry into her voice. "I hope we don't attract the attention of a highway patrolman."

A muscle jumped in his jaw as he considered the possibility.

"Fine. I'll stop at a bathroom—but I'll choose the location."

Twenty minutes later Farley exited the roadway and pulled into the lot of a rest stop. The last of the sun was sinking into the horizon, and dreary yellowed lights on poles flickered to life, causing moths to circle in a frenzy. Once he parked his truck, she reached for the door handle.

"No. We'll sit and wait until the ladies' room is empty. Once you're inside, I'll stand outside and keep anyone else out."

She had to fight not to let her deflation show. It was as if he'd read her mind. When she saw they were at a rest stop, she'd planned to tell everyone in the restroom Farley had kidnapped her and to call the police. But he was a step ahead of her.

As they sat there, two different ladies went separately into the facility.

In the pickup, she and Farley waited until both women got into their cars and left.

There were three big rigs and one sedan still in the parking lot. A man exited the passenger car and headed to the building. While they sat, there wasn't any sign of life at the tractor-trailers.

"Okay," he said. "Sit tight. I'll come get you." Within seconds he was at her door. "Let's go."

She slid from her seat.

He locked the truck, then grabbed her arm. "Remember, if you screw up, I'll have no problem dumping anyone, including innocent people. Don't be stupid."

She nodded. "You've nothing to worry about. I won't put our child in danger."

The tan stucco building had a huge *V*-shaped overhang, no doubt to block the relentless summer sun. In the coolness of fall, the projection blocked the sparse autumn leaves swirling to the ground.

There was a bulge under Farley's shirt on the right side of his waist. The lump was the handgun he was never without, and she knew he meant every word he'd said about using it.

She started for the ladies' room.

"I'm going in with you."

She stopped and turned to face him. "What if there's someone in there?"

"I'll double check. Then I'll wait at the door."

Foiled again. She'd hoped a woman was driving one of the big trucks in the parking lot and that the female trucker was in the restroom. That plan was ruined. They both entered the bathroom.

Farley satisfied himself there was no one inside. "I'll be waiting out front."

"Okay."

As soon as he was out of sight, she searched the sink area, hoping to find a forgotten lipstick or eyeliner—anything she could use to write on the wall. There was nothing. She scanned the floor and even checked the stalls but met with the same results.

She didn't have much time. She used the facilities then looked for a painted object where she could scratch a message using her fingernail. Unfortunately, the state was ahead of the game in rest-stop vandalism. None of the steel surfaces lent themselves to being etched, at least not by a fingernail.

She had no choice but to return to Farley. When she came out of the restroom, he wasn't in sight. *He must have needed a pit stop too.* She looked across the parking lot. The lone sedan was gone, but the semi-trucks were still parked. The weird dim lighting from the poles left pockets of darkness across the vast asphalt.

The pickup was empty. *Run, Amber, run! Now is your chance—get away. Run to the trucks and get help.*

Her gaze scoured the men's room area. No sign of Farley. *Go!* She took off running toward the big rigs. As she got farther from the building, she increased her speed. The big rigs were thirty yards away when, through the dim light, she realized several men were standing between two of the trucks—and one of them was Farley.

48

KAREN

Karen had been with two RHD detectives for over an hour. They'd allowed her to text Brian to alert him she was being interviewed. She asked her cameraman to contact the assignment editor at KABR and advise them of the situation.

One of the detectives had a pinched face like a rodent. The other man was stocky with dark brown eyes. He'd introduced himself as Detective Romero.

She'd wanted to keep Roy's confidence and not tell the investigators that Amber's husband didn't know the location of his wife. But the more they questioned her, she realized the cops weren't playing around and she'd better disclose everything she'd uncovered.

Karen related going to the Buckner home to interview Amber, but Roy's wife wasn't there.

"It's your understanding Roy has no idea where his wife is and he hasn't seen her since she left for work last night?"

"Yes, that's correct."

"And yet you have word Mrs. Buckner was kidnapped? Who told you that? Roy?"

Karen couldn't help the huge sigh that escaped her. "I *explained* already. After finding Seth Farley's posting on Facebook, I made the assumption he's connected to Amber Buckner's disappearance. It makes perfect sense to put two and two together."

The detective with the pointed rat nose snorted. "It's that kind of reasoning that gets people into trouble, especially the press."

Detective Romero shook his head. "Did you share your theory with Roy?"

"I mentioned it to him, yeah."

"What did he say?"

She shrugged. "Nothing, except he was sure she was fine."

The investigators exchanged a glance.

"Thank you, Miss Watson. We'll be in touch if we have any further questions."

"Do I need to have someone walk me out?"

Rat Boy stood. "I'll take you to the elevator."

Karen rose from her chair. The pointy-nosed detective held the door open for her. As she passed Detective Romero, she thought she heard him whisper to his partner, "I'll get started on the search warrant."

49

ROY

After Roy filed a missing person's report on Amber, Detective Johnson finally left, giving Roy time to put a plan in place.

He stuffed a backpack with a several changes of clothes and a few toiletries. He had to wait for the night watch shift to arrive and take their position outside his house.

A little before 8:00 p.m. there was a knock at the door. Two different fresh-faced uniformed officers stood on the porch and stated they were the night watch security detail.

He invited them in and said he already had a fresh pot of coffee going. After the cops got their cup of joe and exchanged phone numbers, they moved to go back outside.

"Hey, guys, since you'll be out front, the door will be unlocked. That gives you access to the head, and you can grab more caffeine. I'll leave some fruit and chips out too." He grinned at the younger men. "Be sure one of you stays awake so Farley doesn't get inside to slit my throat."

The officers laughed, but the fact was Roy knew how graveyard cops were usually sleep-deprived. Working all night took a toll. Add in being subpoenaed to court a couple of times a week when you should be asleep, and officer was bound to be tired.

Sitting in a patrol car doing nothing for twelve hours parked in front of another cop's house would be torturous. It was unlikely either of them would stay awake the whole shift.

He wasn't worried, though. He wouldn't be there.

After double-checking everything he'd crammed into the backpack, Roy turned on a light in the kitchen and set out the snacks for the security detail. He then headed to the bedroom. He couldn't look at the bed. The mental images of Amber and Farley having sex made Roy want to puke—and want to kill his former partner.

But there was work to do. In case the security detail got nosy, Roy retrieved spare pillows from the closet and placed them underneath the covers, shaping them like a person sleeping. His handiwork wasn't great but it would fool someone glancing into the room.

Roy went to the living room and peeked out the window at the black and white backed into his driveway. There was a glow on both officer's faces—reflections from their phones screens they kept below the dashboard level, but nonetheless, they were illuminated. "Stupid kids," he muttered. *If Farley wanted to pick them off, he'd have no problem completing a head-shot with the light their screens provided.*

Roy stood for a second not sure if he should tell them they were making easy targets of themselves. He took his phone out of his pocket and dialed one of the guys in the patrol car.

"Gentry," the kid answered.

"Hey, the lady across the street called. She wondered if I knew there were two men in a car sitting in my driveway using their cell phones. I guess she figured out what you were doing but didn't notice you were cops. Anyway, I wanted to give you a heads-up you're lighting yourselves up."

"Roger that. We'll be more careful."

I bet. "Be safe, and don't hesitate to come and get coffee and snacks. I'm turning in now."

"Roger." The line disconnected.

"Okay, you millennial masters, you're on your own," Roy said to no one.

He slung the backpack over his shoulder and left his house through the back door. He walked across the grass, hoisted himself over the fence and dropped into his rear neighbor's yard.

50

SETH

Seth had just bought some weed off one of the truckers when he noticed the driver's attention fixated on something over his shoulder. He turned.

Amber jogged toward them.

At least she wasn't running away. But it annoyed him she'd exposed herself to outsiders. She slowed to a walk and tried to catch her breath.

Seth held up his hand, indicating she should stop. "Honey, I'm almost done here. Go to the truck and wait for me." To his surprise and displeasure, Amber kept walking toward them.

Joining the group, she displayed a dazzling smile. "I saw your mouth moving, but with the traffic from the highway, I couldn't hear you."

Seth clenched his teeth. He wasn't used to orders being ignored, no matter what the reason. "Thanks, guys. Nice talking to you." He grabbed Amber's elbow. "Come on, sweetie. We've got a heap of road to cover before we reach Vegas."

He turned Amber from the men and marched her across the vast parking lot.

As they walked away, she peered over her shoulder at the weathered truckers and gave them another grand smile. "Bye," she said brightly.

"Come on." Seth tightened his grip on her arm and jerked her forward. "What's the matter with you?" He pulled her around to the passenger door and opened it. "Get in." As he walked to his side of the pickup, the men watched them from a distance.

He climbed into the driver's seat. "What the hell was that all about?"

Amber's lower lip quivered. "I came out of the bathroom, and you weren't there. I thought you'd dumped me here. Then I saw you talking to those guys. I was so happy to see you, I guess I got giddy."

"Didn't you notice the truck was still here?"

"I'm sorry. I panicked." She turned to face him. "I was scared."

It was hard to be mad at a woman who freaked out because she couldn't find you and was frightened. He sighed and leaned over the center console. "Sorry I worried you, baby. Give me a kiss."

She smiled at him and met his lips with her own. When he tried to get a little tongue action, she jerked back.

"Hey, what's wrong?"

"You said it yourself. We've got a long way to go."

Less than an hour later, they pulled into a shopping outlet in Barstow. He cruised between the aisles of cars. The light poles were spaced far apart, and the lighting was dim.

Amber scanned the parking area. "What are we doing?"

"We're searching for a pickup the same make and year as my truck. Once we find one, I'll swap out the plates. You'll have to act as my lookout."

"I'm surprised more people aren't walking around," she said.

"Don't complain. This works to our advantage. I should have no problem switching out the plates."

He had to drive to a different parking lot before he found a matching vehicle. Even better, the space next to the truck was empty. He pulled alongside the pickup but left the engine on his own vehicle running.

"What are the odds of finding another brown truck the same make and year as mine? If anyone approaches, you walk out to them and distract them."

"How?" Her tone was incredulous.

"I don't know. Make something up. Ask for directions, ask for money. At least give me enough time to boost the plates. If I can, I'll put my plates on the other pickup."

He climbed out of the driver's seat and paused. He reached through the steering wheel and turned off the engine of his vehicle. His gaze met Amber's. "It looks kind of suspicious to have a truck sitting there idling in a parking space."

She nodded. "Good luck."

"Keep your eyes open for anyone approaching." He pulled out his Swiss army knife, found the Phillips-head screwdriver, and removed the cold plate. While he worked, he wondered about the little voice that had told him not to leave Amber alone with the truck keys. He hated when his internal voice appeared, but he'd learned long ago his inner voice knew what it was talking about.

PART VI

51

———

AMBER

Amber didn't know what Farley and the two semi drivers had been doing, but her gut told her they weren't exchanging chocolate chip cookie recipes. She'd heard Farley tell her to go back to the truck but getting her face seen by the grungy men was her opportunity to be remembered—and hopefully rescued.

The episode also taught her that in front of other people she could resist Farley's orders. He wasn't happy when she'd sidled near him and his semi-driving buddies, but he'd held his temper in check.

Thank goodness he hadn't caught the exaggerated wink she gave the truckers when she'd turned to say goodbye. She'd done everything in her power to get those men to remember her face. Eventually the world would realize she was missing and the more people she could make an impression on, the better.

As penance for her misbehavior, she knew Farley would need reassurance she was still on his team. Pretending to be fearful that he'd left her at the rest stop was so ridiculous Amber felt sure he'd see through her ruse. Instead, Farley had soaked it up. Another piece of information to store away. The guy was starving for love.

With cold plates on his pickup, they pulled into the drive-thru of a popular burger joint.

Farley was more relaxed. She considered asking him to let her go to the bathroom, but he'd never approve because the fast-food spot was packed. Besides, she'd just used a restroom a little while ago. It was better to lie low since she'd been so bold at the rest stop.

Finally, they placed their order and moved through the line.

"We'll eat in the truck as I drive. I want to get to Big Bear as soon as possible." He collected their order and pulled out into traffic. "Unwrap my burger and put the bag of fries on the console."

Amber did as she was told. Once she had the straw in his drink and his food laid out as directed, she unwrapped her own meal and ate.

"You know where the cabin is, right?"

She took a sip of soda. "Yes. It's been a long time since I've been there, but I'm pretty sure I'll be able to direct you with no problem."

He nodded. "Good."

They'd left the Vegas-bound tourists in Barstow and transitioned onto Highway 247, heading south toward Big Bear.

The roadway was much less traveled. Farley turned on the radio to a news station.

After finishing their meals, Amber crumpled the burger wrappers and napkins.

"Fuck," he spat out.

"What's wrong?"

"A CHP unit appeared like a bat out of hell and is sitting on my ass."

Amber twisted in her seat.

"Don't turn around and look at him!"

She spun forward, her eyes locked on the roadway. *Please, God, let him pull us over.*

Farley maintained his pace, which was a few miles below the speed limit. "Asshole is probably running the plate. I bet he has a description of my truck. The only problem is the plates don't match the vehicle that's wanted." He chuckled. "Now what you going to do, Road Ranger?"

Amber sat as still as a cat waiting to pounce on a mouse. *Please stop us!*

"Push your seat back as far as it will go."

"What?"

"Push your seat back. If he stops us, he'll come up to your window. I'll dump him and I sure as hell don't want to hit you."

"Oh my God. You're going to shoot him? You can't do that."

"Stay out of my way, Amber. I've got a plan, and I can pull it off with or without you."

As much as she wanted to be rescued, she wouldn't want the officer to pull them over only to be killed in front of her. In her mind she tried to plan how to warn the officer if he stopped them. But she trembled so badly with fear she couldn't think.

Farley's gaze locked on the side mirror of his truck. "What's it gonna be, Triple-A With a Gun? Let me go about my business or a shootout at the OK Corral?"

52

KAREN

Karen learned that if the story was big enough, there was plenty of money for overtime. After she reunited with Brian, he'd encouraged her to call their producer with the info that a warrant might be served at Roy's residence.

The producer was enthused. "Go sit on the Buckner house and see if detectives show. You've done a great job of getting us the Buckner stories first. Stay with it until we call you off. I'll send another crew to stand by at PAB for any updates."

"Okay. How long do you think we should wait?"

"As long as it takes. Just be ready." There was a pause. "If you pull this off, I think your chances are good you'll be with KABR for a while."

"Good to know. I'll do my best," Karen told her boss.

An hour later, she and Brian sat about one hundred yards away from Roy's house.

Karen had a clear view of the house so if there was any activity they'd get it on video. "The LAPD isn't taking any chances. Did you spot the patrol car parked in the driveway?"

"Yeah." Brian pushed his ball cap over his eyes and slouched in his seat. "Wake me up if anything happens."

Karen frowned, but then remembered she was the cub reporter. She pulled out her cell phone to check what other news outlets were reporting on the cop-killer case.

After a half hour of waiting she thought maybe she'd misheard what the detective had said about getting a warrant.

Exhausted, she shut her eyes for a moment. Next thing she knew, Brian was shaking her arm.

"Wake up. They're here." He started the van and pulled forward. He several houses away from the Buckner home. Brian jumped from their rig and quickly mounted his camera on his shoulder. After jogging across the street, he took a position behind a big tree but still had a clear shot of the front porch.

Karen bailed out of the passenger side and grabbed her mic, ready to give a play-by-play of whatever happened.

Two detectives and five uniformed officers approached the house and spoke to the protection detail in the driveway.

Two officers split from the group and went into the rear yard. The two detectives followed the remaining officers to the front porch. One officer stood to the side of the front door and rapped loudly three times.

"Police department. We have a search warrant."

The evening darkness was so quiet they could easily hear the officer's commands.

Nothing happened.

Karen watched as one of the protection detail officers got on his cell phone. She'd bet her first paycheck he was trying to call Roy. He held his phone for the others to see and shook his head.

A detective stepped to the door. He pounded with his fist.

"Roy! It's Johnson. Open up. We have a warrant." He stepped back. There was no response. He knocked again.

The contingent waited for a few minutes. Two more patrol officers arrived, one of them holding the handles of a large metal pipe used to pop the entry open. The protection detail officer said something, and the officers with the cumbersome battering ram set it down.

Johnson tried turning the knob, and the door swung open.

The uniformed officers flowed into the residence, followed by the detectives. Even from the street, she heard them yelling, "*LAPD. Police Department.*"

A few minutes later a couple of the cops came out of the house and turned to the security detail officers.

Their irritated voices carried to Karen and Brian. "Where the hell is Buckner?"

53

———

SETH

Seth drove below the speed limit. He knew he had no equipment violations that would rate being pulled over by the CHP officer behind him. Without being obvious, Seth kept a close watch on the lawman. They were approaching an exit. If he planned to initiate a traffic stop, it would be soon.

He gripped the steering wheel tighter. The cruiser exited the highway off-ramp. The swapped license plates had done their job. No doubt the officer had run the vehicle, and the pickup appeared not to belong to Seth Farley but to some shmuck, probably from Valencia, on his way to Vegas with Seth's plates on his truck. Seth chuckled. *I'd hate to be that guy when he gets pulled over.*

They'd skirted disaster. He could focus on getting to the cabin. Amber's objections to him killing the cop if it had been necessary disturbed him. He'd better find out just how loyal she was to him.

"You know, there will probably come a time where I'll have to eliminate law enforcement officers who are after us, right?"

From the horrified look she gave him, he'd caught her by surprise.

Blood pounded in his ears. "Why are you looking at me like that?"

"Because"—she paused—"I don't understand why we can't go on with our life together without hurting anyone. Harming a cop goes against everything I've ever known. I'm still married to one."

"How do you think *I* feel? I *was* a cop. It's all I ever wanted to be. But understand this: Just because I have you on my side now doesn't mean I won't carry through my mission."

She twisted in her seat to face him a little more. "What exactly is your mission? Why are you killing LAPD officers?"

"When I got out of high school, I couldn't afford to go to college, so I went into the military. I wanted to be an MP—military policeman. Being an MP in the military would help me get into the LAPD. My dad's a cop.

"After a stint in the front lines of the Middle East, the army did testing and found out I had an aptitude with electronics, so they assigned me to electronics warfare and surveillance." He smiled. "I was pissed because that wasn't part of my plan.

"My life took a twist. I was a natural with the electronics —a military rock star. I got my degree while in the military and after an eight-year hitch, joined the LAPD."

"And how did joining the LAPD transition into killing fellow cops?"

"Did you see that sign? Big Bear, fifty miles away." He took a hit from a bottle of water and wiped his mouth with the back of his hand.

"I was older than most of the people in my academy class. Because of my military experience, they chose me as the class leader. I ran a tight ship. Most of the snowflakes in my class didn't understand they'd joined a paramilitary organization."

Amber nodded. "Roy said something similar about some people he worked with." She shot him a quick glance. "He wasn't talking about you. With your background, I'm sure you were a standout."

Seth snorted. "You'd think so, wouldn't you? Instead, my classmates took every opportunity they could to bad-mouth me with our DI—drill instructor. They told him I was too hard on them. They'd intentionally screw up. Someone would be late from lunch or show up to the shooting range without their ammo bag. The whole class would be punished, and we'd have to do extra PT. It didn't bother me to run an extra two miles or do two extra sets of calisthenics."

"I don't understand what that has to do with killing police officers."

"I'm getting there," he said, inflecting annoyance in his voice.

"Okay. Go ahead."

"We graduate. The divisions I'd requested to work were Southeast, Southwest, and Newton. I wanted to be where the action was. Class leaders *always* get one of their choices. Not me. They sent me to North Hollywood—the friggin' Valley!"

She looked at him with a puzzled look on her face.

He gave a sigh of disgust. "Didn't Roy tell you anything? The south end of town is where real police work is done." He motioned dismissively with one of his hands. "Oh sure, you might catch an occasional burglary suspect or something in the rich part of town, but if you want to deal with the real assholes you work the south end."

"Wasn't it in the Valley, maybe North Hollywood, where they had the bank robbery where the robbers had automatic weapons and the police shot it out with them for over an hour, even though the bad guys had more powerful guns? Wouldn't that be considered action?"

Seth bit at his upper lip, trying not to lose his temper. Amber was pissing him off. "First, that was a one-time thing that occurred over twenty years ago. Second, the real crime is on the south side of the city. Understand?"

She held up both her hands in a position of surrender. "Okay, okay. So what happened when you got to North Hollywood Division?"

"They gave me an asshole for my first training officer. He was a big guy, lazy as shit, and all he wanted to do was sleep. We worked the overnight shift. During the day, instead of sleeping, he'd play golf. He'd come to work dead tired. We'd handle radio calls until after the bars closed, and then he'd go find a hole—a place our car couldn't be seen—and he'd go to sleep and tell me to stay awake so we wouldn't get ambushed." Seth shook his head in disgust. "One night, the sergeant was trying to get us on the radio. My TO was sawing logs. I was wide awake but didn't answer."

Amber gave a short gasp.

"We weren't getting paid to sleep. We were supposed to be working!" Seth hated the fact he had to defend himself, especially since it made him sound like he was whining. "They got every available unit in our division to look for us. They called in an airship and had the helicopter searching the hills to see if we'd gone off the road and into a canyon."

"Then what happened?"

"One of the other officers knew my training officer's favorite holes and found us. My TO heard the other unit and woke up. When he found out everyone was looking for us, he lied and said I'd been asleep too. He and the guy who found us, Luke Tremont, cooked up a story about us patrolling the canyons where the radio signals were often sketchy. His story kept us out of trouble." Seth rolled his shoulders and tilted his head from side to side trying to get the tension in his neck to crack. "From that night on, I was a marked man at North Hollywood."

"But it doesn't sound like the supervisors ever found out you were sleeping."

His arm shot out, and he popped her in the face. "You stupid bitch, weren't you listening? I wasn't sleeping!" He drove both his hands onto the steering wheel.

She brought her hands to her face where he'd clocked her. She scooted as close to the passenger door as she could.

"Why did you make me do that?"

She sat in silence.

"Answer me!"

She still didn't respond.

"I *said* answer me. Why did you make me hit you?" He white-knuckled the wheel trying to keep his anger in check.

"I'm sorry," she whispered. "I didn't mean to imply that I thought *you* were sleeping. I said it wrong."

He rolled his shoulders and did the head-tilt thing again, this time eliciting a loud crack. "I'm glad you realize your mistake. I accept your apology." He nodded at a sign ahead and smiled. "Only twenty-five miles to go."

54

ROY

After Roy hopped the fence into his neighbor's backyard, he double-timed along the side of the house and out onto the street. From there he walked in a more relaxed manner. To a seasoned police officer he'd appear to be a burglar out capering—his dark clothes and backpack were like a neon sign saying: *This guy's a crook. Burglary tools and loot inside.*

He needed to get out of sight. He was close enough to home he felt he could use his cell one final time. When the LAPD pinged his phone it would show he was at his house when he'd last made a call.

He called for a cab to meet him at a convenience store around the corner. He'd have the driver drop him off miles from his destination. He hoped anyone looking for him—detectives or killer—wouldn't think he'd hoof it a long distance to find a place to hole up.

An hour later he dropped his backpack on the bed of his "no questions asked" motel in Van Nuys. He'd paid cash for two nights but thought he'd probably only stay for one. He looked at his watch. Almost eleven. Time to catch some sleep then figure out how the hell he would locate his wife and/or Farley.

Roy grabbed a few hours of rest before a baby started to cry in the room below him. He lay in the dark and thought how crappy it was that an infant was staying in a dive frequented by whores and addicts. *You can't save the world, Roy.*

He forced his thoughts to his current situation. Was it possible that Farley *kidnapped* Amber? Why? Cops were his target, and no other cop's family had been taken.

From the emails he'd found on Amber's computer, it was more feasible she'd run off with Farley. That proposition seemed farfetched, too. But as crazy as it sounded, the evidence pointed to that conclusion.

He thought back to the times he'd worked with Farley. Nothing his boot had said gave him a clue as to where the kid would go if wanting to hide.

He was coming up with nothing. Farley had done an eight-year hitch in the army working with electronic warfare. He'd said he loved his job but he'd always wanted to be a cop. He got his degree, left the service, and became a crime fighter.

The kid might have been a whiz at electronics but he had no common sense. He'd gotten into hot water with his first training officer for sleeping on the job. That incident cost his training officer a ten day suspension—and Farley had received an unsatisfactory rating report.

His second mistake was made on a traffic stop while working with his second training officer, Jerry McMillan. Jerry had advised Farley he'd used the wrong vehicle code section on the ticket. Farley lost it and told McMillan to go fuck off. McMillan had kept his cool and made Farley change the citation. Once the violator was on his way, the two officers got back in the patrol car, and McMillan drove straight to North Hollywood station.

That incident started Farley on the road to self-destruction. McMillian stormed into the watch commander's office saying he couldn't and *wouldn't* work with Farley—the probationer had a bad attitude. The watch commander, reluctant to open a can of worms, instead pawned Farley off on Luke Tremont.

Roy's classmate did his best with Farley, taking things real slow. Luke showed his boot not only the *how* of doing things but also the *why*.

Farley grew impatient with the tedious side of police work. He complained about all the rules and paperwork.

Things went really bad the night Luke and Farley responded to a call of a fight in a bar. They arrested a guy for breaking a beer bottle over his friend's head. Luke had dropped Farley off at Van Nuys Station to book their arrestee while Luke went to the hospital to get the friend's story of what happened.

At the jail, something had gone wrong during the search, and the next thing Luke knew, he was called back to Van Nuys because his partner had cold-cocked his prisoner. The arrestee was knocked unconscious and was transported to the same hospital where his friend was being treated.

After the dust settled, the jail video was reviewed. Farley

had taunted his prisoner and was rougher than necessary prior to the search. The guy had reached his limit and spat in Farley's face. The probationary officer had immediately delivered a haymaker to the handcuffed arrestee, and he'd fallen to the floor like a crash-car dummy.

An investigation had been started into the incident, and the captain called Roy into his office. He remembered it well.

"Roy, I'm sorry," he'd said. "I've got a shitty job for you."

Roy recognized what was coming and sighed. "Yes, sir?"

"I'm assigning Seth Farley to you. You're my best training officer. I know you to be fair and patient. If there's any way to save this kid, I want you to do it. But if he isn't cut out for the job, document the hell out of his performance so there's no blowback when we can his ass."

"I think it's obvious he shouldn't be a cop, Captain."

The captain had shaken his head and sighed. "You know it, and I know it, but we've got to make it clear he's unfit to any judge who reads the lawsuit Farley will undoubtedly file after he gets fired.

"The cops who sue and get their jobs back return just as fucked up as ever, only with a chip on their shoulder. Since the termination didn't stick the first time, they're golden for the rest of their career. Another attempt to fire them looks like harassment."

The captain had placed his hand on Roy's shoulder. "Do everything by the book, document like hell, and pray you don't get killed or fired in the process."

"Yes, sir."

Roy had taken the time to have a long talk with Farley and made it understood that his time with Roy started with a clean slate. The first few days they'd worked together went well. Farley listened to Roy and made fewer mistakes. Roy had given his partner an unbiased weekly review. The positive feedback resulted in boosting Farley's ego and brought out a swagger and bravado the young officer hadn't yet earned. He'd turned "salty"—a word used to describe an officer on probation who thought he knew it all.

Then Farley had forgotten his gun.

When Roy chewed him out, his partner had lost it and said, "If you do anything to cost me my job, you'll pay."

With that comment, Roy felt sure that would be the end of Farley. But the captain told Roy to document the incident and finish out the week. Two nights later, Farley missed the gun on the pimp and they both could have been killed. Roy wrote out a detailed final performance evaluation, and the probationer was assigned to his home until further notice. At that point, Farley was effectively fired.

Lying on the saggy mattress in a seedy motel, Roy thought. McMillian...Tremont...Buckner. All from the same academy class and two of them dead. Was it possible there was a correlation? Cookie and Delgado hadn't worked with Farley. What was their connection? A dull ache pounded in Roy's head.

One thing was for sure. Whatever was going on, Roy needed to find Seth Farley and get answers—even if that meant beating the answers out of him.

55

AMBER

Amber peered into the darkness of the desolate roadway on the way to her grandparents' cabin. Towering pines stood along the sloped shoulder of the road. Heavy snow fell once they turned onto Highway 18 and climbed into the tree line.

Farley used his windshield wipers to brush the powdery flakes away, but more snow filled the glass. "How am I supposed to see where the hell I'm going?"

Amber was full of worry. She hadn't been there in a year and wasn't sure she could direct him to the cabin. The snow and darkness were disorienting, and nothing seemed familiar.

"Am I heading the right way?"

"I think so."

Driving through town, they passed driveway after

driveway that led to darkened cabins sitting back from the street.

"I believe the next road you turn right."

"I hope you know where you're going." They were silent as they drove the deserted street and went higher into the trees. The farther they drove, the fewer cabins they saw.

Another wave of anxiety washed over her. He wouldn't be able to put his truck in the garage. The old Honda her grandparents had owned was still inside. She wasn't even sure it ran. But there was no point in telling Farley now.

"Keep going. I think we'll make another right and that will be their road. They bought forty acres that back up to the forest."

She considered lowering her window to obtain better visibility but didn't dare. She didn't want him to punch her again. "The cabin is at the end of the road, based against the hill."

As snow blew into the headlight beams of the pickup, the flakes resembled amusement rides where rocket ships barreled through the darkness and stars. The effect was dizzying.

"There! I see it." She pointed. "Go straight. Do you see the cabin?"

"Yeah," he said as he edged the truck onto the concrete driveway. Good thing I've got four-wheel drive. We may need it." He parked in front of the garage. "I don't suppose you have a key to this place?"

Amber shook her head. "No. We'll have to break in."

Farley unbuckled his seat belt and stretched. "Let me look at what we're dealing with." He reached behind his seat and grabbed a black canvas bag. He rummaged through it, pulling out a flashlight.

"Just to be safe, go to the door and knock. I don't want some yahoo to shoot me, thinking we're burglars."

Amber's heart beat with excitement. He was sending her out on her own. Could she outrun him in a snowstorm?

"Don't try running off. I'll have my gun on you the whole time. Make one funny move, and I'll drop you faster than a whore can drop her panties."

Stunned that he'd read her mind, she nodded. After exiting the truck, she almost slipped on the icy steps of the front porch as she darted through the falling snow.

She pounded on the door, her teeth chattering. Peering into a window, she was sure the cabin was empty. She ran back to the pickup and jumped inside.

"No one is there." She rubbed her arms, attempting to get warm.

"Come on, then. It's gonna be cold."

Amber's muscles contracted with the onslaught of below-freezing temperatures. Within seconds her teeth were chattering. She needed more practical clothes than the jeans, T-shirt, and sneakers she wore.

Cursing under his breath, Farley led the way to the back of the structure. There was a single door covered by a gabled porch. He shook his head when he saw the door outfitted with glass panes. "This will be a piece of cake."

"It has a deadbolt," she warned.

He used the flashlight to illuminate through the glass. "From what I can tell, it's a nice place. This was a good call on your part."

Yeah, hopefully you'll remember that the next time you decide to hit me.

He used the butt end of the light to break the pane of

glass closest to the door handle. He picked out broken shards of glass before reaching through the hole he'd made. A huge grin broke out on his face. "I'm sorry, but your grandparents weren't too bright. They left the key in the deadbolt."

Amber bristled with his insult of her dead Grammy and Grampy, especially since—against Roy's warnings—she was the one who'd left the key in the lock. But she didn't let her displeasure show. She was freezing and wanted him to get the door open. He did.

He stepped inside with Amber right behind him. She flipped on the lights and closed the door. They stood in a mudroom that led to the cozy galley kitchen.

"Jeez, it's freezing in here too," he said shaking snow from his shoulders.

She moved past him. "Let's get a fire started in the wood stove. It's in the living room."

Careful Amber, don't get cocky. Make him think he is in charge. She hurried into the other room and remembered she and Roy had stocked the kindling box and firewood rack before they'd left on their earlier visit.

While she built a fire, he checked out the rest of the cabin. He stopped at the dining table positioned between the kitchen and the living room. "This is one badass table."

"My great-great-grandfather built it. It's passed through the generations."

"I've never seen a tabletop that thick. What's it made of?"

"Oak. It's so heavy it took five guys to move it in here."

She hated that a sicko like Farley was in her grandparents' home, but at least she was out of that underground bunker. Here she had the advantage. She knew her surroundings better than her captor did.

Even though her lip had swollen from his previous blow, she forced herself to act normal. The more she could make him relax and think she was on his side the better her chances of escape.

He sauntered back to the living room. "This is really a nice place. Two bedrooms, two and a half baths, and a bonus room with a big-screen TV and a pool table."

She tossed a large log into the stove, then stood and rubbed her arms with her hands to warm herself.

"We need to get the stuff from the bunker out of the truck, or everything will be buried in snow." He glanced around the room. "You think there're jackets anywhere?" He shivered.

"I'll look around. My parents cleaned out all the personal effects, but maybe I can find something for us to wear."

She checked the coat closet, but it was bare. Then she scanned the bedroom closets and found nothing. "Let me try the garage," she said.

He followed her to the double car garage holding her grandparents' beloved Honda sedan. There were no jackets.

Farley glared at the car. "Where the hell am I supposed to park my truck?"

"I'm sorry. I forgot about the car."

He shook his head, disgusted. "We'll deal with it tomorrow. Does it run?"

"I don't think so. Otherwise my parents would have sold it."

"Great. Check the car for coats." Farley's tone was sharp. He was getting into one of his moods.

The car was unlocked. All she found in the back seat was an old umbrella and some tire chains. She popped the trunk.

He got there before she did. "Bingo," he said, his mood

lightening. He reached in and grabbed a quilted flannel jacket and slipped into it. "Your grandpa had a good build on him. Fits like it was made for me."

Amber forced herself not to roll her eyes. She wanted to rip her grandfather's jacket right off Farley.

Beneath the flannel jacket, and next to a set of tire chains, was a heavier down jacket. She remembered her mother buying the garment for Amber's grandmother several Christmases ago. Amber eagerly slipped it on, recognizing the faintest scent of her grandma's favorite perfume. Tears filled her eyes. *Oh, Grammy, help me. Help me get away from this madman.*

"Come on. Let's get the truck cleaned out. I'm tired."

Amber suppressed a yawn. She was exhausted. But even through her fatigue, she felt hope. She was on her own turf, surrounded by furniture and memories that belonged to her. The house was equipped for living. That meant there were knives, scissors, and tools available to her. And about four miles away, down in the village, there'd be people. People who might notice a new truck parked in the driveway and wonder who was in the cabin.

56

SETH

Seth and Amber unloaded the truck and stacked the gear in the front room. They placed her two suitcases at the bottom of the stairs.

He added more wood to the stove. "We need to turn on the water. Where's the main valve?"

She shook her head. "It's not necessary. My parents don't winterize because they have people renting the place."

She kept it to herself that they had a local handyman who came by periodically to check on things. "I want a shower, okay?"

He nodded and stood. "Sure. I'll go up with you."

She hesitated, then made her way up the stairs, dragging one bag with her.

He followed with the other bag.

She entered a bedroom.

"Stop." He stepped around her and pointed to the bed. "Sit." He set her bags by the closet.

She sat watching him as he looked in the dresser drawers, the nightstand, the closet, and under the bed.

Once he'd finished, he turned to her and grinned. "Just want to be sure ol' Grandpa didn't have a shotgun or something hidden in here." He walked to the hallway. "Stay put," he said, closing the door behind him.

He searched the other rooms. Not finding anything threatening, he returned to the bedroom and opened the door. "All clear. Take your shower. I've got things to do downstairs."

With Amber occupied, he went to the phone and cut the cord. Just to be sure, he lifted the phone receiver verifying the line was dead. He got his duffel where he had zip ties, retrieved one, and secured it to a crossbeam in the base of the massive oak table. He grabbed his handcuffs and slipped them into his pocket while walking around the cabin looking for potential weapons. He took the butcher-block knife holder full of knives and other items that could be used against him and locked them in the truck.

When he came back inside, he heard her turn off the water.

A few minutes later she came out of the bathroom and stood at the top of the stairs, rubbing her hair with a towel. She wore black sweatpants and a long-sleeved T-shirt.

Standing below, watching her, he felt his dick enlarge as he imagined how soft her skin would feel now that she'd showered.

Something must have shown on his face because she scurried into the bathroom. She also locked the door.

Stupid woman. If I wanted in the bathroom, one swift kick would get me inside. He started up the stairs. "Hey, you comin' outta there? I'd like a shower too."

After a few seconds, she darted from the bathroom and into the bedroom and closed the door. Apparently she'd determined they weren't sleeping together. He grinned and entered the bedroom. The door didn't have a lock, or he was certain she'd have used it.

Her eyes were wide and wary. She watched as he approached. Her back leaned against the headboard. Her knees were bent toward the ceiling, her arms wrapped around them. He wondered if she'd zoom off the bed—a terrified cat. Her eyes were on his, and she didn't notice the hand he had in his pocket.

Although he hated to do it, he took her by surprise and locked the handcuffs on her wrists.

She didn't resist. "You know, this isn't necessary. I won't try to run away. We're a family now."

Seth laughed. "Well, humor me for tonight. I want a good night's sleep." He grabbed her by her upper arm. "Come on."

"Where are we going?" Her voice shook as she got to her feet.

"Downstairs. I've made you a comfortable little bed."

She opened her mouth to speak but closed it, apparently changing her mind.

"Think of it this way," he said as they descended the stairs, "you'll be near the wood stove so you won't be cold overnight."

He led her to folded blankets on the floor. One decorative pillow from the living room was placed on the makeshift bed. A quilt was off to the side for her to cover herself.

"Get down and find a comfortable position. I'll loop one of your handcuffs through this zip tie."

She sighed as she lowered herself to the floor. "This isn't necessary."

"I'm sure it's overkill, if you'll excuse the pun, but I haven't got this place set up properly."

She got into a prone position and nodded.

Keeping tight control of her arms, he deftly unlocked one of her handcuffs and threaded the metal rung through the zip tie encircling the base of the table. Once done, he stood above her. "I promise it will be different tomorrow night. I've kinda gotten used to you sleeping next to me." He walked away then stopped. "Do you want a bottle of water?"

"My hands are attached to the table. I can't drink."

He chuckled. "I guess you're right. Okay, I'll see you in the morning." He climbed the stairs. "Sleep tight."

57

ROY

Thoughts careened around Roy's mind after his sleep had been interrupted. An hour ago, a baby had woken him from the motel room below his. Once awake, he realized there was much to do and little time to get it done.

One of the first things on his list was to buy a burner phone—a prepaid cell phone difficult to track. He wanted to contact that reporter, Karen, and see if she'd located Amber or if she had new info on Seth Farley.

He'd also need wheels. A used-car dealership was within walking distance of his motel. He'd head over there and pick up the most reliable beater vehicle they had on the lot. The car lot wasn't one that'd be likely to call the cops if someone came in and paid cash for a jalopy. *Thank God for the emergency stash of cash he and Amber kept at the house.*

He flipped on the television to the morning news and

shuffled to the bathroom for a shower. A no-tell motel was not the place to linger. Get in, get showered, get out.

With one towel wrapped around his waist, Roy rubbed his hair with another. He stopped in his tracks when he looked at the television. Seth Farley's picture was on the screen. Roy grabbed the remote and turned up the volume.

Holy shit. The reporter related that police were searching for Farley as a "person of interest" in the recent killings of two, and possibly more, law enforcement officers. It didn't take long for Farley's name to hit the airwaves.

Without thinking, he snatched his phone from the night-stand and punched in Karen's number. She'd fill him in with what was going on. He wouldn't have to sit through other BS and commercials. It took him a second to realize why his cell wasn't on. He'd turned it off and removed the SIM card so he couldn't be tracked. *Damn.*

He got dressed in record time. It was still too early for the auto dealership to be open, but he could go to Walmart and purchase the prepaid phone. They opened at the crack of dawn. As a bonus, there was a donut shop along the way where he'd grab a coffee and a bear claw. The car dealer was about a mile farther down the main drag.

Feeling good with his plans, he packed his backpack and headed out.

Right after he bought and set up his new phone, he tried calling Karen. The call cycled immediately to her voicemail. He left a message with his new number and told her to call. He hung around the big box store pretending to be interested in the televisions, but in reality he was watching the morning news.

Roy's stomach dropped as the details of Farley's manifesto

were revealed. The gist of the document related to the probationary officer's firing from the LAPD and how his termination was unfair.

There was no doubt Roy was a target since it was his reports that got Farley fired. But would the crazed cop have gone after Amber instead? *No.*

But those love-letter emails. The stain in the bed. Maybe Farley thought stealing Roy's wife was a worse punishment than death for his former training officer. *And it is. Look at you. Hiding out in a dumpy motel, skulking around like you're the fugitive.*

He needed more information. Was there anyone in the department who might tell him what was happening? Probably not. He was a potential victim of Farley's. Plus, by now they'd likely discovered he'd ditched the security they'd arranged. That wouldn't help things.

His new phone rang. "Hello?"

"Roy, I've been trying to reach you since last night!"

Relief washed over him at hearing Karen's voice. "I'm glad you called. I've seen the news. I don't know what it mea—"

"Listen. Detectives were at your house. They had a search warrant and carried out several computers. And I can tell you they weren't the least bit happy that you'd skipped out."

"A search warrant? Why?"

"Because I think they suspect you in the disappearance of Amber."

"That's ridiculous."

"Is it? Your wife vanished after you two had a blowup about her being pregnant. My cameraman overheard two detectives. Someone named Speakeasy told them that after you found out Amber was pregnant, the tension was so thick everyone just wanted to get away."

"She'd just sprung a baby on me—and all my friends heard it go down. She *knew* I didn't want a baby."

"Look, you've got to go back home or to the PAB and tell them it's possible Farley's got her."

"I can't do that."

"Why not?" Her tone was sharp.

"Because they'd probably lock me up. They're going to find stuff on Amber's computer making it look like I had a motive to kill her."

58

KAREN

Karen listened to Roy's story about romantic emails between Seth Farley and Amber. Then he disclosed the damp towels he'd found in the bathroom and the stained sheet.

No wonder he got drunk that night. His behavior made a little more sense, but he was still acting like a fool. From the beginning he should have told the detectives what was going on. And that's what she said to Roy.

"I couldn't. You don't understand the shame when another cop runs off with your wife. A supposed *brother* who wears the badge betrayed me, and apparently Amber betrayed me too. I don't want to believe she'd run off with Farley. But I need to find her and prove it—either way. If Farley has her and kills her, he could easily say I did it."

"Let's suppose you're right and he kidnapped her.

Wouldn't you rather have the cops focus on finding Farley rather than chasing you all over town?"

"Of course. But if I go to the department, they'll find a way to confine me. They'll probably say they're locking me up for my protection to keep me safe from Farley."

"Don't you trust them to find Amber?"

"Are you married or have kids?"

"No. What's that got to do with anything?"

"Suppose someone kidnapped your mother. Wouldn't you want to be out looking for her, even if the cops were searching for her, too? Would you trust strangers, who don't love her like you do, to follow every lead no matter how small or silly?"

"Probably not. But the police *are* the professionals. That's their job."

"But you'd still be out looking too, right?"

"Yes," she said, reluctance in her voice.

"That's all I want to do. Go out there and see what I can find."

"Where are you going to start?"

"That's where you come in," Roy said. "I'll need your help."

"What do you want me to do?"

"Go back toFarley's house and try to locate his mother or anyone who knew her. I remember Farley told me his mother had lived with him for a few months. If I can find the mother, she might know where he is."

"Okay. I can do that. It's something I'd do for the story anyway."

"Thanks. You'll call me if you get anything, right?"

"Of course. Where are you, and what are you doing?"

"It's better for all of us if you don't know. I'll be in touch."

The line went dead.

59

AMBER

Although she'd positioned herself as best she could to be comfortable while sleeping, Amber woke up stiff and cold. She needed to pee, but before she yelled to wake Farley she wanted to see if there was any way for her to free her hands.

She got into a sitting position facing the table and the crossbar where she was connected by the zip tie. She had a thought. *Maybe I could burn myself free if I heated the plastic enough to start a fire.*

Interlacing her fingers as if she was praying, Amber moved her arms left and right across the thick piece of wood, trying to melt the solid tie around her wrists.

Worried she was making too much noise, she kept glancing toward the stairs, sure that any second Farley would appear. She'd been sawing on the crossbar for at least five minutes. The zip tie wasn't melting or showing any other sign of wear and tear.

She heard the upstairs toilet flush. He was awake. Overnight Amber had tried to devise a plan for her escape. It was clear he didn't trust her yet.

Trying to overpower him had crossed her mind, but he was so much bigger than her, and she didn't want to do anything that might harm the baby. She'd reached the conclusion she'd have to gain his trust then get away. If a good opportunity presented itself, she'd kill him.

Could you kill a person, Amber? I mean really kill someone? "I guess I'll know when the time comes," she whispered to herself.

He came downstairs wearing sweatpants, a T-shirt, and a visible erection. "Morning." His voice sounded husky with sleep. "I've decided you should come upstairs and we'll spend the morning in bed."

She'd made a mistake. The raspy timbre in his voice was desire. What was she going to do?

"Okay. I've been a little chilly. The stove ran out of wood."

He leered at her. "I'll warm you up." He squatted next to her and unlocked the handcuff connecting her to the table. He freed her other hand.

Rubbing her aching arms, Amber was filled with dread. How would she get out of servicing Farley?

"Make some coffee before we go back to bed. I'll stoke the fire."

"Okay." She went into the kitchen and noticed the knife set gone. He'd begun sanitizing the place. She glanced out the window as she filled the pot with water. "Holy crap."

"What's wrong?" he called from the living room.

"It's snowing big time. I've never seen flakes so large. Some are three inches long—they're like feathers floating from the sky."

He joined her to stare out the glass. "This sucks. I'd planned on staying here today and getting things secured. But with this weather, the local cops will have their hands full with cars sliding off the roads and stuff. They won't have time to look for me.

"Hopefully, it's raining in LA. The freeways will be a mess, and most LA coppers will hide anywhere they can to stay dry. I have business down there. I'd planned to take care of it tomorrow, but today looks like the better day."

She shivered at his words. She knew he meant to add another red *X* to the academy class picture. "Maybe you should leave now before the roads get too bad."

"I'm not worried. My truck is four-wheel drive." He nodded at the coffee maker. The brew was done.

She took two mugs out of the cupboard and filled them. For the briefest instant she considered throwing the hot coffee in his face. But if he was leaving her alone at the cabin while he was gone, she'd escape. She handed him his coffee.

"I'm not comfortable leaving you alone. I'll have to secure you again."

Idiot. You should have thrown the coffee in his face. "I promise I won't run away. You can't leave me chained up here for hours. I'll need to use the restroom. In fact, I need to use it now. Please. Please don't handcuff me to the table." She set her mug on the counter and hurried to the downstairs powder room. She didn't want him to see her tears.

A few minutes later she returned to find him going through the drawers and setting aside any cooking tools that might be used as a weapon. There were more utensils on the table than he'd left in the drawer.

He looked at her as she returned. "This is what I've decided. I'll hook you up with the chain, like I did in the bunker. You'll have enough length in the chain to keep the stove going, reach the kitchen and bathroom, and you should be able to sleep on the couch. You'll be set."

"Thank you. I appreciate that. I wish you trusted me more, but I understand." *Besides, if you leave you won't rape or kill me. I'll figure out a way to free myself and end this nightmare.*

"I want to trust you, but you seemed to take the LAPD's side when I told you how they fired me."

She shook her head. "No. I'm not surprised there was a conspiracy against you. It's obvious, with your background, you were much smarter than everyone—probably even the captains. I'm sure it made them nervous." *Careful, Amber. Don't lay it on too thick.*

He smiled at her, then drained his coffee mug and set it down. "I'm glad you explained what you meant." He reached out and pulled her to him and gave her a hug.

The last thing she wanted was to revive his romantic mood. She needed to get him on his way. "You'd better get ready. It will take you almost two hours to drive to LA. That's four hours round trip."

He glanced at the clock on the kitchen oven. "Yeah, and I'll be there a couple of hours."

Amber shivered again. Was Roy going to be his victim this time? When would Farley stop?

"Let's get dressed. You can fix me breakfast while I get my equipment ready."

An hour later, Amber watched from the front window of

the A-frame cabin. Seth carried the black nylon gun case out to his truck and placed it into the back seat of the cab.

Weighted by the chain looped around her waist and attached to the dining table, she watched Farley's truck slowly cut through a foot of snow as he drove away.

For the first time in twenty-four hours she felt herself relax. Then, out of nowhere, there was a flutter in her belly. For the first time, her baby kicked.

60

SETH

Seth didn't like leaving Amber alone at the cabin, but what other choice did he have? He was on a mission. Before going to his truck, he'd tried to start the Honda in the garage. The battery clicked its death knell.

He'd have more time tomorrow to rid their hideout of anything that might make Amber want to return to her former life. She was his now—or at least she'd be his soon.

As he drove, the ass end of his pickup fishtailed when making turns in the relentless snow. Once, he'd almost skidded off the sloped shoulder of the road. Driving during a near blizzard wasn't his forte. As he listened to his truck radio, he was surprised by the big deal the news made of him. They had an all-out manhunt going for him. "Let 'em come. I'm ready."

His thoughts turned to Amber. He didn't know what to

think. Was she playing him, or did she have feelings for him? She'd wanted a baby for so long, then— *bam*—the first time he launches the meat missile into her, she gets knocked up. "That's how a real man makes a family, Roy Buckner," he said to himself. Seth tried to ignore the seed of regret that he probably wouldn't live to see his child.

He'd started his vengeance with one thought in mind: get back at the people who'd stolen his dream of being a policeman. It was a short-sighted goal. How things had changed. He was going to be a father—a more important job. He'd always imagined himself as a good parent, a dad who'd take care of his children, the type of daddy where the kids squealed with delight when he came home from his day of fighting crime.

At the time he'd planned his revenge, he hadn't thought about his desire to be the perfect father. He had to swallow the irony that his first goal had cost him his second and more meaningful of the two desires.

Unless there was a way out. He needed a new plan. He and Amber could escape and go to another country. They'd get new identities. A flicker of hope sparked in his belly. What if he could pull it off?

He got off the 210 Freeway in Rancho Cucamonga and found a strip mall with a big beauty supply store. He bought several cans of spray-on hair color. Once he'd captured Amber, he'd started a beard. There was no need for his clean-cut cop look. He'd add to his disguise by dying his hair. He drove to a gas station and used the restroom to change his neglected buzzcut to dark brown. The change was startling, and he felt comfortable people wouldn't recognize him. But to be sure, he stopped by a Walmart and picked up a pair of low-level reading glasses and a new burner cell phone.

"Okay, Seth. Time to get down to business." He headed back to the freeway that led to LA. Now all he had to figure out was how to contact Roy Buckner without getting himself caught.

His new cell phone rang. There were only two people he'd called and left messages giving them this number. It didn't bode well that ten minutes later one of them was calling him.

"Hello?" Even to Seth, his voice sounded guarded.

"Hey, Seth. It's Mitzi. I've been trying to get ahold of you for days. What happened? You forget to pay your phone bill or what?"

"What's wrong?"

Seth took the next off-ramp on the freeway, pulled into a residential neighborhood, and parked at the curb.

"It's your mom. She's not doing too well. She didn't want me to call you, but I think she needs to go to the hospital."

"What happened?"

"She had a rough date a few nights ago. It was bad. She convinced the motel manager to call her a cab to bring her back here. Me and the cabbie had to carry her into the apartment. I had to tip the driver extra. It's been two days, and she's gettin' worse."

His immediate reaction was to drive to Mitzi's apartment and take his mother to the ER, but it might be a trap set up by the police. But how would the department have found Mitzi or Mom?

He bit his lower lip. "This is what you need to do. Get Nora up and drive her to the Triple H."

"There's no way I'll get her out of bed by myself," Mitzi

whined. "And Hollywood Med Center is closer than Holly-wood Hills Hospital."

"Christ, Mitzi! Do *not* take her to the med center. That place isn't fit for cockroaches." He shook his head. "If you can't get Nora into your car, get an ambulance. Insist that she goes to Triple H. If you have any problems, call me. Oh, and don't mention me at all. Don't tell them she's got a son. Pretend I don't exist."

"Why?"

"Just do it!"

There was a pause. "Should I tell Nora you're coming?"

"No. It will just worry her."

"How long do you think you'll be?"

Seth punched the driver-side window. "I don't know. I'll get there as soon as I can." He hung up. "Mom, your timing couldn't be worse."

He sat in his truck, deciding what was more important: tending to his mother, or killing Roy Buckner.

PART VII

61

ROY

Roy visited the car dealership and bought a mid-nineties four-wheel-drive Toyota Tacoma pickup truck. The pushy used car salesman urged him to buy the older Tacoma truck with four-wheel drive. The only reason he chose the truck over the other cars was that the pickup was equipped with a shell over the bed of the truck. In a pinch, he could buy a piece of foam and a sleeping bag and have a place to bunk.

The vehicle had a manual transmission which Roy had to retrain himself to maneuver. Thankfully, driving a stick was like riding a bicycle—you never forgot how to do it. The clutch was mushy, but he hoped he'd only need the pickup for a few days.

Now that he had wheels, Roy was on his way to the county registrar's office. He hoped he could badge himself a copy of Farley's birth certificate and find out his mother and father's names. If he could find any family members, they might lead him to Farley—and Amber.

Roy waited in line after filling out an application for Farley's birth document.

"I'll need your identification, sir." The clerk was a round woman with at least two decades of dealing with the public etched on her face.

He retrieved his wallet from his pocket and showed her his police ID card.

The clerk's heavily drawn eyebrows lifted. "You don't have a driver's license?"

"I do, but I'm here on business." He slid his license from beneath the clear plastic slot where his smiling face was displayed.

She looked at the name on the application he'd presented. "Seth Farley...why do I know that name?"

"Because he's a cop killer who's on the run, and if we can't find him soon, he'll kill again."

Her mouth formed an *O* as her eyes got as round as a 1050s ingénues. "I heard about him on the news this morning."

"Then you understand why it's important that I get the information. I need it as fast as possible."

"Yes, I do, but it won't be available until after three o'clock this afternoon."

His irritation must have shown on his face.

She displayed an apologetic smile. "Normally we'd mail it to you."

Roy looked at her ID hanging from an LA Dodgers lanyard draped around her neck. "Listen, Patrice, this is an exigent circumstance. People's lives are at risk. Who do I need to see to make this happen before three o'clock?"

The slightest frown tweaked her brow. She glanced right and left and sighed. "You can't tell anyone I'm doing this for you," she whispered. She tapped Farley's information into her computer. "Wait here. I'll be back in a minute."

Roy tried for an air of nonchalance while he waited, although he didn't know why he worried. Everyone in line behind him was glued to the screens of their cell phones.

A few minutes later, Patrice returned with a white business envelope in her hand and a demure smile on her face. "Here you go. No charge. I hope you catch him."

He gave her a wink as he took the document. "I do too. Thanks a lot."

Roy waited until he got into his new truck to look at the certificate. "The mother's name is Nora Farley, and his father is...unknown." He folded up the birth certificate and slid it back into the envelope. Leaning his head against the headrest of his truck, he closed his eyes. He hadn't gained much information. He'd hoped for so much more but only received one clue. Nora Farley.

He pulled out his burner phone and dialed Karen.

She answered fast, but her greeting was terse. "Can't talk now. I'll call you back."

62

AMBER

Amber sat on the couch marveling at the life growing inside of her. She rested her hand on her stomach waiting for her baby to kick again. Nothing happened, but she remained there for another fifteen minutes. She wanted to ensure Farley hadn't forgotten anything or decided the roads were too dangerous and doubled back.

Once assured he was not returning soon, she examined the chain encircling her waist. She'd gone into the bathroom and seen in the mirror he'd used a padlock secured behind her. She managed to twist the links around to her front, but she couldn't get the lock to open.

She shuffled over to the table where Farley had locked one handcuff around the zip tie and attached the second cuff to the last link of chain. If she somehow cut through the nylon tie, she'd be free to walk wherever she wanted—

albeit with at least twenty-five pounds of metal dragging with her.

A noise from outside caught her attention. She looked out the window and saw a snowplow driving up the hill. *Oh my God! Help!* Amber yanked on the links pulling hard as she made her way toward the front door. Ten feet away from her goal the metal strand tightened against her torso. "No, come on!" She pulled on the chain hard, but the hefty oak dining table wouldn't budge.

She watched as the snowplow inched up the road. What should she do? Throw something through the glass? No, if she didn't attract the plow driver's attention, Farley would realize she'd tried to escape, and he'd never trust her again.

Fire! *Start a fire. No, dummy. You'll burn the cabin down with you attached to the table.* Her gaze fell on the kindling bin. She dragged the chain over to the hot stove and opened it. Grabbing two pieces of the thin kindling, she dipped them into the orange glow. She moved as close to the window as the restraint allowed and waved the burning torches in an arc over her head. The wood burned toward her hands, and a few licks of flame danced across her knuckles. As the fire got closer and hotter, she returned to the stove, tossing those pieces into the flames. She pulled out two of the longest pieces of kindling from the bin and lit them.

The snowplow was in front of the cabin. She waved her arms above her head again. "Help me! Help me!" Panic and then despair washed over Amber as the plow moved methodically, rounding the cul-de-sac and lumbering away. She lowered her arms. The driver hadn't seen her. She returned to the stove and threw the burning wood inside.

Tears of disappointment slipped from her eyes. She

collapsed on the sofa and sobbed. After a few minutes, she righted herself. "Crying won't help you. Get off your ass and get yourself free." She rose from the couch and dragged the chain to the kitchen.

She rummaged through the kitchen, finding nothing useful to cut the zip tie. Farley had done an excellent job purging anything worthwhile to her. The bathroom was no help either. Returning to the front room, she sank into the sofa, watching the snow falling faster than before only with smaller flakes. *I'm glad it's not me out driving in that.* "Come on, Amber, think," she urged herself. She scoured the living room for something able to slice through the tough nylon tie.

Her gaze once again fell upon the kindling bin. Could she sharpen one of those pieces of wood into a cutting tool?

"You idiot! Fire! You can melt the zip tie with a piece of kindling." Relief caused tears to fill her eyes. If this idea worked, she might be able to save herself.

Moving as fast as she could considering the bulky links, she knelt near the stove and pawed through the kindling. She needed a segment long enough to melt the nylon, but not so large it would ignite the cabin. She set aside several pieces of wood, then hurried to the kitchen. Finding a roasting pan in a cupboard, she filled it halfway with water. She didn't want the large pot so heavy she'd strain and lose her baby, but she did need water nearby in case her big idea went up in smoke —literally.

Once she'd taken those precautions, another thought hit her. What if she untethered herself and Farley came back? He'd know she was trying to escape. He might kill her. "Who are you kidding? He's gonna kill you anyway."

Be positive. Think of a plan for when you're free from this damn table.

Heart pounding, she placed two pieces of wood on the floor near the zip tie and base. Then she walked over and got another piece of wood. Learning her lesson from trying to signal the plow driver, she slipped on a silicone cooking mitt and gripped the stick in a pair of tongs.

When she opened the door to the stove and leaned toward the flames a blast of heat warmed her face. She stuck the wood into the blaze, and it caught fire.

She walked with haste to the end of the dining table and lowered to her knees, gasping as the burning stick tilted at a crazy angle. "Don't fall. Don't fall. Don't fall."

Amber held the flame to the tie. At first, nothing happened. Slowly the nylon melted, but her piece of kindling dwindled. She grabbed one of the other bits of wood she'd staged and lit it with the remainder of the old one. Once the new piece was burning, she released the tong's grip on the used fragment. It dropped into the roasting pot with a sizzle.

She placed the new stick into the tongs and held it to the zip tie. The melting restraint fell from the table base. The loose handcuff clattered to the floor as well. Using two fingers to pick up the shriveled restraint, she dropped it into the water. She let out a loud whoop and pulled herself to her feet.

"Okay, Amber, you won't get far if you can't remove the chain," she said to herself. After lifting the links that rode her hips like hip-hugger jeans, she examined the padlock. "But that's the question. How to get it off?"

63

———

KAREN

Karen stood outside the Buckner residence, doing a live shot as detectives and lab techs went back and forth through the front door behind her.

"For the second time in mere hours, LAPD detectives have returned to the home of Roy and Amber Buckner. It appears they've expanded their search as we've seen police personnel coming out of the house with large bundles wrapped in brown paper. It's hard to speculate what might be contained in those packages."

Karen listened through her earpiece as the anchor at the station asked if she'd seen any sign of Roy or Amber.

"No, I haven't. Police sources say they won't discuss the whereabouts of the Buckners due to safety concerns."

The anchor then advised viewers that KABR would keep them updated as more information became available.

Once Karen was clear from her live shot, she hurried to the news van. Her cameraman, Brian, broke down his equipment while talking college football with a cameraman from a competing television station.

Enclosed in the quiet vehicle, she pulled out her cell phone and dialed.

"Yeah?"

"Roy?"

"I didn't think you were ever calling me back. I've got someth—"

"Listen to me first," she said. "Detectives are at your house with another warrant."

"Ah, jeez. I was afraid of that."

"They've got lab technicians going in and out. I'm not happy about that since I was in there a few days ago. My fingerprints are bound to be inside."

There was silence on the other end.

Karen shifted in the seat. "What are you doing?"

"I need to find Farley before the LAPD does. And Amber too—if she's with him."

"And do what? Beat him up because he stole your wife?"

"No, but if that's what happened, I want to hear it from her. I can't believe Amber would run off with a head case like Farley. And if she isn't with him voluntarily, then I'll be the one to send him to his maker."

"I think it's time for you to get home and let the police do their job."

"I won't do it, so let's move on. Did you go by Farley's house, looking for the mother?"

Karen realized how foolish she'd been getting so involved

with Buckner. She'd become part of the story if she wasn't careful.

"Yes. There was no one home. If the neighbors knew or saw the mother, they're not talking."

"Are you still willing to help me? I have new info."

Karen sighed. "I don't want to be a principal in this story."

"I understand. But I'm trying to find my wife who was brainwashed or kidnapped by a psychopath. Don't you want to be the first reporter on the scene when Farley is located?"

She had to give Roy credit. He knew what carrot to dangle in front of her.

"What? What do you need from me now?"

"I obtained a copy of Farley's birth certificate. His mother is Nora Blair Farley." He gave her Nora's birthdate.

"What about the father's info?"

"Unknown." There was a pause. "Karen, I'm sorry I wasn't upfront with you from the beginning, but I need your help here. The only hope I have of finding Farley first is through his mother. I can't access the internet without the authorities knowing my location. Even the libraries ask for ID now. Please use your resources and find out what you can about Nora."

Karen was so involved in the case, she had no choice but to bring the story full circle—and the sooner, the better.

"I'm not promising results, but I'll do my best. If I have any news, I'll be in touch."

64

AMBER

Amber lugged the chain around her waist out to the garage. After flipping on the bare overhead light, she shivered in the frigid air. The snow was still falling. *When had Farley left? A little after nine.* She glanced at a clock above her grandfather's workbench. *Almost noon. She'd better hurry. He could be back any time.*

"Now, Amber, how are you going to break this lock?" She'd found that talking to herself calmed her, gave her her confidence, and helped her think. "Thank goodness Farley left slack in the chain."

She walked over to the workbench. A piece of pegboard held the most common types of tools: a hammer, screwdrivers, pliers, and numerous saws.

A hacksaw! That should do it.

Amber took the saw and lifted the padlock up and onto

the flat surface. The chain pulled tight, not giving her enough room to work. A bulky item at the end of the work table caught her eye. It was a heavy vise.

"Clamp the lock into the vise to steady it."

After several attempts, she figured out she'd need to stand on something to get the boxy metal into the grips of the vise. A bunch of old books sat in a box in the corner. Amber piled enough novels to put her above the table and able to affix the lock in the device.

Even when held steady, the saw blade slid off the rounded shackle of the lock. After trying for five minutes, she slammed the hacksaw down. "Damn it!" *Stay calm. You can figure this out. There are other tools.*

Eyeing the items hooked on the pegboard, she reached for the hammer. *I'll beat the thing to death.* After repositioning the cubed metal piece, she drove the tool across the U-shaped hasp. It didn't budge. She slammed it again. Nothing. She tightened the vise grips on the metal, took a deep breath, and hit it again. The latch sprang open.

"You did it, Amber! You did it!" The bulky chain crashed to the cement floor as she released the padlock from the vise. She felt so much lighter she wanted to dance. But there was no time. Farley might return any minute.

Now what? Should she go through the trees in the heavy snow to the nearest neighbor, at least a mile away? Would they even be there? Or should she walk along the road to the four miles to town?

Then she noticed the Honda sitting there. *The battery is dead. You heard Farley trying to start the car this morning.* Not wanting to admit defeat, she slid behind the steering wheel. The keys were still in the ignition. She turned the key. There was the sad ticking sound of a battery out of juice. *Okay. The Honda is out. Now what?*

"I'll have to walk. I'd travel better on foot with snowshoes." She prowled the shelves in the garage with no luck.

She returned to the cabin and looked in the closet under the stairs. There weren't any snowshoes, but she gasped when she discovered a portable power pack. She took the small boxy device and blessed her grandparents when she located the instructions wrapped beneath the cord.

Amber plugged the device into an electrical outlet and scanned the directions. Disappointment washed over her when she realized the charger was designed to inflate a low tire or charge computers and cell phones during a power failure. The device came with clamps to attach to a car battery, but the instructions warned using the charger for that purpose would likely ruin the power pack.

"I don't care if it's ruined. I've got to get out of here," she said to no one.

She planned to drive to the village and find someone to call the police. Her fear was getting stuck in the snow even though the town was only a few miles away.

While the charger soaked up electricity, she searched the closet for boots, gloves, or a hat. She found a pair of rubber galoshes several sizes too large. She'd make them work. With enough pairs of socks, the waterproof footwear was a better choice in the snow than her sneakers.

She'd have to layer the clothing Farley had brought for her. She packed blankets, food, and water in case she got stuck. Then she laid out the clothes she'd wear and tossed the rest of her supplies into the back seat.

Out the window, the snow continued to fall.

Amber paced and kept checking the power level in the charger. The gauge registered near a hundred percent. "Let's see if the car will start."

She donned the clothes she'd set out, clomped to the garage in her oversized boots, and attached the charging cables to the Honda's battery. Climbing into the driver's seat, she said a prayer and turned the key.

65

SETH

Seth pulled into the parking lot of a drugstore. He entered and walked to the back near the pharmacy. After scouting around, he grabbed a stethoscope. He found a rack of plastic gift cards and selected two that were mostly white and had little design on them. He browsed the office supplies and picked up a glue stick. At the register, he added a soda and *People* magazine to his other purchases.

The clerk rang up his order.

"Hey, I'm new to town. Is there a medical uniform shop near here?"

The blonde tilted her head in thought. "There's one at the IC Mall. That's the closest. Just go south on the 215 and get off at Inland Center Drive. You can't miss it."

He paid the girl in cash. "Thanks."

Less than an hour later Seth had everything he needed

for his disguise. He'd bought scrubs and wore them out of the store. Back inside his truck, he sat in the mall parking lot and pieced together the two gift cards into what he hoped would pass for hospital ID. Tearing text from the *People*, he glued it over the logo on each card. He'd even found a picture in the magazine resembling him. It was the right size to put on one of the cards. Once done, he attached the white pieces of plastic to a lanyard he'd picked up in the uniform shop.

"Showtime," he said to himself. He returned to the freeway and drove toward LA. He drove with one hand while holding and manipulating the stethoscope in the other. He wanted it to look at least a little used.

His phone rang. "Hello?"

"It's Mitzi. We're in the ER. They won't let me in with her —told me I'd be in the way—but I can tell they're worried. When are you going to get here?"

Acid burned inside Seth's stomach. Was he falling into a police trap? "I'm en route."

"I don't want to seem uncaring, but I've got to work, ya know?"

Seth sighed. "Yeah, I understand. Do you have money for an Uber?"

"Nah, I'll take the bus. I just gotta get back. You know what I mean, right?"

He thought of the thug he'd seen Nora giving money to the last time he drove down the boulevard. "Mitzi, it's okay. I'll be there soon." He hesitated. "Uh, you and my mom have counted on each other for a while now."

"We're besties. Have been for years."

"You wouldn't hurt Nora, would you?"

"No. Why are you talking this way?"

He sighed. "I got myself into a bit of trouble. I need you to promise, no matter what, that you won't tell the cops we've talked."

Silence filled the line. "I thought you knew me better. In my business, I've learned to keep my nose out of other people's lives. It's called job security. Whatever you've done, my lips are sealed."

"Good. Thank you. Go to work...and be careful."

He disconnected the call, feeling reassured. Mitzi had been Nora's friend, and he suspected more than that, for at least the last three years. If she said she wouldn't betray him, she'd keep her word.

He continued on the 210 Freeway, setting his truck's cruise control two miles under the speed limit. He didn't want some overzealous California road ranger to stop him.

Once he got to the Hollywood Hills Hospital, Seth parked in the paid garage. He slipped his fake ID cards over his head. They'd looked more convincing when he was making them than they did now. They were too clean. He rummaged around in the glove box of his truck and found a permanent marker. He made a test mark on the back of one card and smudged it. That was better. He doctored both cards, then stared at himself in the rearview mirror. "You're a healthcare professional. Walk like one, talk like a one, and people will believe you *are* one."

66

———

ROY

Not having any leads to go on, Roy considered driving by Farley's residence on the off chance Seth's mother would be there. But he was confident the LAPD had plain clothes officers sitting on the house, and he didn't want them to snag him instead of Farley.

With nothing to do but wait for a call from Karen, he was restless. He hoped it wouldn't take the reporter long to dig up information on Farley's mother. Out of his need to kill time, he purchased a second burner phone. When the reporter called, he'd give her the new number. Why make it easy for the department to track him? Not staying in one place and not using the same phone might help. Finally, Karen called.

"I've got good news and bad news," she said.

"Start with the good."

"I'm sure I've found the right woman."

"And?"

"She's been leading a hard life and is currently in a Hollywood hospital."

"Do you know why?"

"No clue."

"How'd you find her?"

"I can't tell you my secrets. Reporters have our sources."

He let her refusal to reveal how she found Farley's mom slide for the moment and instead gave her the number to his new phone.

"Karen, I understand your desire protect your informant, but I need to know everything. I *will* find Seth, and if I wind up dumping him, I'll have to say how I located him."

There was a pause. Her tone was lower when she spoke. "My brother is a private detective. He's skilled at finding people on the internet from open sources—websites anyone can access. I suspect he also gets information on the dark web. But I don't ask too many questions."

"What did he discover?"

"Nora Farley has been arrested numerous times. There were arrests for being drunk in public and theft but the majority were for prostitution."

"Hmm," Roy mused. "I wonder how his mom being a working girl didn't show up in Seth's background check."

"We found the mom through someone named Mitzi Monroe, who posted a message on Facebook this morning. She said she was at Hollywood Hills Hospital with her friend Nora. Monroe tagged Farley's mom in the post. There was a photo of Monroe standing in front of an ambulance along with two paramedics. From the look of the picture, I'd bet Mitzi is a prostitute too."

"Perfect. Thank you. Did the post say what was wrong with Nora?"

"No."

"I hope it's nothing serious so I can talk to her. Thanks, Karen. I owe you one."

"Not so fast."

"What?"

"Try to watch or listen to the news. The LAPD has scheduled another Farley update later today. The word is out you ditched your security detail and the department is furious with you."

"They'll have to get over it. If I catch the asshole, they'll be thanking me."

"I hope you're right."

Over the line, he heard someone yelling at her.

"I've got to run. Be careful, Roy."

"Thanks."

He smashed his old phone, climbed into his truck, and headed toward the freeway. A few blocks before the on-ramp, he pulled into a convenience store parking lot. He hopped out of the pickup and jogged to the side of the building to a fenced area containing the trash dumpster. He tossed the remnants of his phone into the bin and returned to his pickup.

Hollywood Hills Hospital, or the Triple H as it was known, was about twenty miles away. As he drove to the 170 Freeway, he turned on a local news station. The top story was the hunt for Seth Farley. The latest report stated a transient was discovered shot to death in bushes near the scene of Jeremey Cook's murder. Authorities suspected the killer of the police officer stumbled across the fifty-five-year-old homeless man and silenced him.

Farley is killing with abandon. I hope to God Amber's not with him.

The freeway traffic was surprisingly light. Roy tried to figure out what to say to Nora Farley when he saw her—provided he'd get to talk to her at all.

A mention of the LAPD chief on the radio caught Roy's attention. The press conference Karen had alluded to was beginning.

"Good afternoon. I'm Chief Byron Russo of the LAPD. For the past few days we've been searching for one of our former police officers as a person of interest in several homicides. Today I'm announcing we are looking for another individual, a female: Amber Buckner."

Roy's heart missed a beat like a manual transmission skipping a gear. Why were they making Amber's disappearance public knowledge? If Farley had kidnapped her, they were putting his wife in danger. The fugitive might kill her and dump her, fearing she'd be recognized.

"Ms. Buckner was reported as a missing person and is not suspected of any wrong-doing. We have her photograph on display here and on our website. If anyone has seen her within the last two and a half days, please call either our Missing Persons Unit or Robbery Homicide Division with the information."

RHD must have read the emails between Farley and Amber. As Roy was doing, they were probably trying to ascertain if Amber's disappearance resulted from foul play or a consensual relationship.

Reporters shouted questions. "Chief, there's a rumor

going around that one of your officers ran away from his security detail. Can you confirm the information and tell us what is happening?"

"Not at this time."

A different reporter yelled out. "Is it true that the officer who ditched the officers protecting him is the husband of Amber Buckner and you think foul play is involved with her disappearance?"

The chief hesitated. "This is what I *will* say. We're diligently looking for Amber Buckner and we believe there are people out there who have information as to her location. We want to talk to them. It would benefit those people to make themselves available to us."

67

AMBER

"Come on, baby, start." Amber pumped the accelerator pedal and turned the key. The engine slogged out a grinding sound as it attempted to turn over. She turned the key off and waited a second, then tried again.

The grating noise was peppier this time. "Come on, come on. You can do it." The engine finally caught and started.

"Whoo hoo!" She said a small prayer of thanks. Glancing at the gas gauge, she was happy to see the tank was more than half full.

She pushed the button to open the rolling garage door. In the rearview mirror, she realized she had another problem— two feet of snow covered the driveway.

"Shit." Amber got out but left the car running. She feared she wouldn't be able to to get it started again. Looking around, she spotted a snow shovel tucked in the corner of the garage.

Amber retrieved the shovel and used it to carve a narrow path to the street. From there, she worked her way back up the driveway, tossing the powdery snow to the side. After several passes, she cleared a corridor the Honda would fit through.

While her feet kept dry in the rubber galoshes, her toes burned with the cold, even with the layers of socks she wore. Her grandmother's jacket was heavy with the snow that had melted into the fabric.

When she was done, her arms ached, and she was out of breath. She wanted to take a break, but she feared Farley's return. There was no time to rest. If he returned and saw what she'd done trying to escape, he'd kill her. She couldn't let that happen.

And as if to encourage her to keep moving, the baby kicked again.

68

SETH

Seth walked through the automated glass doors and nodded at the security guard behind a podium off to the side. The uniformed man responded with a curt nod of his own.

Seth cruised past the intake clerks safe behind their bullet-resistant shields. Beyond the clerical workers were two double doors that he felt certain led to the ER. He needed a key card to slide through a reader for those doors to open. A hand sanitizer dispenser was posted outside the entrance. He stopped to scrub his hands while praying someone would exit the ER. No one did.

He couldn't stall any longer, so shuffled to the key reader and slid his fake ID card through the slot. He tried it several times, and with each failed attempt, pretended to become more exasperated. There was a click in the lock device indicating someone else had unlocked the door. Seth scanned the intake staff who were busy talking to potential patients. His eyes lit on the uniformed security guy who gave him a small salute.

Seth smiled at the guard and nodded, then entered the ER. *Idiot.*

From his work with the LAPD, he knew emergency rooms usually had a big whiteboard displaying the patient's last name, their stated complaint, and their location.

There she was. *Farley, Room 6.* He saw her complaint of injury was pain to the upper left abdomen. He walked with purpose to the designated room and pushed open the door.

His mother wasn't alone. A nurse was lowering the upper part of the bed to a flat position.

Nora's eyes were closed, and her skin was so pale it was near translucent.

My God. She looks dead.

"An aide should be here any min—" She looked and saw Seth. "Oh good. Here he is."

She hustled to a sink and washed her hands. "They want her in the OR."

Seth wasn't sure what to do. He didn't have a clue where the operating room was. "Got it." The nurse followed as he wheeled the gurney out. Left or right? Which way should he go?

"You're new here, aren't you?"

Seth nodded.

"The OR is on the third floor. Elevators are to the left."

"Thank you, ma'am." Seth swung the bed in a wide arc into the hallway.

"Welcome to the Triple H," the nurse said, following him

out of the examining room. She headed right, toward the nurses' station.

Seth pushed the gurney the opposite way. Midway, he pulled the bed to the side of the wall and leaned over his mother's face. "Mom? It's me. Seth."

Nora's eyelids fluttered open. "Seth?" Her voice was a mere whisper.

"Yeah, Mom, it's me."

"I hurt so bad, son." Her eyes closed.

"They're gonna operate on you. It will make you feel better. I'm taking you there. I promise I'll be there when you wake up."

Nora gave a weak sigh. "I should have listened to you and stopped working a long time ago. I'm going to die."

"No, no! Don't say that."

His mother's face contorted into a grimace of pain.

"We're going to the operating room right now. It's really important you don't let on that I'm your son. Okay? You understand?"

Nora moaned and nodded. "Hurry. Please."

Seth pushed his mother to the elevators and frantically punched at the button. "Come on, come on," he muttered.

Once on the floor to the OR, he wheeled the stretcher off the elevator.

"Hold it," he called out to a woman exiting the locking doors to the surgical unit.

The nurse, wearing scrubs covered in neon cats, held the door open so he could enter.

He positioned the gurney his mother occupied next to the nurses' station.

"Is that Nora Farley?" The nurse frowned as she pounded on the keyboard in front of her.

"Yes."

"We've been waiting for her. Wheel her over there." The nurse pointed to a position next to a wall.

"How long will her surgery take?"

The nurse looked over her reading glasses at Seth. "Why do you care?"

"I don't know if it's in her patient history, but she's a relative of one of the major donors to the hospital. I'm assigned to stay with her and take her to recovery."

The cranky nurse's gaze flicked over to the gurney. "Really? Well, you won't be allowed in the OR."

Seth nodded. "I understand. I need to be here when she gets out of surgery and transfer her to recovery."

"Guess it pays to have friends in high places." She shook her head. "As if we don't have enough to keep us busy." The nurse signaled to another woman wearing scrubs. "That's our spleen removal: Farley," she said, nodding toward the stretcher. "Tell the doc not to screw up. She's a VIP—relative of a big donor to the hospital."

The other woman came forward, taking hold at the foot of the bed.

Seth leaned over his mom and took her hand in his. "Nora, you're going into surgery right now. I'll be here when you get out. I promise."

"Thank you, son," Nora whispered. "I love you."

Seth raised to a standing position. He fought tears as his mother was wheeled away.

"Check in with me in two hours," the bossy nurse said. "If there are complications we'll know by then. I don't expect them to finish any earlier, but give me a cell number where I can call you."

Seth rattled off random numbers that sounded local. The last thing he needed was the nurse calling him. He'd return in ninety minutes.

With time to kill, Seth thought he'd better go out to his truck and stay out of sight. He didn't want some antsy doctor or nurse to get the idea he was there to work.

Seth's stomach growled. He went to the cafeteria and bought two premade sandwiches, a banana, and a bottle of iced tea. He jogged through the rain and into the parking garage.

69

ROY

Roy went through the main entrance of Hollywood Hills Hospital to the information desk and spoke to an older woman wearing a volunteer badge identifying her as Betty.

"Hi, Betty. I'm Officer Buckner from the LAPD, and here to speak with a witness in a case of mine, Nora Farley. I understand she was admitted this morning."

"Do you have identification?"

"Of course." Roy pulled out his wallet and handed her his police ID card.

"Do you mind if I take a photocopy of this? We have to be careful these days."

"Not at all."

Betty rose from her chair and shuffled to an ancient machine on a counter behind her. With the copy of his ID in hand, she returned and sat at her desk. "What was the woman's name?"

"Nora Farley. She was brought to the ER earlier today." Roy hoped his tone wasn't revealing the frustration he was feeling at how long she was taking.

Betty typed into a computer on her desk. "Yes." She nodded as her gaze scanned the screen. "It appears that she's in the OR. Would you like me to call up there and obtain her status?"

"Can you direct me how to get there?"

Betty's eyes widened behind her thick glasses. "You won't be able to talk to her while she's in surgery."

Roy swallowed his exasperation and displayed a patient smile. "No, I know that. I thought I might speak to some of the nurses and find out if Nora disclosed anything of value."

The old woman shook her head. "Oh no, they're much too busy up there to have you trying to ask them questions."

Roy rolled his shoulders back and exhaled. "You're being such a dear, Betty. Could you call the surgery unit and verify when Mrs. Farley might be out of surgery and able to speak with me?"

At his praise, Betty smiled at him. "Of course, Officer." She dialed the phone, and after a short conversation she hung up. "They just took her into the operating room. They expect the surgery to take about two hours."

He stood silent for a minute, thinking. "Okay. I'll be back later. Thank you. You've been a big help."

Roy exited the hospital into the unseasonably brisk and rainy day. Once again he had time to kill. From working Hollywood Division, he remembered a small hole-in-the-wall joint around the corner. Hoping they were still open and serving breakfast, he tugged his baseball cap lower on his face, zipped his water-resistant jacket higher, and marched down the street.

70

AMBER

Amber looked along the road at the path the snowplow had cleared earlier. Because her cabin was the only one on the street, the driver had just cut a single swath. She was grateful he'd taken the time to do that given the cottage was so isolated. The near-whiteout conditions had already deposited at least four inches of powder onto the plowed pavement.

Maybe you should get the chains and put them on the car. Who are you kidding? You've never changed a tire, much less attached snow chains on one. Leave now while you can! Farley could return any minute.

She moved to the front of the Honda and disconnected the power pack from the battery. She tossed it in the back seat with the water, snacks, and blankets. After sliding behind the wheel, she put the car in reverse and guided the vehicle through the corridor of snow she'd shoveled.

Amber rammed the rear bumper into a snowbank as she turned from the driveway. "Damn it. Don't get stuck." She followed the track left by the plow. Several times the tires slid in the powdery white stuff. "Keep moving, Amber. Slow and steady. You're getting away. You're getting away!"

Blood pounded in her ears as she wound her way along the remote roadway. She came to the T intersection. If she turned right, the neighbor's house was two miles away, but there was no guarantee anyone would be home—the neighbors didn't live there full time. If she turned left, she'd need to travel four miles to town. At least there was some certainty there'd be someone to help her. But what if Farley returned while she was escaping? Could the Honda outrun his four-wheel-drive pickup? No.

"You have to take the chance." She turned left.

The snowplow had only cleared a single lane on this thoroughfare—probably because it, too, was isolated. Apparently, the authorities wanted people off the roads and to ride out the storm. Heavy snow covered the single path, telling Amber it was plowed a while ago.

Amber gave the accelerator more gas, and the back end fishtailed to the right. She took her foot off the pedal and turned the wheel toward the skid. The Honda slid to a stop. When she stepped on the accelerator, the car labored to gain traction. The wheels spun, then grabbed and propelled her forward. "Slow and steady, Amber. Slow and steady." She had the windshield wipers set to high, but they struggled to keep pace with the falling snow.

She crawled along for several minutes then began to

climb an incline in the roadway. Amber increased the pressure on the pedal. The wheels spun, but the Honda didn't advance. She tried again—and failed. "Damn." Amber's eyes filled with tears. She hadn't even gone a mile yet.

"Suck it up, buttercup. Looks like you're gonna learn how to put on snow chains." She left the car running so the heat from the engine could help to keep her warm while she crawled on the ground.

She retrieved the plastic box containing the heavy hardware and brought it inside the passenger compartment of the Honda. The instructions were folded neatly on top of the metal links. Amber looked at the diagrams of how to mount the chains onto the tires. Then she pulled on gloves and added another shirt to her bulky ensemble.

Knowing she needed to drive forward to put the chains on, Amber backed up several feet. Because of the incline, the Honda rolled backward but moving forward was out. She took the first two chains from the box and exited the warmth of the interior. Snowflakes blew into her face as she crouched next to the left front tire. She draped the chain over the wheel as the instructions had shown and drove forward to connect the unsecured ends. But when she got out of the car and knelt by the wheel, it didn't take her long to figure out something was terribly wrong. The chains were the incorrect size. They were too short go around the tire.

PART VIII

71

KAREN

At the Police Administration Building, Karen and her cameraman waited in a room on the first floor set aside for updates to the Seth Farley story. Brian sat playing video games on his phone while Karen remained on the fringe of groups of other journalists recounting tales of being a reporter.

The lieutenant in charge of the Media Relations Section entered and stood in the doorway. "May I have your attention, please?"

The room grew quiet.

"The chief will give a brief update on the search for Seth Farley in ten minutes."

Someone yelled. "What about the mayor? Will he be here?"

The lieutenant shook his head. "As far as I know, it will only be the chief. Anything else?"

No one responded, and the lieutenant left.

Reporters sprang into action, checking their microphones, touching up their makeup, and reviewing notes and questions they hoped to ask.

Karen's cell phone rang. She recognized the number as the one Roy had given her earlier in the day. "Be right back," she told Brian. She moved into the hallway.

"Hello?"

"It's me. Any news?"

"Not yet, but soon. We're getting an update in just a few minutes. Where are you?"

"I'm having lunch. Nora Farley was in surgery when I got to the hospital. I'll head that way as soon as I'm done."

"Okay. If there's noteworthy info in the briefing, I'll give you a call."

"Phone reception is crappy in hospitals. I'll call you after I talk to Seth's mother."

"Either way we'll connect later."

"Right."

"Gotta run," she said. "The chief is coming to start the update."

72

SETH

The space where Seth parked his truck faced the hospital entrance. As he ate, he watched people scurrying below through the precipitation.

One man leaving wasn't in a hurry. The bite of sandwich Seth had swallowed got stuck in his throat. The guy wore a baseball cap and black jacket. Seth recognized him right away. It was Roy Buckner, and he was walking to a side street perpendicular to the medical center.

For the first time since he'd posted his declarations on Facebook, Seth was frazzled. Despite his planning, tricks, and disguises, within hours his former training officer had found his exact location.

There was no way Roy had located him through his mother. On his application to become a cop he'd listed both of his parents as dead.

What should he do? From his position in the parking garage he couldn't kill his prey. Roy had rounded the corner. Where had he gone? How did he find him? Was a command post being formed? Panicked thoughts bombarded his brain.

Why hadn't Roy confronted him? Were they watching him right now? He scanned the garage for anyone sitting in a car, then surveyed the hospital roof looking for an observation post or snipers.

It was possible the department was using Roy to confirm that Seth had been at the Triple H and would then call in reinforcements. They might come for him soon.

He'd feel better if he looked around, so he pulled his war bag from the rear floorboard to the front passenger seat. The black nylon duffel contained his two stolen military M-4 rifles, two Glock handguns, and all with extra ammo. It also held his binoculars case, his police radio, and a charger he'd stolen a month before his firing.

He'd go to the roof and use his binoculars to scout nearby streets and parking lots for unusual uniformed presence or a command post.

Before exiting his truck, he affixed a pancake holster to his waistband and slipped on a hooded rain jacket. He stashed two loaded magazines in each pocket, and turned on the police radio to Hollywood Division. If the division were dropping calls, he'd know they were probably being diverted to assist in his capture.

The LAPD thought he wasn't cop material. He'd show them. If things went south, he had stolen military hand grenades in the black duffel.

He exited the truck and sauntered toward the elevator at the center of the building.

He punched the button to go up. When the car arrived, the elevator was empty. He tugged the hood of his jacket further over his head in case there was a hidden security camera in the confined space.

Once he stepped out of the elevator, it surprised him how many cars were parked on the top deck. He moved to the south side of the structure and knelt behind a BMW.

He got his binoculars out and surveyed the hospital roof and streets. His vision was obscured not only by the rain but because of large buildings in his way. From his vantage point, he didn't see any unusual activity. He studied the other three directions, and nothing abnormal came into view.

He supposed it was possible Roy's arrival was a coincidence, but it was improbable.

Fluke or not, he'd take his chances and go back and visit his mother. He wanted to tell her how much he loved her. His gut told him it was the last time he'd see her.

Returning to his truck, he took off the rain jacket and stowed all the equipment except for the Glock at his waist.

He glanced at his cell phone. She should be out of surgery soon. He'd better hurry in case Roy came back.

As he walked to the ER, his thoughts returned to being a young boy and how his mom had told him many times that his dad was a policeman. Police work was in his blood. He'd grown up wanting to emulate the father he'd never known.

But the LAPD, and especially Roy Buckner, feared being outshined. He'd show them how stupid they were. But first, he needed to talk to his mother one last time.

Afterward, he'd bait Roy into following him to the cabin. He could suffer the humiliation Seth experienced when he was told police work wasn't a good fit. He should "consider a new career choice." Seth smiled to himself, anticipating Amber watching her husband beg for his life.

He slowed his walk at the security guard's podium and held up his fake ID. "Hey, bro, my cards still aren't working. Can you buzz me through?" He didn't know how to find the elevators unless it was from the ER.

His "pal," the rent-a-cop, dutifully unlocked the double door to the emergency room. Seth marched through—a man on a mission and not to be bothered—which was true.

He got to the surgical floor, and his favorite cranky nurse seemed to be waiting for him.

"Hey there, hotshot. I arranged a spot in the ICU for Miss VIP. They're less busy up there, and she'll receive more attention. She's been in recovery for a half hour. Although the surgery went well, it's touch and go for her."

Touch and go? I thought they were supposed to fix her. He swallowed. "I'm sure the family will be grateful. Is she awake?"

A new voice entered the conversation. "She's coming to now." The speaker was the other nurse he'd seen earlier. "You'd better get her up to the fifth floor where they can monitor her more carefully." She motioned to him. "Come with me. I'll take you to her."

Seth nodded to the crabby gal and followed the other one.

When he saw his mother, he gasped. Her brassy red hair clashed against the white of her skin—skin so thin every vein in her forehead was visible. Her eyes were shut, and there was an IV in her arm. If it weren't for her shallow breathing, he'd have thought she'd passed.

"I'm not surprised she dozed off again. We lost her twice on the table."

He took hold of the bed. "I'll take her upstairs."

"Good luck, Nora," the nurse said and held open the door for him.

The fifth floor, the intensive care unit, was designed as two ovals separated by a bank of elevators. Each oval had a massive nurses' station in its center. A brunette directed him to roll the bed to a room on the west side of the building.

The woman had a toothpaste-commercial smile and told him to put on a gown and mask before entering. "I'll be right back to get the patient settled."

He didn't have much time to say goodbye. He wheeled Nora inside and positioned her next to the door. An empty bed sat by the window. He mentally made a note to switch the beds so his mother could have a view. Then he bent to put his mouth to her ear.

"Mom? Mom, it's me, Seth." His gaze searched her face.

She pried open her eyes and then shut them.

"Mom, I can't stay long. I'll have to leave soon. I just wanted you to know how much I love you."

She swallowed but kept her lids closed. "I love you too, son. I'm sorry I wasn't a better mother."

"Shhh, Mom. Don't say that. You've been a wonderful mo—"

The door burst open and the smiling brunette charged in with the energy of a Labrador Retriever puppy. "Nora. Nora Farley, wake up."

He jerked to an upright position and frowned.

The nurse bristled at his disapproval. "I need to assess

her. I can't do that if she's asleep." She marched to the bedside computer and typed. "Nora, are you in any pain?" Her voice was overly loud.

Nora tried to shake her head.

"Can you tell me what city you're in?"

"Los Angeles?" Nora's voice was faint.

"Okay, hon, let's get your vitals." The nurse left the keyboard and looked pointedly at him.

"Oh, Mrs. Farley is a relative of one of the hospital's biggest donors. I was directed to bring her a floral arrangement from the store downstairs."

The brunette snorted. "Well, I don't know who was doing the directing, but flowers aren't allowed in the ICU." She input the numbers coming from a blood pressure cuff she'd attached to Nora's arm. "If the family's determined to spend a bunch of money, you can purchase mylar balloons."

A wave of relief surged through him. He wanted the nurse to take his mother's vitals and anything else she needed, and then go away.

When he returned, he'd have a few more minutes alone with his mom. "I'll go to the gift shop." He exited the room, stripping off the protective garments he wore and tossing them in a bin.

Once in the elevator, he hoped he'd be able to return to the fifth floor without going through the security guard in the ER. When he reached the ground level, he saw that the elevators serving the ICU opened to the general lobby.

After making his purchase, he plastered on a smile for the old woman manning the information desk wearing a candy-striper uniform.

Outside his mother's room, he put on the required protective clothing and entered. She was alone. The floating mylar balloons he'd bought bounced against each other with a hollow sound as he shut the door.

She turned her head and opened her eyes. "Seth."

He set the balloons, which had a weight tied to the ribbons, on a rolling table next to the bed. He hurried to her and gave her a kiss. "Hi, Mom. How ya feeling?"

Nora lifted her brows and sighed. "Not great. They said the doc removed my spleen."

He took his mother's hand. "I'm sorry. Tell me who did this to you."

"It's not important now. What's done is done."

"No. He has to pay. What was his name?"

"Son, I don't know. He was a man with twenty dollars."

There was a moment of silence, then he squeezed her fingers. "Mom, I'm in a bit of trouble, and if anyone asks, I need you to tell them you haven't seen or heard from me."

"What kind of trouble?"

"It's not serious. I just need time to set things right."

"Is it something to do with your job as a policeman? I'm so proud of you."

"No, Mom. Nothing like that."

His mom's eyelids were heavy. "Mom, I have to leave. Remember that I love you."

Nora nodded, her eyes closed.

A noise at the door was followed by the voice of the loud nurse. "Sir, wait. You must wear a gown and mask before going in there. They're in that wooden cabinet."

Someone was coming.

He had to hide. He whirled a room-dividing curtain from against the wall around the empty bed. He yanked the sheet and blanket down, and climbed inside, facing the door. He pulled the bedding to cover his legs and torso. If the nurse came in along with the visitor, he'd be discovered. He'd have to do whatever it took to escape. He eased the Glock from its holster and held the gun on his stomach.

73

ROY

After eating a greasy omelet and soggy toast, Roy trudged back to Hollywood Hills Hospital. He didn't know what information he expected from Nora Farley. He hoped she'd be able to tell him something helpful in finding her son—and Amber if she was with him.

He had to go through the whole charade of flashing his ID card to get access to the surgical unit and Seth's mother. His subterfuge of working a case was worth it if he found his wife.

On the ICU floor, he met with Nora Farley's nurse, a vivacious brunette with a big smile. "If she doesn't want to talk, don't force her."

"I won't," he promised.

"I've got to take a peek at another patient, but Nora Farley is in the room three doors down on the right."

He hurried to the room she'd indicated. His hand was on the doorknob when she hollered for him to put on a gown and mask. She directed him to a cabinet right outside the door.

As he entered the room, he noticed a large curtain divided the room. Apparently the other bed was occupied. Which patient was Nora?

The woman in the closest bed slept.

Should he go ask the nurse? Maybe the person behind the curtain was awake.

The woman before him stirred and stretched, then placed her hand on her belly. The hospital bracelet she wore was visible. He'd take a peek at the band.

He approached her and leaned over. The name said Nora Farley. Seth's mother didn't look well. In fact, she looked near death.

"Padre? Is that you?" Her voice was little more than a whisper.

He drew back and scrutinized the woman's face. Finally, the face and name connected. "Nadine?"

"How've you been, Padre?" Breath. "Still on the job?"

He stared at the woman, not believing the frail woman in the bed was Nookie Nadine—*and* Seth Farley's mother. "I can't believe I'm seeing you after all this time."

Deep breath. "Life throws us surprises." Breath. "Like this. I have surgery, and you walk in." Another deep breath. "I didn't think I'd ever see you again."

He nodded. "Yeah, it's crazy."

"How long has it been, fifteen—twenty years?"

"It's been a long time."

"You see any of the other guys?" Breath. "Speakeasy, Fast Eddie, and the rest?"

Roy's mind flashed to him and his friends reminiscing at his house about their wilder days. Then to Luke's murder—a killing committed by her son. "Every now and then."

"You boys sure knew how to party."

"We were young and stupid. After the first few years, most of us settled down."

She offered a weak smile and took a deep breath. "You were settled when I met you. That was the problem. Judy? Janice?"

"Jennifer," he said. "I was married to Jennifer."

"I 'member now." She sighed and closed her eyes, then opened them. Deep breath. "Then you got divorced—and I got pregnant." She looked at him. "You *did* know I got pregnant, right?"

Roy tensed. "I'd heard rumors but nothing definite."

"You didn't wonder what'd happened to me? You knew how I felt about you. I told you—"

"Funny, but I mentioned you the other day." Realizing how lame he sounded, he added, "But I should have taken the time back then—"

"Why are you here now?" Deep breath.

"It's regarding Seth."

She gasped, and her watery eyes widened. "You don't know him. What do you want with him?"

He ignored the buzzing of his burner phone. "Nadi— Nora, I *do* know Seth. I was his training officer for two months. He's a smart kid, but not cut out to be a cop. I'm sorry to tell you that. I'm the reason he was let go."

"He got fired?"

"Well, he left the department of his own accord. We call it leaving in lieu of being fired."

"Oh." Breath.

"Have you seen him recently?"

She turned her head away. Deep breath. "No. I haven't seen him in a long time."

"Where would he go if he was in trouble? Friends, a favorite vacation spot?"

"What kind of trouble?" Her weak tone carried an edge.

"I don't have time to go into it, but it's serious. Do you know where he is?"

Deep breath. "I'm not sure I'd tell you if I did."

His phone vibrated again. *It must be Karen. She must have news.* Roy looked at the woman who'd partied herself into a hard and sordid life and now wanted to protect her son.

"If he comes here, please tell him to turn himself in. If he leaves, call the police and tell them he was here."

"What has he done? Tell me."

"He's killed people, Nora. And I think he has my wife."

74

SETH

Lying in the hospital bed hidden by the draped divider, Seth's heart and mind raced. Seconds before, Roy had left the room.

It made sense now. The trumped-up rating reports of Seth's performance as a cop were personal. Roy hid the fact he was Seth's father. Afraid his son would discover the truth, Roy saw to it he was as good as fired.

This changed things. The punishment he'd pronounce on Roy was no longer about destroying his dream of being a policeman. The death sentence was payment for abandoning his mother and leaving her alone with a baby to raise. All those missed birthdays, Christmases, and school events denied to him by his absent father.

Roy had used Nora and tossed her away like garbage. Her life was ruined while he lived in a big house in a nice neighborhood and married a younger woman. A woman who now carried *his* child. *The Freudian head-shrinkers would have a field day with this family tree.*

He'd make Roy pay by luring his dad to the cabin to see with his own eyes his *son* had stolen Amber *and* impregnated her. Something Roy couldn't accomplish.

Understanding washed over Seth. *Of course, Roy didn't get his wife pregnant. He probably got a vasectomy after impregnating my mom. When he married Amber, he didn't tell her.*

He leaped from the bed and ran over to his mother's side. "Mom, I need to go." He leaned and planted a kiss on her forehead.

Disbelief filled her face. "Where'd you come from? What have you done?" She took a deep breath. "A man was here and said you've killed people. Tell me it's not true."

"He's a liar. You know that better than anyone else. He'll pay for ruining our lives. I have to go. I love you."

"Seth, wait—"

He dashed out of the room hoping he'd be able to catch up to Roy.

75

AMBER

Amber looked at the two-inch gap between the ends of the snow chains and wanted to scream—and she did. Farley wasn't around to hear her. No one was nearby. Tears fell from her eyes and froze on her cheeks. She wished she had a hammer or something to pound the hell out of the car. *Grammy and Grampy, why put chains in the trunk that don't fit the tires?*

She wiped snowflakes from her lashes. If she could just connect one side of the chain, the added traction might propel the car up the incline. She had to reach the village. She'd never make it walking. She was wet and freezing already.

She returned to driver's seat to warm herself. The heat caressed her face and frozen hands. "Brrrrr," she said, rubbing her arms. "Okay, Amber. You're in a tough spot. But you've gotten through worse than this, so you'll get out of this too. Think."

She considered tearing material into strips and tying the ends of the chain together. She looked through the clothes she'd brought with her and flung them aside. Thinking of warmth, each piece was made of thick fabric. She had nothing to cut the cloth and only her teeth to rip it. Nothing was suitable.

She needed wire or something. The taillights had wire, but she faced the same problem—no cutting tool.

She returned to the back seat and thrust her hand into the pockets attached to the rear of the front seats. Feeling around, she prayed for a bunch of pipe cleaners to appear. She pulled her empty fingers out of the compartment, overcome with defeat...until she saw the telescopic umbrella tucked into a cup holder in the back passenger door.

Despair turned to hope as she grabbed it and brought it into the front seat of the car. She opened the device, excited to see the metal ribs attached to the canopy by only a few threads. She pulled a rib with one hand and pushed on the nylon fabric with the other and ripped it free. Little tufts of cloth stuck to the metal, but it wouldn't affect what she hoped to do with it.

Amber grasped the rib at the middle and rapidly bent the piece back and forth. When it snapped in half, she smiled. "One down, seven to go."

She sat in the car's warmth and bent the base of the metal back and forth, fatiguing the pieces to where they broke from the device. Each section was about eighteen inches long.

From the passenger seat, she grabbed one of the tire chains she'd brought inside the car so she wouldn't be dealing with ice-cold materials. Draping links over the steering wheel, she looked at the best way to attach her makeshift extension to the device.

From her earlier attempt, she knew three inches was needed to join the ends together. She planned to affix one end of the metal to the chain. Then she'd weave the rib through the links, still having enough of the metal to loop it over the tail end. If it worked, hopefully the umbrella rib and the chain would last until she drove into the village.

By the time she finished her MacGyver-inspired fix, Amber's swollen fingers ached and two of them bled. *If I get these fastened on the tires, I can get out of here.*

It took her longer than she wanted to fasten the chains on the front wheels of the Honda, but the makeshift devices did attach. Although she'd pressed the umbrella ribs as smooth as she could, she worried a sharp rogue fragment might pierce the tires. In the driver's seat, she said a quick prayer, then stepped on the accelerator. To her amazement, the car rolled forward and climbed the incline.

76

———

ROY

As soon as Roy got outside the hospital, he called Karen. "What's up?"

"You're in big trouble, Roy."

He stopped walking to the parking garage and stood beside a light pole. "Why? What happened?"

"The chief of police has announced that you're a person of interest in the disappearance of Seth and your wife. The LAPD is asking for the public's help in locating you. They've posted your picture everywhere and asked the public to call a tip line if they see you."

"That's crazy."

She sighed. "Not according to the chief. They're saying evidence points to Seth and Amber having an affair and that you found out. Now the two of them are missing."

"Farley murdered four police officers and a transient in the bushes by the freeway."

"They think you're trying to frame him for those incidents."

He laughed.

"Don't laugh. They're serious."

"Yeah? Well, they're dead wrong. I couldn't have shot Luke Tremont. I found him after he crashed his car. Witnesses saw me holding Luke's body."

"No one challenged the chief. My colleagues were too focused on you becoming a suspect. You're the big story of the day." Karen paused. "You'd better come up with a plan to find Farley and clear yourself. And you'd better do it fast."

He didn't say anything.

"Roy, are you there?"

"Yeah, I'm here. You know this is BS, right?"

There was a slight hesitation. "I wouldn't be helping you if I thought you were capable of murder. What did you learn from Farley's mother?"

He shook his head. "She looked near death. She's had surgery, but I doubt she'll last the day. She claimed she has no clue where he is."

"What are you going to do now? It will be harder for you to move around. If they spot you, they'll bring you in for questioning."

"I guess I'll hole up for a while and hope Farley comes after me."

"Listen, why don't Brian and I come to the hospital and do an interview with you? We'll get your side of the story on tape. You can explain everything."

"Yeah, that's just great. You and your camera won't bring any attention my way."

Karen was quick with her reply. "Then tell me where."

"An exclusive story with me could seal the deal on you getting a permanent reporter job, right?"

"It couldn't hurt." She hesitated. "I *have* tried to help you."

That was true. He owed her. "Don't bring your news van." He gave her the name and location of the motel he'd booked for the next couple of nights. "It'll take me forty-five minutes to get there."

"No worries. We've got to go to the station and pick up my car."

"I'll be in room eight."

"Okay. See you in an hour."

77

SETH

After charging out of the hospital, Seth almost walked past Roy standing by a light pole, speaking in an animated manner on his phone.

Diverting his direction, Seth circled behind his former training officer and took a seat on a bench placed on the opposite side of a circular driveway. From this position he had a clear view of Roy, who was still talking.

As he looked at his father, Seth wondered if he should kill him right there. *No. You have a plan. Stick to it.*

He must be humiliated just as I was. They said I could quit or be fired. Everyone in the station knew what the captain was telling me. When I walked out of the office, no one met my gaze. I held my head high.

They were wrong. I've been killing cops for months, and yet they needed me to spell it out for them on the internet.

Roy ended his call and headed to the parking garage.

Seth waited until his former partner had gone fifty yards and then he rose and followed. He smiled when his father took the stairs rather than risk being ambushed in an elevator. *Police training at its finest.* The tactic made following him harder, but he knew he was up to the task.

He needed to find out where Roy was staying. From there he'd be able to lure his prey to his demise, but he'd have to do it fast. The saying *karma's a bitch* was appropriate for his dad, and Seth couldn't have been happier.

Arriving at the base of the stairwell, he watched Roy go to the floor above where Seth's pickup sat. He sprinted up the steps and jogged to his truck. Once inside, he angled the rearview mirror to see the vehicles descending the parking garage. Two cars passed by, both driven by women. The third vehicle was a Tacoma truck with his father behind the wheel. He waited until the pickup had circled to the level below before starting his own truck.

Once out of the structure, he spotted the Tacoma pickup waiting to turn left. There were three cars between Roy and him. Even so, because they were both in pickup trucks, he worried the cop might glance in his mirror and spot him. Seth grabbed a baseball cap and slung it over his head, pulling the bill low on his forehead.

The light changed, and the Tacoma transitioned to the 101 Freeway going north, leading to the San Fernando Valley.

Roy lived near there, so he'd probably stay in an area where he felt comfortable.

Traffic, as always, was thick. But at least the vehicles were moving at a steady clip. Once they passed through the Cahuenga Pass, the cars thinned out. After they'd passed

Universal Studios, he was surprised when the truck transitioned to the 170 Freeway. It was a ballsy move considering that Roy worked at North Hollywood Division and he'd be driving right through. If by some fluke he pulled next to a North Hollywood patrol car, the cops inside would recognize him.

He stuck with him, keeping at least three cars between him and the Tacoma. They exited the freeway at Sherman Way, and Seth grinned when Roy turned into the parking lot of a cheap motel frequented by druggies and whores.

"Well, well, well. You've come down in the world...Dad." He drove past the entrance to the driveway but pulled to the curb and parked. He exited his truck and jogged toward the flop joint.

78

———

KAREN

As Karen drove her small SUV along Sepulveda Boulevard, her gaze scoured the business signs for the motel where Roy was staying.

Brian, in the passenger seat, was checking emails on his phone.

"You know, you could help me find this place."

Her cameraman didn't shift his eyes from his glowing screen. "Yeah, I could, but then you'd think I'm condoning your actions. This Roy guy could be a serial killer and playing you."

"My gut is telling me he's been truthful."

"When you're in jail for aiding and abetting a fugitive that will be a great defense."

"A person of interest. Not a fugitive. I'm under no obligation to call anyone."

"That may be true, but you don't have to help him evade the cops." Brian looked up from his phone. "I've been to this flop joint before on a story. It's up ahead on the left a hundred yards."

She shifted her focus farther up the street. She cruised into the center turn lane and stopped, waiting for opposing traffic to clear so she could enter the motel property. Glancing in the horseshoe-shaped parking lot, she searched for Roy's truck he'd described to her earlier. It was backed into a parking space in the corner.

Something else caught her eye. A man wearing a light-weight jacket and a baseball cap walked fast from the motel. What grabbed her attention was the fact the man's pants were powder-blue scrubs. But it was more than that—he seemed familiar. She watched through her side mirror as he got into a pickup truck parked on the street and pulled away.

"Brian!"

Her passenger jumped. "What's wrong? You scared the hell out of me."

"I think that was him."

"Who?"

"Seth Farley. He walked out of the parking lot, jumped in a truck, and drove off."

"Are you sure it was him?"

"Maybe eighty percent. He looked like the picture the LAPD has posted."

She jerked the steering wheel to the left and, seconds later when there was a break in traffic, she made a U-turn. She sped down the boulevard in the same direction that Farley had gone. "He's in a brown pickup."

Brian leaned forward scrutinizing the traffic ahead of them. "Is that him in the right lane getting ready to turn?"

"I think so. That's the only one I see. What should we do?"

"Call the police," he said. "Let them deal with him."

Farley's truck turned and entered the freeway on-ramp going south. With several cars between her and Farley, she followed.

She bit her lower lip. "But I'm not sure. What if the cops come, get him out of the truck, and it's not him?"

"Then they'll tell Joe Schmo it was a mistake and send him on his way."

"But I'll be the laughingstock of the news business."

The cameraman frowned at her. "What is it you want to do?"

"Follow and pull up next to him. You can casually glance and confirm it's him."

Brian snorted. "Yeah, and then he'll shoot me from the safety of his truck. You forget he sits higher than us. He'll look inside your car and see my camera behind our seats."

"I've got my jacket on the back seat. Throw it over the camera." She eyed the hoodie he wore. "Toss yours on it too."

"This guy is armed and dangerous. I know you want the job, but I'm not willing to get killed in the process."

She gripped the wheel tighter. "I understand. Let's confirm it's him, then call in the cops. Should we switch positions and I'll be the one looking at him?"

Brian shook his head. "No. We'll lose him." He made a forward motion with his hand. "Hurry and get this over with." He unbuckled his seat belt, and struggled out of his hoodie and tossed it on his equipment. Then he reached to the rear seat and snagged Karen's jacket and draped it over the remaining exposed parts.

She increased the pace of the car a little at a time. Farley was in the third lane and driving the speed limit. She moved over into the second lane from the center of the freeway. Traffic went faster. As she gained on the brown truck, Farley shifted again.

"He's transitioning to take the Ventura Freeway," Brian said. "Get over a lane."

"Not a problem." She eased her SUV in behind Farley's truck. She slowed her pace, allowing two other cars between her SUV and his pickup.

Once they were on the same freeway heading east, there were more cars. It took her time to position her vehicle next to the brown truck.

Coming alongside the driver's door, Brian casually looked up and right. He kept his expression neutral and turned to Karen before he spoke. "It's him."

She eased her foot off the accelerator allowing the pickup to edge ahead of them a half of a car length. She picked up her phone from the cup holder on the center console and dialed. "It's me. Thank God you answered. I'm with my cameraman, and we spotted Farley walking from the parking lot of the motel where you're staying." There was a pause. "We're on the freeway following him."

Brian's face contorted in outrage. "Are you crazy? We've got a serial killer in front of us. We need to notify the police. Screw Buckner. He can't do anything."

She tuned out her cameraman's wrath and listened to Roy's questions.

"Are you sure it's him? Is Amber with him?"

"Yes, I'm sure it's him. No, I think he was alone."

"*Where are you now?*"

She paused. "The Ventura Freeway. We're coming up to..." She looked at the next freeway sign. "Azuza."

"That's wrong. We just merged onto the 210 Freeway and are approaching Arcadia," Brian spat out.

She started to relay the message, but Roy had heard Brian's correction. "Okay. We'll call you if anything changes." She disconnected. "He's on his way."

"Karen, I'm calling the authorities. Farley is wanted for multiple murders. If we don't notify the cops, we'll have blood on our hands if anyone gets hurt."

Her cameraman was right. She'd done everything she could to give Roy a chance to find his wife. She nodded. "Make the call."

Brian talked to the 911 operator, giving them the license plate of Farley's truck, the direction of travel, and their perception that he was alone.

Karen continued to follow.

Within minutes, two California Highway Patrol SUVs, lights and sirens blaring, flew past Karen's vehicle.

She and Brian watched as the CHP units moved in behind Farley.

The brown pickup accelerated—and the chase was on.

79

ROY

The phone call from Karen shot a surge of adrenaline through Roy's body. As he listened to her recounting how she'd spotted Farley on the street, Roy gathered his few belongings and threw them into his backpack.

As he ran toward his pickup, he skidded to a stop. *How had Farley found him at the motel, and why hadn't he tried to kill him?* Roy eyed the truck. *His former partner was a veteran. Could he have rigged Roy's Tacoma with explosives?* He set his gear on the bumper, then walked around the perimeter of the vehicle. He inspected the door locks for tampering, wheel wells, and bumpers. Nothing appeared out of place. He looked for newer fingerprints or smudges. Last, he climbed under the pickup and examined the frame, fuel tank, and exhaust pipe. Everything appeared normal.

After crawling from beneath the vehicle, he pulled his

possessions off the bumper and opened the driver's door. He checked for tampering inside, including the ignition and dashboard, and scanned underneath both the gas and brake pedals for a fuse device. Not finding anything suspicious, he popped the latch for the hood. His inspection of the engine compartment disclosed nothing alarming. But that didn't mean the car was safe. He returned to the driver's seat, said a quick prayer, and started the vehicle.

He burned rubber out of the parking lot and headed toward the Ventura Freeway. He needed to make up a shit-load of time. If Amber wasn't with Farley, it meant that he was probably returning to where he'd left her.

Roy sat at a red light when his cell phone rang. Karen. "Yeah, where are you now?"

Her cameraman responded. "He's running and the cops are chasing him. We're trying to stay with them but Farley's doing over a hundred. We're following the cop cars as they join the chase."

"Where are they?"

"Still on the 210 going through San Dimas."

"I'm never gonna catch up. Keep me posted." Roy disconnected the call and focused on his driving. The one thing he knew for sure was that every police officer in the southland would listen to the pursuit. If it were televised, they'd park someplace and stream it live on their phones. Anyone who wore a badge wanted to be involved in the chase and arrest a cop killer.

Since he knew the police were preoccupied, Roy gave his truck more gas and sped faster. The sooner he caught up to Farley, the sooner he'd see Amber.

80

SETH

Seth had known it would come to this. Talk about bad luck. He'd walked into the parking lot of the fleabag motel where Buckner was staying, and a couple of vice cops were talking to a whore. He *thought* he'd eased out of the inn's courtyard without being seen, but the herd of CHP units pursuing him indicated otherwise.

Traffic was a nightmare, and he opted to pass slower vehicles on the right shoulder rather than invite the possibility of getting boxed in the center divider. At least if pressed he could exit the freeway and flee on surface streets. Just in case that scenario became a reality, he took his personal cell phone and powered it on. In the meantime, he dug around the duffel on the seat next to him. He pulled out a handgun and placed it on his lap. He grabbed three fully loaded extra magazines and set them against his war bag. Using a GPS app, he requested directions to Amber's grandparents' cabin.

His police training had taught him one thing well—always know where you are. When he and Amber had pulled into the driveway, he'd noticed the street address branded into the logs. The numbers were hard to forget— 5150—the section of the California Welfare and Institutions Code allowing officers to involuntarily detain someone if they were gravely disabled or a danger to themselves or others.

Sweat rolled down his face despite the wintry temperatures outside. He wanted to turn on the air conditioning, but he needed every horse in his engine to help him get away. He turned on the radio to a local news station. They were broadcasting the pursuit but weren't saying they were chasing *him*. It wouldn't be long before they'd be identifying him by name.

He'd caught a break with the weather being so blustery. No helicopter pilot in his right mind would fly in the low visibility. But Seth also knew the media could be relentless when it came to a big story, and he was one of the biggest of the year. Some news jockey would put a bird in the air. Hopefully the copter would crash.

Seth wondered if he'd become a notorious legend, much like Charles Manson—or would the world see him as a victim of an LAPD conspiracy? A scheme orchestrated by his training officer who happened to be his father. When the facts came out, the travesty done to him might even spark riots. It was unfortunate he wouldn't be around to enjoy his vindication.

Ahead he saw a CHP vehicle parked on the on-ramp waiting for him to go past, or maybe to throw out a spike strip to puncture his tires. He forced his way into the congestion and over to the thin shoulder along the center divider. While drivers were prohibited from traveling on the emergency strip, by doing so he could pick up speed as he approached Rancho Cucamonga. The gridlock had thinned, and a look in his rearview mirror revealed four CHP units plus another five patrol vehicles from different municipal and county agencies. This wasn't good. He was running for his life, but he'd never give up. Three miles before the transition to Highway 330—the road leading to Big Bear and Amber—he moved out of the emergency shoulder and back to the freeway lanes.

He eyed the bottleneck in front of him, figuring out his next move. Weaving through the cars, he rolled down the passenger window of his truck. The brisk air cooled his sweating skin. Another glance at the rearview mirror showed the patrol cars gaining on him. "Come on, boys. Bring it."

He positioned his pickup in the number two lane, abutting the fast lane of the freeway. To the far right, a big tanker-truck cruised along going at least sixty-five miles per hour in the "slow" portion of the roadway.

The transition sign for Highway 330 showed he had a mile to go. The driver of the fuel truck was oblivious to the fleet of cop cars trailing his rig. Seth smirked. More likely the operator of the tanker had formed the opinion he didn't want to get involved.

"Too bad for you, fucker."

Seth raised his gun, aimed at the fuel truck driver's head, and fired.

PART IX

81

KAREN

Karen followed the fleet of patrol cars in pursuit of the brown pickup. Farley was three football fields ahead of her and Brian. Between her SUV and the truck, there were at least ten police vehicles, and each on-ramp they passed, another cop car joined the hunt. When that happened, she decreased her speed and dropped behind the latest addition to the chase. Traffic behind her must have assumed she was part of the chain because they kept their distance.

The only time she could see Farley was when he changed lanes. "What do you think he'll do, Brian?"

"No clue. My guess is the cops will just let him run out of gas."

"I thought they might box him in when traffic was bad, but since the gridlock thinned out, he could go for a while."

"He's moving from the fast lane into the number two lane," Brian said.

A few seconds later, a gasoline tanker at the far-right side of the freeway went out of control, veering across the highway and colliding with several law enforcement black and whites. As the police cars spun and crashed into other vehicles, the fuel truck overturned, blocking all lanes.

Karen's instincts kicked in. She stomped on the brake pedal and scanned her rearview mirror to be sure traffic behind her saw her stopping. "Oh my God!"

More police cruisers slammed into each other attempting to avoid hitting the upended truck and the other disabled police units.

As soon as their car came to a stop, Brian twisted around in his seat and grabbed his camera.

She looked at her cameraman. "What are you doing?"

"Getting film. We're the first news team on the scene." He turned and viewed the traffic behind them. The lanes were blocked. "See if Farley was in the wreck. I'll shoot video of the tanker. Then come back, and we'll get the story on tape." He opened the door, placed the camera on his shoulder, and jogged to the overturned big rig.

She grabbed her press credentials from the center console and locked the car, taking the keys with her. Thankful she was wearing flat-heeled boots, she dashed past Brian and the wreckage, which was a hundred yards ahead. Four of the patrol cars had avoided the collision.

The officers not involved in the accident sprinted toward the immobilized police units, yelling, "Hey, you okay?"

Karen skirted around the stopped and crippled cars and

bolted past the toppled fuel truck. The eastbound lanes were empty except for a couple of vehicles that had pulled to the right shoulder. But there was no brown pickup. She turned to the tanker. No one seemed concerned about the driver's condition.

As if reading her mind, an officer jogged beyond crashed cop cars and climbed the side of the cab. He dropped inside the broken driver window. A minute later he pulled himself outside and stood on the cab of the wrecked semi.

She called to him. "How is he?"

"Lady, get the hell outta here. This thing could explode."

She waved her press pass that hung from a lanyard around her neck. "Karen Watson, KABR News." She nodded at the eighteen-wheeler. "Do you need help with the driver?"

"Nah, he's dead." The officer gazed at both sides of the interstate, which were completely stopped. "What a friggin' mess." He jumped from his perch on the big rig and jogged to her. "If I were you, I'd get your car and find a way off this damn freeway. It'll be closed for hours." He pulled out his radio and alerted someone that the driver of the fuel truck was deceased.

She turned to see Brian filming some officers assisting the others injured in the crash. She hurried that way so she and her cameraman could film their report.

Additional citizens were out of their autos and converging on the accident scene.

A female officer approached the growing crowd. "Folks, we need you in your vehicles. Safely clear a path for the fire department and ambulances to go through. Be careful. There are people walking around the freeway." She paced back and forth making a pushing motion. "Return to your cars. Do it now."

Reluctantly, the stunned drivers, almost all taking videos with their phones, complied with her order.

"Ma'am, that includes you," the officer said, looking at her.

Karen pointed to her press credentials.

The uniformed woman rolled her eyes. "Okay, but stay out of the way."

Brian was setting up to film.

Her cell phone rang. It was Roy.

"The news says there was a tanker explosion on the 210 north of Redlands. Is that true? Where's Farley?"

"It didn't explode, it overturned. The driver is dead, and the freeway is completely blocked. I don't know where Redlands is..." She searched for signage to tell her where she was. "We're near the interchange of the 210 and the 330 highway. As for Farley, he got away. I looked for his truck, and it's not here. I'm sorry."

"Did you say you're close to the 330 highway?"

She peered at the nearby signs. "Yes. That's what the sign says."

"I think I know where he might be going."

"Where?"

"I'll let you know when I've found him."

"Roy, that's not fair—or safe. The guy wants to kill you. Tell me where you're heading so, if you run into trouble, I can send help."

Silence filled the line. Then he spoke. "I'm not sure, but he may be on his way to Big Bear Lake. Amber's family has a cabin on a good chunk of property there. Don't alert anyone until I confirm he's there."

"If you think that's where he is, we should notify the police in Big Bear, right?" Silence. "Roy?"

He'd hung up.

82

SETH

Seth stomped on the accelerator and let out a whoop as the gasoline-hauling tanker swerved across the freeway, taking out at least two cop cars. Viewing the event through the rearview mirror, he wanted to see a fireball, but the truck had merely crashed and overturned.

He listened to the directions from his cell phone, and exited at Highland Avenue and went east. After a few minutes, he was on highway 330, heading up to the mountains and Big Bear where Amber was waiting at the cabin for him. The mess he'd made on the freeway probably had every first responder for miles trying to untangle the chaos. But he still needed to stay alert in case a forest ranger or some other local yokel tried to apprehend him.

Heavy snow fell as he drove up the winding road filled with hairpin turns. The weather added another hour to his thirty-mile drive. He wondered if he should try to boost a different vehicle in Running Springs, a mountain town twenty miles from Big Bear. His pickup made him a marked man.

Rounding a sharp turn along the ridge ahead of him, he saw a lone vehicle coming his way from the opposite direction. He pulled his truck to the side of the road at an angle as if his auto were disabled. He waited. Seconds later, he heard the car approaching.

A mid-sized red SUV outfitted with tire chains rounded the corner. The vehicle slowed seeing Seth waving his arms for the driver to stop. *Shit. It's a kid. Suck it up. It's you or him.*

The red car stopped, and the driver's window slid down. "You need help?"

Seth grinned. "Yes. Yes, I do." He brought his right arm up and shot the teen in the ten ring. *Like shootin' fish in a barrel.*

He originally intended to shove the driver over the roadside embankment, but he realized that once his pickup was discovered with the body nearby, they'd know the make and model of the vehicle he was driving. It was better to dump the remains where they would take longer to find.

He pushed the kid onto the center console, but he was still in the way. Worried someone else might come along, he pressed the button to unlock all the doors and dashed around the car to the passenger door. He opened it and then ran to open the rear hatch. Returning to the corpse, he grabbed it underneath the arms, dragged the dead teen to the cargo area of the SUV, and tossed him inside. He covered the corpse with a blanket he found in the cargo hold.

Out of breath from rushing around in the heavy snow, he returned to his truck. There he gathered his duffel bag and the rest of his arsenal in their nylon cases and dumped them on the rear seat.

He drove back along the highway he'd just come from until he turned into and through an open gas station on the outskirts of Running Springs. He didn't want the police to follow the SUV's tire tracks and learn the car had made a U-turn and returned toward Big Bear.

Later, on the edge of Big Bear Lake, with dusk fast approaching, he drove past the Fawnskin Market. A sheriff's deputy sat in his police unit watching traffic on Shoreline Drive. Seth was grateful he'd procured the red SUV.

In a few minutes he'd turn onto the road leading up the canyon to where Amber waited for him in the cabin. He couldn't wait to tell her that Roy was his father. Then it was time to lure dear old dad to his execution.

83

AMBER

Amber drove at a crawl along the canyon's steep and windy roads. The Honda's windshield wipers pounded a steady rhythm. In her mind, the left-right cadence intoned: *Get help. Get help. Get help.*

The single swath cut in the whiteness made it clear the snow removal resources were being used in a more populated part of the resort town.

At one point, her makeshift chain extension pulled apart. She'd been lucky and only a single side of her self-engineered work had come undone. It had taken ten minutes to fix it, and she'd worked at a frantic pace because time was running out before Farley's return. Her goal was to make it to Shoreline Drive—a major artery around the lake. She'd be sure to find someone else crazy enough to be out in the storm, or better yet, a police officer. Her heart beat faster because she knew she didn't have much farther to go to reach the main road.

Between the swishes of the wipers she thought she saw a car in the distance. *What if it's Farley?* She strained to see if the vehicle was a brown truck. Relief flooded through her when she realized the auto was red. Not only that, but the vehicle was coming toward her.

She pulled the Honda as far to the right of the plowed section of the path as she could. She'd let the driver get closer and then get out of her car. The other car would stop, and she'd ask them to take her to the police. *You've done it, Amber. You're safe.*

While she waited for the car to reach her, she glanced around the Honda to determine if there were items she'd need to take with her. She grabbed her gloves, slipped them on, and got out. Even the frigid cold couldn't dampen her spirits as she raised her hands above her head and joyfully crossed them back and forth.

Through the falling snow she tried to glimpse the driver to gauge their reaction to her signal. Amber's arms dropped to her side and her elation fizzled upon realizing the person driving the red SUV was Seth Farley.

84

ROY

Roy wasn't an overly religious man, but someone was watching out for him. Karen's phone call provided him enough time to shift his direction from the Ventura to the 2 Freeway, offering him a different route to Big Bear. He'd add miles to the journey, but with the 210 completely closed, he'd be ahead overall.

He knew Farley was responsible for the truck crash on the freeway. His former partner had wiped out his pursuers and built a barricade against anyone from immediately following him. The fact the accident occurred just before the turnoff to Big Bear was what made him think of the cabin. Most likely, law enforcement would assume Farley had continued on the 210 to double back on the San Bernardino Freeway into the Los Angeles area.

Since Roy had thought of the isolated cabin in the woods,

Amber might have considered it an ideal place to hide too. That Farley was alone when Karen saw him in his truck led Roy to believe the pair were staying at the family dwelling and his wife had remained behind. But the question he couldn't answer: Was she there willingly or not? But if she'd mentioned the home in Big Bear, she must have done it voluntarily.

Another explanation of why Farley might be alone—he'd killed Amber. But Roy wouldn't allow his mind to dwell on that possibility.

He fought the traffic until he got through Littlerock. Out in the high desert, he made good time.

If Amber was there against her will, his plan was simple: kill Farley and rescue his wife. But if she and Seth were everything their love letters suggested, Roy's decision was more difficult. And that didn't even take into account the baby issue.

He'd been lax in showing Amber how much he loved her. He wasn't the kind of guy to shower his wife with flowers or jewelry. But he was a man of his word, and on their wedding day when he'd recited his vows he meant them.

The thing she'd understood was that he'd provide for her to the best of his ability and protect her, annihilating anyone who caused her harm.

But maybe the lack of tangible displays of affection had resulted in her love wavering...and she'd found new passion with Seth Farley. Could Amber have fallen for a psychopath?

Roy's stomach churned at the thought. If that were the case, he'd soon be making life-altering decisions for all of them.

85

AMBER

Amber stood unmoving, snow swirling around her. The red SUV came to a stop. Farley got out, slamming the door.

"What the hell is going on? Are you *running* from me?" He reached out and slapped her across the face—hard.

The blow jolted her to realize everything she'd gone through had been for naught. He was real. She had to convince him she wasn't betraying him.

"I...I'm not running from you. I was scared. I started bleeding. I wanted to find help or a doctor."

He grabbed her arm, and jerked her toward the passenger side of the SUV, and opened the door. "Get in."

After he'd banged it closed, she sniffed the air. The car smelled foul. Looking around, she saw something covered by a blanket in the cargo area. A wet red stain had formed on the cover. She felt light-headed with the realization that a body lay beneath the tan fabric. *Was it Roy?*

She watched as Farley turned off the Honda's engine, locked the car, and pocketed the keys.

He plopped into the driver's seat and put the SUV in gear. "You must think I'm stupid. I don't know how you got the Honda working, but I'm sure it took a hell of a lot of work." He eyed her belly. "You took the chain off yourself too. You've been a busy lady. You're not fooling me one bit. You were trying to get away. You know it—and I know it." He chuckled. "No matter. We're arriving at the end of watch for you and your hubby." He laughed again. "I'll enjoy this."

Apparently, it wasn't Roy beneath the blanket. But then who was it? She tried to gather her wits and come up with a way to placate Farley.

With four-wheel drive and the chains on the SUV, he drove easily to the cabin and pulled into the open garage. "Get out—and don't even think of trying to escape."

"I told you. I was bleeding. I was afraid of losing our baby." She exited the car and started toward the door connecting the garage and cabin.

He got out and grabbed his duffel bag. "Cut the bullshit. I'm not sure you *are* pregnant. You've proven yourself to be resourceful. Maybe you faked the pregnancy test."

She stopped short and turned to face him. "Get another one and I'll take it again. Go on. I dare you."

He marched over to her, and with his beefy hand, grabbed her chin, forcing her to look at him. "You are not the one in charge here. I am. If you think I'm leaving you alone ever again, you're wrong—dead wrong."

He looked at the heavy chain coiled on the garage floor—a snake ready to strike. "Pick that up. I'll make your leash shorter. Hope it reaches to the bathroom, or your hubby will find you a stinky mess."

She bent and picked up the dreaded hefty links.

He held the door open for her as she dragged the chain past him. Once inside, his gaze scanned the wood stove and the burnt pieces of kindling and the remnants of the melted zip ties. He shook his head. "Good thinking to use the fire to get free. I won't make *that* mistake again."

He went to his duffel and returned with a pair of handcuffs.

Did the guy have an endless supply in his bag?

He grabbed the chain and wrapped it around her waist, fitting it more snugly than it had ever been before. He secured the shackle using one of the handcuffs, with the other cuff dangling loose. He looked at her. "Let's see you burn your way out of that."

His stomach growled. "I'm starving. You can make me some food. I'll leave the chain free from the table until after we've eaten. Boy, do I have a story to tell you."

She found canned chili and vegetables in the pantry and heated them on the gas stove.

The last thing she wanted to do was eat. But she needed to keep up her strength and feed the baby. Drained, discouraged, and depressed, she sat across from him at the table.

"I've got big news for you."

Amber looked at him.

"I saw Roy today."

Her eyes widened.

He smiled. "I knew that'd get your attention." He spooned another mouthful of chili into his mouth. "He was at the hospital visiting a woman. A woman who happened to be my mother."

"I don't understand. Why would he go see your mother? How does he even know her?"

His head bounced like a bobblehead doll. "Yeah, that's where the conversation *really* got interesting."

She hated his smug grin and the hint of laughter in his eyes.

"Dear old Roy and my mom knew each other way back in the day. In fact, about twenty-five years ago. The significance of that time frame shouldn't be lost on such a smart gal. Remember how I mentioned my dad was a cop?"

She gasped.

"Are you seeing the picture now? Your husband is my father. That bun in the oven you're carrying is his grandson."

"That can't be true. Roy has never abandoned his responsibilities."

"Oh, but he did. He left my mother to fend for herself with a baby in tow. She's led a life that no woman deserves to live. Meanwhile, my *father* has been livin' good and married —twice. He didn't give a rat's ass about my mother or me."

He rose from the table and paced. "I started this whole thing as revenge for the people who were responsible for my firing, and those who laughed and joked about me. The pièce de résistance was supposed to be me humiliating Roy by killing him while you watched."

He stopped pacing and whipped around to face her. "But this is even better. Now I get to tell daddy dearest, not only am I smarter than he is, but I own his woman too. I may even screw you in front of him. Then I'll share with him that you'll be the mother of his grandchild." He laughed and rubbed his hands together. "I can't wait to give him the news. Let the games begin."

86

KAREN

The freeway was still a mess, but the highway patrol was doing a great job of getting the eastbound traffic lanes clear. In the meantime, with her phone charging, Karen called her boss. He was none too pleased to learn his cub reporter and cameraman were involved in a high-speed chase with a murder suspect...until he heard Brian had fresh video of the aftermath.

The news director ordered them back to the station, but Karen said she had a tip that might lead them to Farley. "The thing is, we need a news van. The story is about to explode."

"What do you have, and where'd you get it?" He sounded weary.

"I got it from a confidential source, and I promised I wouldn't disclose."

"If you want a van, you're gonna tell me."

Brian took the phone from her and put it on speaker. "There's word Farley may be holed up in San Bernardino County. I believe the info is solid. No one else knows—yet. If someone can bring us a news truck and me another camera, they could drive Karen's car back to KABR along with the tape I filmed. We can head to the mountains with the news van—oh, and be sure chains are in the van."

"I don't like it. You two are running amok out there. You're gonna get hurt."

Karen rolled her eyes at Brian.

"We'll need law enforcement's help," he said, "but we need to be closer before notifying them. If we contact them too soon, the whole thing will be over before we arrive. Besides, the informant didn't want us to contact them until it was confirmed Farley was there."

"Is Karen up to it?"

"She's the one who got the story. Listen, you need to hurry and send the van."

There was a long silence. "Okay. But you two better deliver."

Brian shot a look at her. "We'll do our best."

87

ROY

Roy's travels had him driving the "back" route to the ski resort towns of Big Bear, Lake Arrowhead, and Running Springs. The drive was long, but the reduction in traffic made the extra distance a smart move. He hoped it wouldn't be his last good decision.

Roy passed the Big Bear airport while snow caused near white-out conditions. Another mile and he was turning up the canyon toward Amber's grandparents' lodge. He'd gone a short distance on the isolated road when he saw a vehicle pulled over to the side.

"That's the Honda from the cabin." His heart beat with excitement. He knew Amber's parents wouldn't visit, and he doubted the place was rented. Amber must have been there... or a thief stole the car, ran out of gas, or got stuck in the snow.

Closer inspection caused him to stare at the chains on the

tire. He exited his truck and walked to the driver's front wheel. He bent over, not wanting to kneel in the piled drifts.

"What the hell?" Crudely woven pieces of wire were hooked through the chain. Rising, he wiped a layer of flakes off the driver's window and peered into the interior. A box filled with blankets, snacks, and water sat in the rear seat. Whoever was driving thought they might get stuck. He stomped to the passenger side. The tire chain was the same crude configuration.

Snow spilled inside the hiking boots he wore, chilling his ankles. Someone had jury-rigged a pair of chains to fit the Honda. Seth? Amber? Both? Where were they?

He looked harder at the roadway. Another vehicle had traveled up the road toward the cabin. Numerous scenarios filled his mind, none of them good. *The only way to find out what's going on is to get on up there.*

88

SETH

Seth watched Amber clean up the dinner dishes. He recalled the events of the day. The cops had found him. Could they have put a tracker on his pickup? Had they discovered his truck on the side of the road? Were they following him now?

He slid from his chair and motioned her to come over to him. She wiped her hands on a dish towel and stood before him. He connected the other end of the chain around the base of the wood stove using another set of handcuffs. "You try to get away again, you'll have plenty of burn scars to show for it."

Satisfied she was contained, he shuffled to his duffel which was beyond her reach. He rummaged through the bag, and his fingers grasped what he was looking for. Night-vision goggles. He put on his jacket and boots.

"I'll be outside for a bit." He grabbed the rifle he'd staged at the back door and slid the sling over his shoulder, leaving his hands free.

Amber looked at him and eyed the goggles hooked to his belt. "Where are you going?"

"I want to check the perimeter. I won't be long."

He stepped onto the deck. Fitting the eyewear over his head, he adjusted the straps and inhaled the frigid air. The snowfall had dwindled to random drifting flakes. As he peered into the darkness, nothing unusual was revealed. He walked toward the tree line behind the cottage. He'd go out to the woods, climbing higher to get a better view of the terrain. Snow crunched beneath his feet as he walked.

He explored the woodland, each pass going deeper into the forest. There was no evidence law enforcement had been in the area.

He heard a vehicle before he saw it. A truck had turned onto the road leading to the cabin. The driver pulled to the right of the plowed section of roadway and killed the lights. Seconds later a person exited the driver's door. The individual was too far away to determine gender, but he figured it was a man.

Seth descended a few yards lower on the hill.

Not unexpectedly, the figure walked toward the dwelling. Seth's heart raced as though he'd just completed the obstacle course at the academy. The arrival of a lone person didn't convey a coordinated operation to capture him. Could it be Roy Buckner? *Hell, I didn't even have to lure him up here.*

Hidden behind the thick trunk of a towering pine, he monitored the figure deviating off the roadway and trekking into the forest. Seth's hands were freezing. He blew on them, tucking them beneath his armpits to keep his fingers nimble.

Through the trees he caught glimpses of the man. He was positive the visitor was male, and Seth was sure it was Buckner. He lost his prey but relaxed when he spotted Roy doing what *he* was doing—using a tree trunk for cover while keeping an eye on the cabin.

After five minutes, Roy was on the move again. He walked with stealth, which Seth found hilarious since he'd been spying on him since he left his vehicle. Roy skulked nearer to the log home, exploiting tree trunks as concealment.

He was in a good position to keep tabs on his former partner unless he continued farther west. The building would block the view. It wasn't a problem. No matter what Roy did, with his night-vision goggles and the high ground, Seth had the advantage.

The prey traveled to the edge of the trees along the driveway. If he wanted to reach the cabin, he'd have to cross the open path Amber had shoveled on the driveway. And that's just what he did.

Seth chuckled to himself, thinking Roy resembled a squirrel darting across a road. Halfway, he'd dropped to his knees, statue still. Then he rose to his feet and sprinted the rest of the way, flattening himself against the side of the garage.

After a few seconds, Roy stepped to the pedestrian door.

Seth studied him as he gripped the doorknob and twisted it to see if the door was locked. It was.

Now what, Dad?

As if in answer, Roy edged toward the log siding, and placed his hands at each temple, and peeked into the kitchen window.

Seth knew Amber's chain wouldn't reach that room.

Roy crept to the front of the cottage where the windows were floor to ceiling.

Seth moved a few trees over to keep his eyes on his father.

Once again, Roy put his hands up to his head. He took a quick peek through the bottom corner of the glass and then withdrew. He let out a long breath, his condensation rising into the air.

He must have seen Amber.

Roy looked through the window again—this time longer. Apparently bolstered by seeing his wife, he advanced to the front porch.

89

AMBER

Sitting on the couch, Amber stared at the fire glowing behind the glass door of the wood stove and contemplated how to get herself free. Her failure to escape made her a dead woman. Farley hadn't bought her account that she thought she was losing the baby. It *was* a lousy excuse. But she'd been so busy running she hadn't thought of a cover story. The frustration was overwhelming. She'd almost gotten away.

But here she sat chained—again—worrying that Farley would contact Roy and trap him. Once her husband was dead, he'd turn on her.

She'd tried several times to snag the black duffel Farley had put beyond her reach near the rear door of the cabin. She knew guns were in the bag. She looked around the front room for something—anything she could use to hook the satchel and draw it to her. She bit her lip in frustration. *Think, Amber, think!*

A soft knock on the front door caused her to jump and interrupted her thoughts. She hurried to the entryway. The solid wooden door didn't contain a peephole. Was this Seth testing her?

"Who is it?" She said the words softly.

"Amber, it's me, Roy."

"Oh my God." She unlocked the door and flung it open. It *was* Roy. She launched herself at her husband's chest as he wrapped his arms around her and held her tight. She closed her eyes and thanked the heavens he'd found her.

"Isn't this a touching scene?"

She froze. Farley. Opening her eyes, she saw her captor had the end of his rifle pressed against the back of her husband's head.

"Take your hands off her. Don't be stupid. If I shoot and kill you, she's next."

Roy removed his hands. He turned, and Farley jabbed the muzzle deeper into Roy's skin.

"Now get your hands in the air. Where's your piece?"

She had her gaze locked on her husband in case he motioned with his eyes he wanted her to do something.

"Right side."

Farley adjusted the position of the rifle stock under his arm but kept the muzzle against her husband's head. He reached with his left hand to slide Roy's pistol from the holster on his waist.

Roy spun, yanking Farley's hand from his pistol. While he was grasping for his gun, Amber watched horrified as Farley fired the rifle and Roy fell to the floor.

90

SETH

Seth looked at Roy lying on the front porch and got angry. *Damn it, I killed him. No chance of vengeance now.* He slung the rifle over his shoulder, removed Roy's gun from the holster, and stuck it at the back of his waistband. He stepped farther out onto the stoop, looking to see if anyone had heard the shot and was coming to investigate.

Down on her knees, Amber bent low over Roy, examining his wound. She took off one of her several shirts and placed it on the injury.

"Is he dead?"

"No, but it's not good."

"Head wounds always bleed and look bad."

She rose. "We'd better get him inside, but we need to wrap something around his head."

"I'm not carrying him."

"Well, I can't move him by myself. Now, if you took the chain off me, I might be able to drag him."

He looked at her and smiled. "Nice try. It stays on, and you stay attached to the wood stove." Roy was bleeding all over the place. Seth stepped over his body and marched to the kitchen where he found several dish towels. Returning to the entryway, he pulled a knife out of his rear pocket and cut a small tear in each of the towels. He ripped them into strips and dropped them on Roy's stomach. "Here. Bandage him up, and we'll drag him into the front room."

It didn't take her long to dress the wound. Once she'd finished, he grabbed Roy underneath one arm and motioned she should take the other.

She gripped his bicep but couldn't even lift his shoulder off the floor.

Seth sighed and shooed her away. He moved behind his father and lifted him up under the arms as he'd been taught in the academy. The mannequin he'd dragged as a recruit weighed one hundred sixty-five pounds. Roy outweighed the dummy by thirty.

He grunted and finished the job, dropping Roy's upper body on the hardwood floor near the stove.

"You shouldn't have dropped him. We don't know the damage he's suffered."

"Who gives a shit? The man cared nothing for my mother or me. I intend to kill him. I just didn't want it to go down this way." He eyed the blood on the porch. "I'll get a bucket and rinse that away. You clean the mess in here."

He was careful not to leave any of the firearms within Amber's reach. He couldn't trust her. He'd seen the joy on her face when she'd opened the door. She'd never looked at him that way. He'd have to kill her. Tough luck for their baby, but Amber wouldn't be a good mother to his child anyway.

He grabbed a bucket from the garage, and when he came back, he saw that she'd placed several pillows from the couch under Roy's feet. He remembered from his first aid training the position was standard when someone was unconscious.

She had paper towels and cleanser and was doing a good job.

"How likely is it he'll wake up and we can give him the news about our bundle of joy?"

She glared at him. "I don't know, but it won't be tonight. He could be in a coma." Her eyes filled with tears and she bit her lips, he assumed to keep from crying.

"Okay, this is what we'll do. I'll rack out on the couch. You'll be hooked to the table again like you were before." His gaze fell on Roy. "I'll zip tie his hands and feet, and he can sleep or die right there."

He didn't need more than a blanket, and Amber's blankets were still on the floor. She asked him to bring bedding from one of the rooms upstairs to make a bed for Roy. He considered refusing, but he wanted his former partner to wake up. He wanted his father to pay for abandoning him and his mother and humiliating him further by getting him fired.

Roy needed to be in good enough shape to experience and understand the pain *he* had suffered. Roy needed to be shamed in front of his wife. Seth stomped upstairs and retrieved blankets and a pillow. One thing he knew for sure: there was no joy in killing a half-dead man.

PART X

91

AMBER

Amber didn't know if while she'd examined Roy's wound he'd heard her whisper for him to play dead. His injury, while worse than a graze, hadn't involved penetration of the skull. If he was acting, he was giving an award-winning performance.

She'd taken two of her own blankets and added them to the few that Farley had brought from upstairs. She gently rolled him onto each of his sides to smooth the fabric beneath him. Several times when Seth wasn't looking she'd taken her husband's hand and squeezed it, but he hadn't responded.

"You about done there? I'm bushed and want to sleep."

She cast a worried glance at her husband and nodded.

"I have to go to the bathroom," she said, glancing at the chain attached to the base of the wood stove.

Farley shot her a look of disdain.

"Don't blame me, you're the one who knocked me up. The baby is pushing on my bladder."

Wordlessly, he unlocked the handcuffs securing her to the heating element.

She dragged the links with her to the small bathroom. As she did her business, she thought she saw a flash of light out the frosted window. She sucked in a breath. Maybe someone was coming to help. More likely it was lightning or space junk falling to Earth.

She moved over to her bed by the table, and Seth used handcuffs to chain her to the table base.

"Good luck if you think you'll get free from the table." He motioned to the couch with his head. "I'm gonna be sleeping right over there."

92

ROY

Before he'd passed out, Roy had heard Amber whisper to play dead. It was easy. He'd closed his eyes and was out. Now he was awake, and his whole head throbbed. He'd kill for some water. But he wasn't sure of his situation. Was his wife nearby? Where was Farley?

He tried to bring his hands to the pain in his forehead but discovered his wrists were tied together and resting on his stomach. His feet were bound at the ankles. He forced himself to open his eyes to just a slit. With limited vision he could make out a form snoring on the sofa. Farley.

The warmth and glow from the wood stove were over his right shoulder. Where was Amber? He listened between Farley's raucous snorts. Roy couldn't hear his wife but sensed she was nearby. When his eyes closed he almost drifted off again.

Small metallic clinking sounds reached his ears. The sounds came from behind him. He strained to look over his shoulder, but daggers of pain shot through his head and neck.

The faint noises increased in speed. From the stove's glow, he saw his wife crawling toward him. With her hand, she maneuvered a heavy chain wrapped around her waist, controlling how the thick links fell against one another and the floor. The clinking of the metal hadn't awakened Farley.

Minutes later she was leaning over him. Using gestures, she indicated she was handcuffed to the table.

He let out a sigh, then made motions asking about guns.

"*Too far,*" she mouthed.

He held up his index finger, signaling he had a plan. He raised his zip-tied hands and tried to motion with his head. His efforts must have hurt because he fell back and closed his eyes. After a few seconds, he offered his bound wrists to her.

"*What?*" she said silently. "*I can't undo your hands.*"

Roy frowned. He used his right pinky to tap on his right front pocket.

"*What? What do you want me to do?*"

"*My keys. Get them.*"

Amber glanced at the sofa to assure rhythmic snores still ensued.

He lifted his right hip toward her, and she removed his key ring.

She held them so he could see. Then she saw it. The handcuff key. Her face lit up with a huge smile.

He gave her a nod, communicating she should open the handcuffs securing her.

Amber crawled in a precise and quiet manner to the base

of the table. Using the glow from the stove as light, it took her several attempts before getting the metal cuffs unlocked and freeing the chain. She turned to him with another smile and held both of her thumbs in an upward position.

Outside an amplified voice cut through the night. "Seth Farley. This is the San Bernardino Sheriff's Department. We have the cabin surrounded. Come out the front door unarmed and with your hands in the air."

93

SETH

Seth leaped from the couch pistol in hand, hit the floor, and low-crawled to where he'd secured the rifle from Amber's reach.

Amber fiddled with the chain attached to the table base, probably trying to get herself free.

Seth slung the long gun and his black duffel over his shoulder. He dropped next to Amber.

She stared at him with an owl-like gaze.

He unlocked the handcuff securing the chain to the table and pulled her to her feet. Then he grabbed her around the waist and pulled her along with him, chain and all. He stopped at the bottom of the stairs.

Roy, leaning first on his elbow, fought his way to a sitting position.

Seth pointed the handgun at him. "I'll finish you off right

now."

Outside another announcement broke the quiet of the forest. "Seth Farley. You have ten minutes to surrender. Release the others inside the cabin."

He looked at his former training officer and laughed. "Do they really think that BS will work on me?" He lowered the gun to a forty-five-degree angle.

"Let Amber go," Roy said. "She had nothing to do with you leaving the department."

"You're right. She didn't. *You* forcing me out of my job started this. You lied regarding my abilities as an officer and you and your friends laughed about it. My first two training officers, Jerry McMillan and Paulo Delgado, told everyone I wasn't cop material—and all the rest of those sheep cops believed it." Seth snorted. "Then the captain assigned me to you. You watched me like I was a gangster and documented piddly shit that didn't matter. You never wrote the good stuff I did." He shook his head. "But that's not what this is about. This is personal. This concerns you and me."

"What? What did I do to you, Seth? I tried to help you."

"You left me. You're my father. You turned your back on me. Me *and* my mother."

"*What?* Have you lost your mind?"

"I was in my mom's room at the hospital. I listened to you talking to her. Even on her deathbed you shut her down. You couldn't stand to hear her say she loved you."

"You're crazy. I knew your mother, but we were never together in...in that way."

"Liar! I heard her. You got divorced, and she got pregnant. That's what she said."

"I'm telling you the truth. I never had sex with her."

Why was his father still denying the relationship? "She told me my dad was a policeman."

Roy looked away and then back at him. "She dated a lot of cops, Seth."

He started to raise his gun again, but Amber put her hand on his arm.

"Don't argue with Seth," she said. "And you should know…I'm pregnant. I'm having his baby."

If Seth remembered nothing else in his life, he'd remember Roy's reaction to Amber's words. His face paled, and his gaze shifted to stare at his wife.

"I'm sorry if you find this shocking," Amber continued, "but it wasn't anything Seth or I expected."

"Ambe—"

She held up her hand. "Don't try to change things. Seth gave me the one thing you couldn't—a baby." She turned to him. "We should help Roy to the front door. He now understands how I feel."

"Just a damn minute," Roy said. "Don't help me anywhere. None of this makes any sense."

"It's time for you to go. Seth and I are in love and are starting a family. Something you obviously don't understand or want."

Amber placed her hand on Seth's arm encircling her waist. "Let's put him on the front porch. We don't need him any longer. It's you and me together—until the end."

He looked into her eyes. She seemed so sincere. But he remembered she'd tried to escape and lied to him about losing the baby. He knew she *was* pregnant. He'd felt the swelling of her belly while holding her close. But that didn't mean she wasn't lying to him now.

The front window broke, and a loud concussion blasted their ears while a flash of light blinded them. It sounded as though the flashbang canister had landed near the couch. He gripped her tighter. "Come on," he said, yanking her up the stairs.

Roy struggled to get to his feet, finally rising to his knees.

As Seth pulled Amber to the second level, Roy fell in a heap onto the floor.

94

KAREN

Brian drove the news van while Karen called the San Bernardino sheriff's office to tell them Farley might be heading to Big Bear. She also advised that Roy Buckner was en route to a cabin owned by Amber Buckner's grandparents, but she didn't know the address.

The dispatcher had asked a bunch of questions regarding the location, most of which she couldn't answer.

By following responding law enforcement, Brian found the area of the cabin. He pulled the news van onto the side of the main roadway leading to where Farley was hiding.

She scanned the area. Ahead of them, two sheriff's SUVs blocked the road. Inside their vehicles, the deputies eyed them with curiosity. After a few minutes, they returned their attention to their in-car computers. Beyond the blockade of sheriff black and whites, a half dozen other law enforcement cars were parked leaving space for vehicles to pass.

"This won't work. We've got to get closer," she said.

"And how do we do that? They're blocking the only road to the cabin."

"I don't know. Give me a minute to research." She pulled out her phone.

Brian appeared to go through emails on his cell.

"Okay, this will suck, but I've figured it out. If we walk west in the forest a little way, that puts us below an unpaved hiking trail. We wouldn't have to hike very far north to intersect with that path. It runs from the trailhead east of our current position to the mountain and circles around the property to the cabin." She leaned over and held her screen out to him. "See?"

He scrolled on the device, then released it and gave her a sour expression. "You want me to hike a half mile uphill through two feet of snow with thirty pounds of equipment on my shoulder?"

"That's just to reach the trailhead. Taking the trail, we'd be close after another quarter mile." She smiled. "But at least it stopped snowing."

He shook his head.

She sighed and made a face. "Okay, I get it. We're going to lose out on the biggest story of both of our careers because of stupid snow."

Headlights reflected through the van's rear windows. "More troops to the party," Brian murmured.

A Fish and Game truck along with a couple of plain-wrap police vehicles and an ambulance pulled to the barrier of

SUVs. One deputy exited his black and white and went to talk to the game warden.

"I've got an idea," she said. "Get your camera and be ready to go." She hopped out of the van and bolted to the ambulance. The young driver lowered his window as she approached.

"Hi there. I'm Karen Watson with KABR News. My cameraman and I could use a lift to get near the cabin. Can you take us?"

He averted his eyes. "Uh, well, I don't think—"

"I'll do an interview with both of you on the dangers of your job."

"Sure, we can take you," the passenger said. He had the confidence of a seasoned veteran EMT. "Grab your guy and hop in the back. The only stipulation is if someone gets hurt up there, you'll find your own way down."

She gave him her oft-practiced television smile. "It's a deal. Thank you." She turned to the van and waved to Brian.

95

ROY

Never give up. Never give up. The more you sweat up here, the less you bleed on the street. Never give up. The old academy adages replayed in Roy's head while he struggled to stand.

The flashbang caused afterimages which fouled his vision, but Roy didn't care. Farley had Amber, and no matter what his wife had said, he knew she'd been lying. The chain around her waist had told him that. Everything she'd said and done was to get him away from Farley. Roy had seen through her speech, but what about the lunatic holding her?

The kitchen window shattered, and another flashbang went off. Simultaneously, the front door burst open and eight heavily armored officers rushed inside. Four of them descended on him yelling for him to put his hands in the air. The remaining four surrounded him, providing 360-degree coverage with rifles at low-ready.

Once the team realized he was bound, they patted him down for weapons, hoisted him on their shoulders, and sprinted out the front door.

"No! No, go back. Farley has my wife!" Roy struggled against his fellow rescuers.

"We'll get her, bud. We'll get her," one of them said.

The team ran to a turnout behind a small hill where an ambulance was parked. EMT's waited outside the rig beside a gurney. The officers laid him on the crisp sheet and stepped aside while the medics assessed him and took his vitals.

Out of the corner of his eye, he caught someone with a camera taking video. Then he saw Karen. He motioned her to him.

"He's got Amber in there against her will. She's convinced him she wants to be with him."

"Okay, Roy. Okay. Don't worry about that now. Let the medics take care of you and trust the SWAT team to do their job."

"How did you find us?"

"You told me the cabin was on a lot of property. The local cops thought of several possibilities, and this was one. When a Honda registered to this address was found abandoned on the road, it wasn't hard to figure out."

"We've got to get her. He's delusional and ready to die. Farley thinks *he* got Amber pregnant." The ramifications of what he'd just said hit him. *Could that be true?* For the first time during the ordeal, he felt faint. "But then, he also thinks I'm his father. He's nuts." He looked desperately at the reporter and the officers who stood nearby.

"Roy, hold still. We're trying to get your blood pressure," said one of the EMTs.

An LAPD patrol SUV barreled to the ambulance. Detective Johnson exited the passenger door. He frowned when he saw Karen next to the gurney with Brian filming.

"You and your cameraman need to take a break," Johnson said.

Karen looked at Roy.

He gave a slight nod.

She and Brian walked away.

"Farley's got Amber. She's chained up in there. You've got to help her."

"I've been in touch with the incident commander. They're working on a plan now."

"Make them work faster. He's gonna kill her!"

"Roy. They're doing everything they can. Let them do their job. I have news for you. While you were on your solo adventure, we served a couple of search warrants at your house. We collected DNA."

"I know. I saw it. Farley's DNA on the sheets on our bed."

"Yes. You're right on that account. But guess what else we discovered."

"I don't have time for games. What'd you find?"

"You and Farley are related."

"That's bullshit no matter what his mother or the DNA says. I did not have sex with Nora Farley. I am not Seth's father."

"No. You're not. However, based on the DNA, you *are* his half brother. It appears your father had a...relationship with Farley's mother, Nora."

"That's a lie," Roy said. But as soon as the words were out of his mouth, he knew the detective's words were true. It made sense. Nadine was a staple at cop bars long before he'd come on the job. It was possible his father could have run across her—and bedded her.

Roy turned to his side, leaned over the gurney, and dry heaved.

96

AMBER

With them both at the top of the stairs, Farley spoke to her, but Amber's ears still rang from the flashbang. She couldn't make out what he was saying.

"What? I can't hear you," she yelled.

He pulled her into the bedroom that faced the street and turned her to him. "You said you loved me, right?"

She nodded.

"This is where you prove it." He dragged her near the window and pushed her to the carpet. "Together we'll get up there and kill one of the cops. I think they came and rescued Roy, but if we spot him and can get a shot, we will."

How much more she could take from this psycho? She wouldn't shoot her husband or anyone else. And yet she nodded.

Farley smiled and pulled the rifle off his back. "Let me do

a quick peek and try to pick a target." He moved beneath the window and popped his head up to survey the scene below. He slumped to the floor. "I can't see a thing. I need my night-vision goggles. Get them for me," he said, nodding toward his duffel.

She crawled to the black nylon bag he'd dropped next to the bed. Reaching inside, she grabbed the device she'd seen him wear when scouting the property earlier. There were also several round objects she recognized as hand grenades. She snatched one and shoved it between her pregnancy-swollen breasts.

"What are you doing over there?" Suspicion edged Farley's voice.

"Being sure I get the right thing. I don't know what night-vision glasses look like." She squirmed to him and handed him the goggles. "When we're out of here you'll have to train me on this stuff."

He smiled at her. He put the device on and poked his head in the window. "Well, this sucks. No one's exposed. There's nobody visible to shoot."

"Maybe we could make a run for it out the back," she offered, turning away and pushing the grenade more securely between her boobs.

"No. But the guys in the rear won't expect us to attack that side. Good thinking, Amb. Let's check out the other bedroom."

He started for the hallway but turned to verify she was coming.

He doesn't trust you yet. She stood and scuttled to the bedroom across the hall. This room faced the backyard of the cabin. The forest's edge was a mere twenty feet away.

He made a beeline to the window. With his goggles still in place, he looked into the dark. A slow smile filled his face. "These guys are sloppy. One idiot is smoking." He raised the rifle to his shoulder.

"Wait!"

Startled, he turned to glare at her.

"I thought we were doing this together."

His expression changed to an approving grin. "Come on over, baby girl." He held his arm out, welcoming her to his side.

"Let me do it," she said, reaching for the rifle.

"Really?"

"Yes."

He didn't give her the firearm. "I'll hold the gun and get the cop in the sights. But you'll have the honor of pressing the trigger."

Amber swallowed her disappointment that he wouldn't trust her with the rifle. "Okay."

He took her hand and placed it on the stock. "Put your finger on the trigger, and I'll tell you when."

Her heart pounded. What if he put his hand over hers and made her fire the shot?

His head was bent as he looked through the scope. "Ready? Set. Now."

Amber inhaled and sneezed as she squeezed the trigger. She prayed her fake sneeze sounded believable.

"You stupid bitch." Farley pushed her aside. He lifted the rifle and blindly fired several shots out the window.

"I'm sorry. I'm sorry. I couldn't help it."

He shoved her to the ground and raised the rifle like a club.

She curled into a fetal position and drove the grenade deeper into her cleavage. "The baby. The baby. He doesn't deserve this."

He slung the rifle over his shoulder then yanked her by her upper arms to a standing position. Then he punched her in the face.

Amber fell back to the floor and nearly passed out from the blow.

He jerked her to her feet and backhanded her again.

This time she stayed upright. She tasted blood. He'd beat her to death.

"Farley," called the amplified voice outside, "let the woman go."

"Fuck you," he yelled to the outside. "She's my ticket out of here." He grabbed Amber and pulled her in front of him, grabbed his pistol from his waist, and held the muzzle to her head. He sidestepped, dragging her across the framed opening, then dragged her to the floor. "I'm not dumb enough to give a sniper a shot at me."

He lowered the gun and pushed her away, still keeping her in his sights. "Sit in the corner."

Like a five-year-old on a time-out. She moved as directed and seethed. *Don't do something stupid. Your chance will come.*

Farley backed to his black bag, unslung the rifle, and leaned it against the wall. He pulled a military vest out of the duffel and put it on. He put one of his M-4s over his shoulder and grabbed the other rifle and slung in front of him. He reached back into the satchel, drew out two hand grenades, and hooked them to his body armor. Next, he stood in the opposite corner from her, out of the line of fire from the window. He turned to her.

"This is the end of the road for us. I used you to lure Roy here. He got away, lucky bastard. I'll never be able to make him feel the humiliation and abandonment I felt. But I *can* make him suffer." He paused and looked at her. "Come here."

Amber's heart pounded like a jackhammer. She swallowed but didn't move.

"I *said* come here."

"No."

He cocked his head at her. "What'd you say?"

"I'm not going over there so you can pull me in front of the window and shoot me."

He unholstered the pistol at his waist and pointed it at her. "I could kill you right now."

She forced sadness onto her face. "I thought we were in this together. I've been loyal. You gave me the baby I always wanted, and I thought we'd be the family *you* desired. I've stuck with you this whole time, not alerting anyone, even though I had opportunities. "You want to make Roy suffer? Let him see us happy together with our own family. We don't just have to have one child."

"That'll never happen. I've killed people. If I get out of this, I'll be going to prison for life."

"Then let's get married, and I'll visit you. I'll hire you a good lawyer. We can make this work." She rose and ran her hands over her breasts as she walked toward him. "We'll have conjugal visits," she said, stopping toe-to-toe with him. She slipped her right hand inside her blouse and curled her fingers around the grenade. As she brought the explosive out from her shirt, she used her left hand to caress his face, blocking him from seeing her actions. She wormed her right arm along his neck, then hooked her left arm over the other shoulder.

Resting both her arms on his shoulders, she leaned in to kiss him. She deepened the kiss while pulling the pin—then dropped the grenade down the back of his shirt and pushed him away.

Taking a deep breath, she jumped out the broken window into the night.

97

KAREN

Six months later...

"Good morning, everyone. As you can see, I'm here at Northridge Hospital, and we're on Buckner Baby watch. As you might remember, Amber Buckner was kidnapped six months ago by disgraced LAPD Officer Seth Farley. He took Mrs. Buckner, who was pregnant, to a cabin in the woods near Big Bear Lake. Farley was responsible for the deaths of six people during his reign of terror as he sought vengeance for being forced out of the LAPD. Amber single-handedly dispatched her captor using a hand grenade. She then leaped from a second-story window to save her own life as well as that of her child."

Karen took a breath and looked behind her toward the

hospital. "Today is a much happier day. Amber and her husband, Roy, expect that baby to arrive any minute. The Buckner's promised me they'd send a signal to let the world know when their bundle of joy is here."

She listened to a question from the anchorman back in the studio, then replied. "Yes, I have a special connection with this story as the incident was my big break into TV news, and for that fact, I'm forever grateful."

The anchorman said how pleased they were to have her at KABR.

Karen smiled. "Thank you. I'm thrilled to be a part of the KABR family, and I'll let you know as soon as we get word on the Buckner baby. All I can say is that if the parents are any indication of the child's tenacity, that baby will be one tough kid."

98

AMBER

"Okay, Amber, it's time to push," the doctor said.

Amber looked into the eyes of her husband and bore down as a contraction racked her body.

Roy gripped her hand. "Push, Amb, push."

"Aghhhh!"

"He's crowning, we're getting the head," said the doctor.

"Aghhhh!"

"You're doing great, honey," Roy said, adjusting his grip as she squeezed his hand.

"We've got one shoulder." A few seconds passed. "Two shoulders. One last push...and...we've got a boy." The doctor held up the slick and flushed baby, then placed him on Amber's stomach, where the doctor clamped and cut the umbilical cord.

Roy leaned in and gave her a tender kiss. "He's perfect, and he's ours."

Amazed at the fitful cry that came from the bundle on her belly, Amber reached out and pulled their son up toward her face.

The baby immediately quieted.

"I'm your mommy, and I love you very much," she said, sticking her pinky finger into her son's grasp.

The newborn held onto her finger with surprising strength.

A nurse swooped in and spirited the baby away to wash him and get his vitals.

Roy went to the window and released a dozen blue balloons into the sky. He eyed the dozen pink balloons still in the corner. "I guess those can go to the woman in the next room. She's having a girl."

She looked up at her husband. "No regrets about us having a baby?"

"None," Roy said, returning to her and smiling. "I thought the only way to protect a child from an absent father was to never have the child in the first place. I couldn't have been more wrong."

"And we agree upon the baby's name?"

Roy nodded. "It couldn't be more perfect."

"Can we be good parents after what we've been through?"

Roy looked at her. "You're a titan, a woman who single-handedly took out a serial killer. We've got this. We'll continue our counseling. That will make us stronger." He lifted her hand and kissed it. "The dark days are behind us— nothing more than collateral damage to the life we've left behind."

Amber smiled up at her husband as the nurse brought their freshly washed baby and placed him in Roy's arms.

"Today we start our new life," Amber said. "You, me, and little Gage Marvel Buckner."

AUTHENTIC CRIME…ARRESTING STORY

Many things can spark an author's imagination. We never know when or where we'll get a nugget of inspiration to use for a story.

If you're reading this section before you've read the story, STOP! Read the story first. I'm about to reveal an important element in Collateral Damage.

SPOILER ALERT

I'm sure some of you are wondering where I got the idea for having Amber make snow chain extensions out of the metal ribs of an umbrella. Here is where that idea came from.

One day I was getting a massage (I have a bad back). I was telling the masseuse the plot of my story. Not much of the story was written, but I knew at some point my heroine would be snowed in at a cabin in the woods. I told Jessica (the masseuse) that I needed to make this gal suffer in her attempts to get away from the cabin. We brainstormed ideas but didn't come up with anything right for the story.

When my massage was over, I went to the lobby to pay. Jessica was talking to her next client, an elderly woman. We all related experiences we'd had driving in the snow (I live in Idaho).

The older woman related a story from many years ago when she got stuck on a snowy road.

Two men stopped to help her. They attempted to put the snow chains she had in her trunk onto her tires—but the chains were too short. The two men used the ribs of an umbrella to make extensions for the chains. The woman said she had just a few miles to go and the jury-rigged chains got her to her destination…And I had a scene for my story.

I'm always listening to other conversations for snippets of dialogue I might use, or experiences that sound good for one of my books. And that is one conversation that fell into my lap and solved my dilemma.

Don't miss out on any of my new releases. Sign up for my electronic newsletter and get in on the fun. Sign up for my newsletter here: www.KathyBennett.com

I'm sure other readers would like to know what you thought

about *Collateral Damage*—and frankly, I would too. Please consider leaving a review wherever you purchased this story of revenge, death, and tenacity.

Warm regards,

Kathy Bennett

ACKNOWLEDGMENTS

I give thanks to Keith Bushey for his knowledge about hand grenades and the roadways leading to Big Bear Lake. Any mistakes regarding these elements of the story are purely mine. I also appreciate his willingness to have an off screen cameo appearance in the story.

ABOUT THE AUTHOR

Hi there!

I'm Kathy Bennett.

A little about me—I worked for the LAPD for twenty-nine years. I worked eight years as a civilian employee, and I served twenty-one years as a police officer. While most of my career was spent in a patrol car, I also worked at the police academy as a firearms instructor, promoted to the position of a field training officer, then worked in the "War Room" as a crime analyst. I promoted again, this time to the position of Senior Lead Officer—where I was in charge of a basic car area within a geographic division. I've done a few stints undercover and was honored to be named Officer of the Year in 1997.

In my spare time, I started writing romance books. However, I wasn't really cut out to be a romance author—I'd forget to write the romance, but I was always killing off one or more characters. After a few years, I realized I'd better write what I know: Authentic Crime... Arresting Stories. (Yeah, that catchy phrase is a part of my brand.) One of the books in my Deadly Thriller series, *A Deadly Blessing*, was chosen by Barnes and Noble as one of the best original books of the year.

I live in Idaho with my husband, who is also a retired LAPD officer. We have two entertaining and energetic

Labrador retrievers, and two cats who aren't nearly as active or amusing, but they're loved just as much. I like to garden, exercise, and spend time with our daughter and her family. Life doesn't get much better than the one I'm living.

I'm always interested in my readers. Drop me a line and tell me a little about yourself or what you thought about *Collateral Damage*. You can reach me here: kathy@kathybennett.com, and know that I *do* write back—and it's me—not an assistant.